HIGH-FLYING PRAISE FOR AWARD-WINNING AUTHOR SANDRA HILL AND HER NOVELS

THE CAJUN COWBOY

"Hill will tickle readers' funny bones yet again as she writes in her trademark sexy style. A real crowd-pleaser, guar-an-teed."
—*Booklist* (starred review)

"An intoxicating addition to her Cajun Bad Boys series."
—*Publishers Weekly*

"A pure delight. One terrific read!"
—*Romantic Times* (four stars)

"Sandra Hill's writing is fabulous. Look forward to a book by her because it will be a great read."
—*The Literary Times*

"Ms. Hill has a marvelous way of weaving a story chock-full of frivolity, sensuality, and delight . . . Her talent for comedy brings a unique quality that entertains."
—*Under the Covers*

more . . .

TALL, DARK, AND CAJUN

The
Red-Hot Cajun

Also by Sandra Hill

Tall, Dark, and Cajun
The Cajun Cowboy

The
Red-Hot Cajun

Sandra Hill

NEW YORK   BOSTON

Warner Forever is a registered trademark of Warner Books.

Cover design by Shasti O'Leary Soudant
Cover photography by Herman Estevez
Book design by Giorgetta Bell McRee

Warner Books

Time Warner Book Group
1271 Avenue of the Americas
New York, NY 10020
Visit our Web site at www.twbookmark.com

Printed in the United States of America

First Paperback Printing: April 2005

10 9 8 7 6 5 4 3 2 1

This book is dedicated with much love to my good friend and critique partner Cindy Harding. Cindy has the most extraordinary talent for putting sensory detail in a book, and she's always berating me, "But how do they smell?"

Cindy does all the day-to-day work on her farm, runs a bed-and-breakfast on the side, for a while was an interior decorator, which she still continues as a hobby, is raising five children, and still manages to write. Someday, she will win a prize for her literary fiction; it is that good.

Most of all, I admire the love Cindy and her husband, Jeff, have for each other. Many times readers ask if the love we portray in romance novels is realistic. What I see with Cindy and her husband and family convinces me it can happen, even in this cynical world.

Thanks for all your help, Cindy.

The
Red-Hot Cajun

Chapter 1

The long hot summer just got hotter . . .

"That Richard Simmons sure is a hottie."

Whaaat? René LeDeux put down the caulking gun he'd been using to chink the logs of his home-in-progress and stared in astonishment at his great aunt Louise Rivard, who'd made that astounding announcement. Tante Lulu, as she was known, lounged on a hammock in the front yard, cool as a Cajun cucumber.

He wore only cargo shorts, a tool belt, and heavy work boots in deference to the scorching heat of the hottest summer in Louisiana history. He swiped his forearm across his brow, as much to gather patience as sweat before speaking. "Tante Lulu! Richard Simmons is not a hottie. Not by any stretch of anyone's imagination."

"He is in mine. Whoo-ee! When he wears those short shorts, I just melt."

Now that was an image he did not need. He tried picturing his seventy-nine-year-old great aunt in hormone overload. Talk about! But it did explain her attire: a pink headband encircling tight white curls, a red tank top with the logo Exercise That!, purple nylon running shorts, and white athletic shoes with short anklets sporting pink pom-poms on the back. She was a five-foot-zero package of wrinkled skinniness, the last person in the world in need of a workout. The fact that she was a noted *traiteur,* or folk healer, while at the same time being a bit batty, was a contradiction he and his brothers had accepted all their lives.

He adored the old lady. They all did.

He started to walk toward her and cracked his shin against the big wooden box in the middle of the porch. "Ow, ow, ow!" he howled aloud, while inside he screamed much fouler words and hopped about on one foot.

"I tol' you ya shoulda put yer hope chest inside," Tante Lulu said as she raised her head slightly to see what all his ruckus was about. "Doan wanna get rain or bird poop on it or nuthin'."

Actually, inside wasn't much better than outside when it came to René's raised log **house**. He had the roof and frame up, but no windows, only screens. It was all just one big room with an unfinished loft, aside from the bathroom, which was operational thanks to a rain-filled cistern. A gasoline-operated generator provided electricity for the fridge and stove. Except for a card table and two folding chairs, a bookcase, and a bed with mosquito netting, there was no furniture. That's the way he liked it. It would do till the construction work was completed.

Of course now he had a hope chest to add to his furnishings. And the midget-sized plastic St. Jude statue sitting in the front yard, another of Tante Lulu's "gifts." St. Jude was the patron saint of hopeless causes. René was no fool. Tante Lulu was giving him a message with both her gifts.

"Auntie, there is something I need to say to you. My life is in shambles right now. I quit my job. I'm burned out totally. Don't even think of trying to set me up with some woman. I am *not* in the market for a wife."

Whenever his great aunt thought it was time for one of her nephews to bite the bullet, she started in on them. Embroidered pillow cases, bridal quilts, doilies for chrissake. She was a one-woman Delta Force when she got a bee in her matchmaking bonnet.

Right now, he was the bee.

Tante Lulu ignored everything he said and continued on about the exercise guru. "Charmaine is gonna try to get us tickets to go see Richard—I likes to call him Richard or Dickie—next time he comes to N'awlins."

Dickie? Mon Dieu!

"Mebbe I'll even get picked fer one of his TV shows."

That was a hopeless wish if he ever heard one. He hoped. *St. Jude, you wouldn't! Would you?*

Charmaine was his half sister and as much a bubble-head as his great aunt. The prospect of his Tante Lulu doing jumping jacks on TV was downright scary. But then, she and Charmaine had entered a belly dancing contest not so long ago. So, not out of the realm of possibilities.

"Mebbe ya could go to his show with us. Mebbe ya could meet a girl there. Then I wouldn't have to fix you up."

Yep, that's my dream date, all right. "Don't you dare try fixing me up."

"And Charmaine's gonna get me the latest video of 'Sweatin' to the Oldies' fer my birthday in September. You want she should get you one, too?"

"No, I don't want an exercise video. Besides, I thought Charmaine was planning a big birthday bash for your gift."

"Cain't a girl get two gifts? Jeesh!" She eyed him craftily. "Actually, I'm hopin' fer three gifts."

At first he didn't understand. Then he raised both hands in protest. "No, no, no! I am not getting leg shackled to some woman just to give you a birthday present. How about I take you to the racetrack again this year for a birthday gift, like I did last year?"

She shook her head. "Nope, this birthday is a biggie. I'm 'spectin biggie gifts." She gave him another of her pointed looks.

"No!"

"Of course, I might be dead. Then you won't hafta give me anythin', I reckon."

He had to laugh at the sly old bird. She would try anything to get her own way. "I'm only thirty-five years old. I got plenty of time."

"Thirty-five!" she exclaimed. "All yer juices is gonna dry up iffen ya wait too long."

"My juices are just fine, thank you very much." *Jeesh! Next, she'll be asking me if I can still get it up.*

"You can still do it, cain't you?"

He refused to answer.

"I want to rock one of yer *bébés* afore I die."

"No. No, no, no!"

"We'll see." Tante Lulu smiled and saluted the St. Jude statue. "Remember, sweetie, when the thunderbolt hits, there ain't no help fer it."

René had been hearing about the thunderbolt ever since he was a little boy hiding out with his brothers Luc and Remy from their alcoholic father. Always, they would hot-tail it to Tante Lulu's welcoming cottage. The thunderbolt pretty much represented love in the old lady's book.

He had news for her. He might own a townhouse in Baton Rouge, but this piece of land was all the love he needed, even if it was just a weekend or vacation place. In truth, it was all the love—meaning trouble—he could handle at the moment. To say his life was in chaos was an understatement.

He'd recently quit his job in Washington D.C. as an environmental lobbyist, burned out after years of hitting his head against the brick wall that is comprised of the oil industry, developers, sport fishermen, and levee builders who are destroying the bayou he was so passionate about. Up to thirty-five miles of the Louisiana wetlands were sinking into the Gulf of Mexico each year. In some places, the coastline had already retreated thirty miles. But environmental protection cost money. Estimates were that billions would be needed over the next fifty years. But the U.S. government had expensive problems of its own—terrorism, poverty, you name it—and Louisiana was a poor state due to fiscal mismanagement, corruption, and loss of oil and gas revenues. For every battle René had won to protect the Louisiana coastal wetlands, he'd lost a war.

In his lifetime, he had been a shrimp fisherman, every type of blue collar worker imaginable, a musician (he played a mean accordion), an environmental advocate and lobbyist. Hell, if he ever finished his doctoral thesis, he could probably be a college professor as well.

But there was no point to any of it. He was a failure in

his most important work: the bayou. The fire in his belly had turned to cold ashes. For sure, the *joie de vivre* was gone from his life.

So he'd hung tail and come back to Southern Louisiana and resumed work on this cabin—or fishing camp as they were known thereabouts—in one of the most remote regions of Bayou Black. He loved this piece of property, which he'd purchased ten years ago. It included a wide section of the slow-moving stream. To the right of the cabin, the stream forked off in two directions, separated by a small island that was home to every imaginable bird in the world, including the graceful stilt-legged egret. The only access to the land was by water plane or a three-day, grueling pirogue ride from Houma. No Wal-Marts. No super highways. No look-alike housing developments. No wonder he'd been able to buy it for a song. No one else had wanted it.

"I think I hear a plane." Tante Lulu interrupted his reverie. "Help me offa this thing. I'm stuck."

He went over and lifted her out of the hammock and onto her feet. The top of her head barely reached his chest.

"It mus' be Remy," she said, peering upward.

His brother Remy was a pilot. He'd brought Tante Lulu here yesterday for an overnight visit, promising to return for her today.

But, no, it wasn't Remy, they soon discovered. It was René's friends, Joe Bob and Maddie Doucet, who could best be described as aged hippies. Both of them had long hair hanging down their backs, black with strands of gray. At fifty and childless, they were devoted to each other and the bayou where generations of both their families had lived and "farmed" for shrimp. They were quintessential tree huggers, and they couldn't seem to accept that René had dropped out of the fight . . . for now.

"Lordy-a-mercy! It's those wacky friends of yers," Tante Lulu said as they watched the couple climb out of the rusty old water plane and anchor it to the shore by tying ropes from its floats to a nearby live oak tree.

Tante Lulu calling someone wacky was like the alligator calling the water snake wet. But they *were* eccentric. Like, right now, J.B. wore his old Marine camouflage fatigues; the only things missing were an ammunition belt and rifle. Maddie wore an orange jumpsuit that had a former life on either an airplane mechanic or a prisoner. Probably a prisoner. She and J.B. had both served time on occasion when their participation in peaceful protests had become not-so-peaceful. J.B. was a well-decorated soldier who had come home to emerge as a "soldier" in domestic causes.

"Holy crawfish! Where do those two shop? Goodwill or Army Surplus?" Tante Lulu whispered to him.

He had no time to answer or warn his great aunt to be nice. Not that she would ever deliberately hurt anyone . . . unless she perceived them to be a threat to her family. She did have a tendency to be blunt, though.

"Hey, Joe Bob. Hey, Maddie. Whatcha doin' here?" Tante Lulu asked as they approached.

Yep, blunt-is-us. René groaned inwardly but smiled. "J.B., Maddie. Good to see you again so soon." *Whatcha doin' here?*

They didn't smile back.

Uh-oh! The serious expressions on their faces gave René pause. Something was up.

"What's up?" he asked.

"Now, René, don't be gettin' mad till you've heard us out," Maddie urged.

The hairs on the back of his neck stood up on high alert. "Why would I get mad at you?" The last time he'd lost his temper with them was two years ago when they'd used their shrimp boat as a battering ram against a hundred thousand dollar sport-fishing boat out on the Gulf. The sport fishermen's crime: hauling up almost extinct species of native fish as bycatch, which meant they just tossed them back into the water, dead. It had taken all of his brother Luc's legal expertise to extricate J.B. and Maddie from that mess.

"You've got a lot of work done since we were here last week," J.B. remarked, ignoring both his wife's and René's words. The idiot obviously made polite conversation to cover the fact that he was as nervous as a cat in a room full of rocking chairs.

"Forget the casual bullshit. What's going on?" René insisted on knowing.

It was Maddie who answered. "Remember how you said one time that what we need out here in the bayou is some celebrity to get behind our cause? Like Dan Rather or Diane Sawyer. TV reporters or somethin' who would spend a week or two here where they could see firsthand how the bayou is bein' destroyed. Put us on the news, or make a documentary exposing the corruption."

Man oh man, I hate it when people quote back to me stuff I don't recall saying. "Yeah," he said hesitantly. "So, did you bring Dan and Diane out here? Ha! Like that would ever happen!"

"Well, actually . . ." J.B. began.

René went stiff.

Tante Lulu whooped. "Hot-diggity-damn!"

It was then that René noticed how J.B. and Maddie kept casting surreptitious glances toward the plane.

"What's this all about? What's in the plane?"

"Jumpin' Jehosephat! They musta brought Dan Rather here," his great aunt said, slapping her knee with glee. "Great idea! I allus wanted to meet Dan Rather. Do ya think he'd give me an autograph?"

"It's not Dan Rather," Maddie said, her face flushing in the oddest way. Odd because nothing embarrassed Maddie. Nothing.

This must be really bad. "Spit it out, guys. If it's not Dan Rather"—he couldn't believe he actually said that—"then who is it?"

"Oh, *mon Dieu*! It mus' be Diane Sawyer then. I allus wanted her autograph, too. Betcha she could introduce me to Richard Simmons."

"What're you wantin' with that flake Richard Simmons?" J.B. asked.

Tante Lulu smacked his upper arm. "Bite yer tongue, boy. He's a hottie."

"Are you nuts?" Maddie asked.

"No more'n you," Tante Lulu shot back.

"Unbelievable!" René said, putting his face in his hands. After counting to ten, he turned on J.B. "Is there a human being on that plane?"

J.B. nodded.

There is! Sonofabitch! I sense a disaster here. A monumental disaster. And I thought I was escaping here to peace and tranquility. "Why is that human being not getting off the plane?" he asked very slowly, hoping desperately that his suspicions were unfounded.

"Because the human being is tied up." J.B. also spoke very slowly.

Tied up? Holy shit! Holy freakin' shit! I'm getting the mother of all headaches. St. Jude, where are you? I could use some help.

A voice in his head replied, *Not when you use bad language. Tsk-tsk-tsk!*

It was either St. Jude, or he was losing his mind. He was betting on the latter.

A celebrity who could do a TV documentary, that's what they hinted at. "A network TV anchor?" he finally asked, even though he was fairly certain they weren't that crazy. Best to make sure, though. "Did you kidnap a major network TV anchor?"

"Not quite," Maddie said.

Not the answer I want to hear. He sliced her with an icy glare. "What the hell does 'not quite' mean?"

"Not from a major network. And she's not an anchor, more of a news analyst." She glanced at her husband and said, "I told you René would get mad."

Mad doesn't begin to express how I'm feeling. "What the hell does 'not from a major network' mean?"

"She's on Trial TV. And you don't have to yell."

You haven't heard yelling yet, Maddie girl. "She? You kidnapped a female TV celebrity?" His headache had turned into a sledgehammer, and visions of lawsuits began doing the rumba in his brain.

Trial TV.
Celebrity.
Female.

He looked at Tante Lulu, and Tante Lulu looked at him. At the same time they swung around to the dingbat duo—who were holding hands, for God's sake—and exclaimed, "Valerie Breaux!"

"Yep," the dingbat duo said.

"You kidnapped Valerie 'Ice' Breaux?" René choked out. "The Trial Television Network regular? My sister-in-law Sylvie's cousin?"

J.B. and Maddie beamed at him, as if he'd just congratulated them, not raised a question in horror.

"Why her?" he asked through gritted teeth. Valerie Breaux was such a straight arrow she would probably turn her mother in for tasting the grapes in the supermarket. Even worse, he and Val went way back, and not in a good way.

J.B. shrugged. "She was available. She's from Louisiana. I heard she had a crush on you at one time."

"You heard wrong. Valerie Breaux can't stand my guts."

"Oops," Maddie said.

"Maybe you could charm her," J.B. advised. "You can be damn charming with the ladies when you wanna be."

"Charm that!" he said, giving J.B. a finger. Luckily Tante Lulu didn't see him.

"She's the answer to our prayers," Maddie asserted.

"Oh, no! She cain't be the one," Tante Lulu wailed, now that the implications of their conversation sank in. "I won't let that snooty girl be the one. She's so snooty she'd drown in a rainstorm. I remember the time she asked me iffen I ever looked in a mirror, jist cause I tol' her she could use a good girdle. She's not a Cajun, even if she does have a Cajun name. Her fam'ly likes ta fergit that Breaux skeleton in their closet from about six generations back, which makes her only one-tenth or mebbe one-twentieth Cajun. Nope, she's a Creole. Her blue blood's so blue she gives the sky a bad name. She looks down on us low-down Cajuns. All them Breaux in her family do. Take her back. I doan want her to be the one fer René. St. Jude, do somethin' quick."

René's jaw dropped open. He wasn't sure which surprised him more. That his friends considered Valerie Breaux the answer to their prayers, the woman who'd called him a "crude Cajun asshole" more than once in their years of growing up together in Houma. Or that Tante Lulu feared this woman might be his soul mate. As if the Ice Princess would let him touch her with a ten-foot pole, let alone his own lesser sized pole! Not with their history. Not after the infamous, uhm, incident.

They'd been fifteen. There'd been a party. He'd been perpetually horny, like most teenagers. She and her girlfriends had been sucking up sickeningly sweet Slo Gin Fizzes. Suffice it to say, he'd somehow found himself naked with Val in someone's bedroom. Suffice it to say, he became a member of the Hair-Trigger Club that night. Suffice it to say, she still retained her virginity after the fiasco. If all that hadn't been embarrassing enough, she'd jumped off the bed afterward and spewed pink barf all over his instrument of non-pleasure. Teenage hell, for sure!

He blushed just thinking about it, and he hardly ever blushed.

Could life get any worse?

Yep!

J.B. had waded out to his water plane and was now

carrying the "answer to their prayers" over his shoulder. She was squirming wildly but unable to say anything because, of course, the goofballs had duct-taped her mouth shut. That should merit at least one felony count, on top of the others for the restraints that bound her wrists behind her back and her ankles together.

But that wasn't the worst thing of all . . . or best thing of all, depending on one's viewpoint. And René's viewpoint right now was fixed on Valerie Breaux's bare white behind.

She was going to kill them all for that indignity alone, after she'd filed every legal charge in the world against them.

The Trial TV celebrity wore what could probably be called a *Sex and the City*-type power suit, which meant it had a very short skirt. A very short skirt that had ridden up with all her struggles, exposing her thong panties.

And thus the sun shone bright on Valerie Breaux's buttocks.

Very nice buttocks, by the way.

"Is she moonin' us?" Tante Lulu wanted to know.

"I never could figure out why women want to wear those thong thingees," Maddie mused. "Seems to me they'd be mighty uncomfortable, up in your crack and all."

"I like 'em," J.B. said.

Maddie probably would have hit her husband if he hadn't had his hands full of Valerie. Instead, she suggested, "You wear 'em then, honey." *Honey* was not said as an endearment.

René felt like pulling his hair out, one root at a time,

over the irrelevance of this chitchat. Meanwhile, Valerie's tempting tush was waving in the wind.

J.B. turned slightly and René got a good look at Valerie's face. Her shoulder-length, wavy black hair hung loose all over the place, but still he was able to see her dark Creole eyes, which flashed angrily. Against the duct tape, she screamed something that sounded pretty much like, "Flngukkk yuuuaauu!" It probably wasn't Howdy.

Grabbing a knife out of his toolbox, he walked over and lifted her off J.B.'s shoulder. She was unsteady on her high-heeled feet, but he managed to stand her against a tree and cut away the restraints. He saved the duct tape for last.

Once the tape was off, the first thing she did was shimmy down her skirt. Then the fireworks began. "René LeDeux! I should've known you'd be behind these shenanigans."

"Hey, I had nothing to do with this."

"Save it for the judge, bozo."

René glanced over at the St. Jude statue and murmured, "Now would be the time to perform a miracle 'cause I sure am feeling hopeless."

He could swear he heard a voice in his head answer back, *You're on your own, big boy.*

Chapter 2

Once a rogue, always a rogue . . .

When Valerie Breaux had lost her job last week as trial news analyst at TTN, she'd thought her life couldn't get any worse. But being dropped, practically butt naked, practically in the lap of René LeDeux, her worst nightmare, well, that had to rank right up there with life's defining moments of misery. She and René were the same age and had gone to the same Houma, Louisiana, schools for twelve years, every minute of which the rogue had chosen to torment her with his teasing ways. Then there had been that one humiliating incident, even more humiliating than this.

Someone was going to pay.

"You are going to pay, big-time, mister," she told René, who stood there looking hunky and way too roguish, as usual, in his skimpy attire. And a toolbelt! Holy moley, he looked like some model for a beefcake calendar. He had really broad shoulders and a really small waist and hips. Hell, her behind was probably bigger than his cute little butt. *God above! I've landed in hell and I am looking at the devil's butt.* His black hair was over-long, and his dark Cajun eyes danced with wickedness. She was in big trouble, and it had nothing to do with being kidnapped.

"I did not have anything to do with this, Val," he said, smiling at her.

"First of all, do not call me Val. Second, do not freakin' smile. Third, whose property is this?" She gave a sweeping glance to the raised cottage-in-progress and the remote bayou property.

"Mine," he admitted.

"Aha!" she said. "Two miscreants kidnap me off the Houma airport parking lot and deliver me to your property. Won't even let me get my briefcase out of my car or use the ladies' room first. I'm thinking they are the accessories and you are the perp. Take a guess how that would look in a court of law."

"Not so good, but I swear I had nothing to do with this." His sincere-sounding words were belied by his grin. He was probably picturing her bare behind.

"Good grief! I think the thunderbolt is hitting," Tante Lulu pronounced dolefully. The old lady's name was Louise Rivard, but everyone called her Tante Lulu. "The air's practically sizzlin' with electricity between you two. I shoulda never come here with the hope chest. I shoulda left St. Jude at home. I shoulda waited till next year to help you get a nice Cajun girl. St. Jude, iffen you forget that uppity snob ever came here, I'll say five novenas . . . mebbe even ten." Tante Lulu was sitting on an old stump, moaning her misgivings about thunder and saints or something. Dopey, as usual!

"What is she blabbing about?" Valerie asked René. His great aunt—well-known throughout Southern Louisiana for her outrageousness—was true to form today, her tiny body encased like a teenybopper's in an exercise outfit, despite her being older than dirt.

"She thinks the thunderbolt of love has hit me and that you're the one."

"The one what?"

He waggled his eyebrows at her.

"You're kidding."

"I'm warnin' ya, René, honey, iffen ya warm up a snake, it's gonna turn 'round and bite you, sure as shootin'."

"I have no intention of warming up anything," he protested.

Tante Lulu gave Valerie a disgusted look of resignation. "Well, if yer the one, yer the one. Doan suppose ya have a bride quilt yet? No. Tsk-tsk. Guess I'll hafta start sewin'."

It was hard following the train of Tante Lulu's thoughts, if she did in fact ever think in a logical manner.

"On the other hand, mebbe I should stay here and try to break the love spell. Guess I better call Remy and tell him not to come fer me today. Holy sac-au-lait! It's hotter'n 'n a goat's butt in a pepper patch t'day." She was already reaching for René's satellite phone on the porch. "Lordy, Lordy, Valerie 'I am perfect' Breaux in my family! Charmaine'll eat 'er alive. Or mebbe she'll eat Charmaine alive. We gotta stop this thing afore it explodes."

It took several moments for Valerie to digest everything the old lady rambled on about. When Tante Lulu ended her phone call to Remy with a "Bye-bye, sweetie," Valerie wagged her forefinger at the looney-bird. "Old lady, don't you dare sew anything for me. As for love spells, forget about it. I am immune."

"No one is immune once the thunderbolt hits," Tante Lulu pronounced.

To J.B. and Maddie, who cowered in the background trying to be invisible, Valerie ordered, "Take me back to Houma immediately . . . right after I use the bathroom." Before they had a chance to balk, she inquired of René, "You do have a toilet in this dump, don't you?"

He nodded, not at all pleased by her reference to his home as a dump, which was mean of her. But she was in a mean mood.

"Please don't tell me it's an outhouse. That would be the final indignity."

He sneered and said something foul under his breath. But he steered her up the steps. He was probably ogling her butt; humiliating as that prospect was, she wasn't about to give him the satisfaction of checking.

The inside of the cabin was one large room with very little furniture. Exposed log walls and open rafters. Hardwood floors. Basic kitchen. Unfinished loft. Great ambience if you liked rustic, which Valerie did not. She thought of her small apartment back in Manhattan with its doorman, its elegant antiques, and access to all the amenities the city had to offer.

The contrast in their abodes correlated to the differences in their personalities. He had always been earthy, raw, and wild, while she'd been poised, ambitious, and in control, even at a young age.

I wasn't always that way, she thought all of a sudden, surprising herself. *There was a time when I would go fishing on the bayou with Papa. Lazy days spent lolling about. Eating our catches over an open fire with crusty French bread we bought on the way at a roadside market. Coming home late, grubby and tired. But so very, very happy. Even when Mother launched into us when we re-turned to her nice pristine house.* That was before she turned eight. Before her father, Henri Breaux, had left her and her mother behind in Louisiana and hightailed it off to France to lead the good life. He never came back.

The next eighteen years, till she'd graduated from law school, had been spent under the thumb of her rigid, and sometimes abusive, mother, Simone Fontenot Breaux, a Houma realtor. All of the Breaux women, whether they were Breauxs by blood or marriage, were ambitious, per-fect, and cold as ice. If they weren't born with the ice gene, it was beaten into them. Val knew that all too well.

All men are pigs, Valerie. Stop whining over your no-good father. All men leave in the end. Be independent. Work hard. Keep your emotions in check. Stop being a baby. You are a Breaux. Act like one.

My God! Why was she thinking about all that now? Water under the bridge. Such maudlin thoughts just be-cause Tante Lulu pushed her buttons! She shook her head, calling herself back to the present.

René pointed her toward a closed door. Once she'd re-lieved herself, she washed her hands. Glancing at her image in the mirror over the sink, she couldn't help a lit-tle squeal of distress over her appearance. Rummaging in the drawer of the sink vanity, she found dozens of foil packets—disgusting man!—under which she discovered a brush and rubber band. She made quick work of pulling her hair back tightly off her face into a high ponytail. She had no makeup to cover the red marks around her mouth caused by the duct tape. Brushing the wrinkles out of her gray silk Donna Karan suit, she sighed. It was the best she could do.

There was a saying in the South that animals sweated, men perspired, and women glistened. Well, in this 115-degree heat, with about 90-percent humidity, it felt like a hothouse, and Valerie was glistening like a greased pig. Not a nice picture!

When she emerged, René stood at the kitchen counter pouring two glasses of iced sweet tea. He handed one to her, taking in her appearance with a disconcerting, way-too-wicked, head-to-toe scrutiny. That's the way he'd always been. Wicked. Crude. Disconcerting.

He'd probably looked at her the same way when they were teenagers. Why else would she have let him talk her into having sex with him? *Hah! Who am I kidding? I was probably the one who propositioned him, fortified with all that booze.*

He leaned back against the wall, still watching her closely. As if he could read her mind. *Good Lord, I hope not.*

She sat down in one of the folding chairs, making sure her skirt didn't ride up too high in case he noticed.

Yep, he did. His eyes fixed on her legs.

"I liked your hair better loose," he said lazily.

"Well, golly gee, that will certainly make me let loose," she replied. "Should I run back in and change it for you?"

He ignored her sarcasm and switched subjects. "So, what's new, babe?"

"Not much, *babe* . . . other than being kidnapped."

"Still working for Trial TV?"

"Nope." She took a sip of the cool beverage. "You still working as a lobbyist?"

"Nope."

"This is some conversation." She set her glass down on the counter. "Why aren't you still working in DC for the Shrimpers Association?"

He shrugged. "I quit."

Now, that surprised her. She'd never expected René to amount to much. Over the years, when she came home on occasion, she heard of his being a shrimp fisherman, an accordion player in a low-down bar band, lots of dead-end jobs. Then, a few years ago, she'd been shocked to hear about his working as an environmental lobbyist. She had to admit, she'd been impressed. She didn't ask him for details of his resignation now, though, because she didn't want him to think that she cared.

Not that he volunteered any further information. After a long silence, he said, "Why aren't you still with Trial TV? I would think that's a primo spot for a girl like you."

She bristled. "One, I am not a girl anymore."

He grinned in the most sinful way as if to say that he knew very well she wasn't a girl anymore . . . and that he liked the woman she'd become.

"Two, it *was* a primo spot. Three, screw that 'girl like you' crap. And four, I got fired."

"Oh, hell! I'm sorry, Val." She must have glared because he immediately said, "I mean, Val-er-ie." She would have been better off with his calling her Val, because the way he said Val-er-ie sounded silky and sensual on his tongue—the way a man might murmur her name in the midst of hot sex. Not that she'd had hot sex in a long, long time. If ever.

"What happened?"

A younger legal eagle was waiting in the wings to take my place. I refused to compromise on an ethical issue. I have an attitude problem. The ratings are down. Pick one. That's what she thought, but what she said was, "It's all part of the game."

He wasn't buying it, she could tell.

"Well, this has been fun," she said, standing. "You'll be hearing from my lawyer."

Just then a loud motor roared outside.

She looked at René, and the expression on his face immediately alarmed her.

"They wouldn't!" he bellowed with disbelief and ran for the door. She followed closely behind.

The water plane was taking off, up into the air, and Tante Lulu was standing on the stream bank waving them off.

"Come back here! You have to fly me back to Houma," Valerie shouted, her voice shrill in her own ears.

"You ain't the boss of this op," Tante Lulu said, then explained, "Op is short for operation amongst government agents. Not that we're government agents. We're our own agents. Fer protectin' the bayou." She beamed as if she'd just been named CIA Jane.

"I . . . want . . . to . . . leave," Valerie said, real slow so her message would get through to Tante Lulu.

"You . . . ain't . . . gonna," Tante Lulu said just as slowly.

Valerie shrieked her outrage.

"Now, don't get excited, *chère*. I'll call my brother Remy to come for you," René assured her. He was searching around the porch, swearing something about "killing" and "dingbats" and his "worst nightmare".

Hah, she had dibs on the "worst nightmare." "Quit dawdling around. Where's your damn phone? Give me the thing, for God's sake. I'll call someone to come get me. I don't want anything more to do with you or your wacko family or friends."

"Oops!" he said finally, after walking up and down the length of the porch.

She did not like the sound of that "Oops!" Nor did she like the weak, apologetic smile he cast her way. "Don't tell me."

"They must have taken my phone."

"I told you not to tell me. I swear, you are going to be on a chain gang for years when I'm done with you."

"It's not my fault."

"I am going to sue the ass off all of you."

Tante Lulu walked up to them. "Not to worry, Valerie. They'll come back fer you once ya agree to help us."

"Us?" René asked. "*Us?* Since when did you get involved, Tante Lulu? Or me, for that matter?"

She ignored his question and slapped her knees with delight. "Holy crawfish! This is almost as much fun as watchin' a Richard Simmons show. Is anyone in the mood fer gumbo? I'm thinkin' I'll go in an' make us a pot of gumbo fer supper. Bein' an agent makes a body hungry."

Valerie was not going to ask what she meant about Richard Simmons. And she was not going to discuss some freakin' bayou menu choice, either, or Tante Lulu being an agent, secret or otherwise.

"You know, Valerie, yer gonna get grumpy lines around yer eyes and mouth if ya keep frownin' like that,"

Tante Lulu offered as she walked past them and into the cabin.

"Grumpy? Killing is a legal defense in some parts of Louisiana, you know!"

Tante Lulu just laughed.

Valerie raised her hands into claws behind the woman's back.

"Holy crap, Val! You look just like Lizzie Borden must have just before she raised her axe."

She took several deep breaths. As good as it might feel, losing control was not the answer. *Calm down, Valerie,* the voice of Simone Breaux echoed in her head, like a toothache that would not go away. *Temper tantrums gain you nothing. Perhaps an hour in the closet will help you control your emotions. Maybe next time you'll get an A in math. We do not settle for B's in this family.* Inhaling and exhaling, Valerie finally got her racing heartbeat back to normal.

Slowly, she turned and bared her teeth at René, who was the only half-normal person in this schizo-drama, and that wasn't saying much. "How do I get out of here?" she asked.

"Damned if I know."

"Stop kidding around."

"I wish I were."

"Is there a boat?"

"A pirogue," he said, pointing to a canoe that was typically used in low bayou streams. "But it would probably take three days to get to Houma in that thing. I'm not tryin' it."

"Me neither," Tante Lulu called from inside the cabin where she was rattling pots and pans, openly eavesdropping. "No way am I goin' on a three-day boat ride through the swamps. Not even if Richard Simmons wuz paddlin' my canoe."

Richard Simmons again. "What is it with your aunt and Richard Simmons?" Then, "Never mind." She waved a hand in the air, as if it to dismiss the topic entirely. "Don't you usually keep in touch by phone? How long before someone gets worried and comes to check on you?"

"I don't know. A day or two. Maybe a week. Unless . . ."

"Unless what?"

"Unless Tante Lulu got involved. Unless she called Remy and told him not to come till she says so. Then there's no guessing when anyone would show up here. I'm guessing a week."

A meaningful silence rang out from inside the cabin.

"Why would that old biddy get involved?"

"I already told you. She might think that, if we're stuck here together long enough, we'll fall madly in love. The ol' love thunderbolt thing."

"Or I might be wantin' to stop the bolt from happenin'," Tante Lulu suggested from inside, no longer silent.

"A *week*?" Val screamed, a long, loud wail of frustration. "Nooooooo!" About a thousand birds screeched and chirped and flew up out of the island. Folks probably heard her in Big Mamou. She sure hoped so.

"Well, that about peeled the bark off every cypress tree within a mile," René remarked, hitting the side of his head with the heel of his hand as if to clear it.

"Good," she said. Then she yelled toward the inside of

the cabin, "Is there anything good to eat in there, Ms. Rivard?"

"'Course they is," Tante Lulu answered. "I brought a batch of *beignets* with me."

René was staring at her with concern. He probably worried that she was going off the deep end with this quick change of subject. He reached out a hand to pat her forearm.

She slapped his hand away. "I've been on a diet the past ten years, to maintain the perfect TV image. Lot of good it did me!"

Who the hell cared now? Desperate times called for desperate measures.

"If I'm going be trapped in hell for the next week," she informed René, "I'm sure-God not going to be on a diet."

More information than any healthy male needs to know . . .

"I haven't had sex in two years."

Val surprised him with that astounding revelation after walking, barefooted, out onto the porch with the screen door slamming behind her. She had one of Tante Lulu's beignets in one hand and a bottled water in the other. Sugar coated her lips, which she proceeded to lick.

Lick, lick, lick.

Good thing I am immune to this woman's charms.

And, really, any more sugar and she is going to be bouncing off the walls like a kid on Kool-Aid.

In the past two hours, she'd eaten just about everything in sight, straightened out his kitchen cabinets and the fridge, color coordinated his ragtag batch of towels, alphabetized the several dozen books on his small bookshelf, and wanted to put tiny labels on all his tools, except he had no tiny labels handy. Thank God!

Even Tante Lulu was going a little crazy with Val's anal-obsessive need to organize the world. Actually, a little bit *crazier*, René corrected himself, since Tante Lulu was already a little bit crazy.

So Tante Lulu played a Richard Simmons cassette tape, full blast, and did jumping jacks all over the cabin. Talk about! He didn't think Val would ever recover from that sight. Neither would he.

After that, Val decided to rummage through his hope chest, which caused Tante Lulu to about have a fit. "Those are fer René's bride. Iffen you doan plan on bein' that bride, then keep yer paws off his stuff." Val just laughed.

That's when Tante Lulu wisely decided to take a nap till dinner was ready.

And now Val brought up sex, *pour l'amour de Dieu*. The woman was driving him batty.

Could she possibly be thinking about that one little piddly unimportant time we were together?

I hope not.

He'd done his best over the years to put it behind him, to forget it had ever happened. But a small part of him wanted another shot, to prove he was better. But that would be trouble on the hoof. Totally, absolutely, out of the question.

"I beg your pardon," he said with as much lack of interest as he could muster. *Two years?* Meanwhile his you-know-what jumped to attention with no lack of interest.

In fact, *it* was definitely interested. It had been two weeks since he'd had sex, but weeks were like dog years on the male testosterone thermometer. At least, that's what his older brother Luc always used to say. Luc had been the expert to all the boys in Houma ever since about age twelve when he'd pilfered a copy of *Penthouse* from the shelves of Boudreaux's General Store. *Two years?*

"Listen, bozo, I haven't had sex in two years," she repeated.

"I heard you the first time," he grumbled, setting down his chinking tool. Without thinking, he reached for the bucket of water he used to clean his tools, and dumped it over his head, hoping to cool his blistering body . . . and his *other* tool. Val's provocative remark was probably some wiseass lawyer strategy for putting a guy off-balance before coming in for the kill. He was definitely off balance, but he'd be damned if he'd let her win in any battle.

After he finger-combed his hair off his face, he looked at her. *Two years?* "And you are sharing this information with me because?"

She stared at him with seeming fascination as water dripped from his hair and face onto his bare chest. Then she shook her head with a shiver of distaste. That was more like it. Valerie Breaux considered him on the same level with slugs, snakes, and other slimy creatures, and always had. Except for that one time, when her judgment had been colored by pink Slo Gin Fizzes. "I just don't want you to get any ideas," she explained, leaning her head back to chug down about a pint of fluid.

"About what?" *Two years?*

"Sex."

"With *you*?" *Two years?*

"No. With that toad over there. Jeesh! Maybe you are dumb as a brick, like I always thought."

René gritted his teeth and counted to ten, then added another five for good measure. Val was still drinking. He watched her long neck with each gulp she took. But he wasn't looking any lower. Uh-uh. She'd taken off her jacket, and her white silk blouse was unbuttoned down to never-never land. Never-never for him, anyhow. "I wouldn't be getting ideas if you hadn't brought it up." *Get a grip, guy,* he advised himself. *I sound like a pathetic goofball.*

"You kidnapped me. I wouldn't put anything past you."

"I had nothing to do with this . . . forced vacation."

She stiffened, morphing quick-as-a-lick into lawyer mode. Greta Van Breaux was about to give him a blistering legal dissertation on his choice of words. "Kidnapping, big boy. That's a federal crime."

"I was not involved in that," he argued.

"Okay, then. Accessory before the fact. Aiding and abetting. Obstruction of justice. Compounding a felony. Battery."

"Battery?" he interrupted her list of charges, some of which could probably stick.

"I was restrained and bruised. Look at my mouth. It's still raw from the tape."

"Battery by duct tape?" He hooted with disbelief.

Her face turned pink, but she lifted her chin high. *I am in deep shit.* "Maybe I'll just plead insanity."

"There you go," she agreed, way too easily.

He decided to try to lighten her mood. "How many

lawyers does it take to screw in a lightbulb?" he asked, then answered himself, "One. The lawyer holds the bulb while the rest of the world revolves around her."

"Oh, God! I'm in the middle of hell and I'm being subjected to lawyer jokes."

"Do you know what's wrong with lawyer jokes, honey? Lawyers don't think they're funny, and the rest of the world doesn't consider them jokes."

"Are you trying to annoy me? Or are you just trying to change the subject?"

"Yeah. The latter." *Two years?* "Okay, I'll bite. What does your non-sex life have to do with me?"

"You have a reputation."

"For what?" he asked indignantly.

"Smoothness."

Man, that's just what J.B. said. Who knew? Maybe us LeDeux men have a smooth gene. He smiled at that idea.

Val made a low growling sound at his smile.

He kind of liked her growl. *Yep. Pathetic.*

"Just don't think your silly smoothness will work with me. In fact, considering my weakened state, don't even try it. I'll find some way to add it to the charges against you, which are compounding by the minute."

Leaning back against a porch post, he grinned. He couldn't help himself. "I make you weak?" *Two years?*

"Get a life. I'm weak because of the heat and the stress of being kidnapped. I was a jury consultant before I got that Trial TV job. And a defense lawyer before that. A good one. The best defense is a good offense. When I told you that I haven't had sex in two years, I did it to forewarn you. I am not in a good mood."

"Horniness does that to a person sometimes."

"Don't be cute with me."

He winked at her.

"I am going to nail your sorry ass to the nearest Angola wall, Mister Smooth."

"What? Smoothness is a crime now?"

"You are not now and have never been attracted to me. And vice versa."

"Well, actually, there was that one time," he blurted out before he had a chance to cut the motor on his tongue.

"Aliens must have stolen my brains. Don't you dare bring that up now."

"Okay," he readily agreed, putting his hands up in surrender.

"Does the word *repulsive* ring any bells in that hollow head of yours? Just know, any change on your part now will be immediately transparent to me."

René winced inwardly. *Whoa! Wait a minute. She just told me that she was a jury consultant at one time. Don't they study people's body movements and stuff? Can't they tell when a person is lying? Can't they practically read people's minds? I better be careful.* In as offhanded a tone as he could manage, he inquired, "You've got me all figured out, huh?"

"Yep." She sank down into a cushioned Adirondack chair and propped her legs up on the rail.

If he were out in the yard, he would probably be getting a *Basic Instinct* peek at her thong . . . again. "You know, you've had it in for me ever since I talked you into showing me your Barbie underpants."

She gave him one of those "Get real!" looks that women are so good at. "I was seven freakin' years old. And you were already showing your true colors, especially when you blabbed to all the other kids at Our Lady of the Bayou School afterward." She saw that he was about to defend himself and raised a hand. "And, puhleeze, don't try to tell me that you reciprocated by flashing me your Superman's. Once a jerk, always a jerk."

Sometimes the dumb things men did came back to bite them in the butt; in this case, years of payback from Val for that one little peek at her Barbies. From that point onward, Val had become a world class pain in his ass. At the time, it had seemed worth it.

But, jeesh, René had forgotten about those superhero briefs. Tante Lulu had given him and his brothers their own individual sets one particularly bleak Christmas when their father had been absent on one of his alcoholic binges. Those were the days before Valcour LeDeux had sold out family lands to the oil companies. The alcohol still flowed after that, just a better brand of booze. But that Christmas, Tante Lulu had taken the boys into her Bayou Black cottage and made them feel secure, even if only for a week or two. And among her gifts had been the silly briefs. His had been Superman, Luc's had been Spiderman, and Remy had gotten The Hulk. He'd worn his till they'd practically fallen apart.

"Yoo-hoo! Earth to René!"

"Huh?" he said, coming back to the present. He shook his head to clear it, which caused water droplets to fly about. "You were the one who started it all by becoming a world-class snitch. In fact, that was the nickname us guys gave you back in elementary school. We could always rely on you to report all our bad deeds back to Sister Clothilde."

She shrugged. "There were plenty of them."

"Well, it's been great chatting about old times, darlin', but I've got work to do."

"What am I supposed to do?"

He eyed her carefully to see if she was serious. She was still in her thong-peeping position, which gave him ideas he wouldn't dare suggest to her. Like, *How about another shot?* "How do you feel about hard on . . . uh, hard labor?" *Mon Dieu, I'm losin' my friggin' mind.*

"You mean the kind you're going to do?"

"No. I mean chinking logs."

She glanced down at her carefully manicured nails, painted a creamy white color. "Not in this lifetime."

"Why don't you go for a swim?"

She arched both eyebrows at him. "Are you suggesting I go jump in the creek?"

"Precisely." *Maybe I'll jump in, too. Maybe we can both cool off together. Maybe we can do something about that two-year business. Maybe I can show you the staying power I've perfected over the years.*

"Maybe I will. Just to cool off, till the plane comes back. I'm sure your goofball friends will realize the legal danger they've placed you in, and hightail it back here before nightfall."

"Oh, yeah. For sure." *I wouldn't bet on it.*

Chapter 3

Beware of snakes with Cajun accents . . .

Wearing a pair of René's black boxer shorts and a white BITE ME Bayou Bait Company T-shirt knotted at the waist, Valerie walked down to the stream and proceeded to wade in, waist-deep.

The slow-moving water was deliciously cool. Despite its tea color—from centuries of bark from submerged trees—it was pure enough to drink. She splashed water on her arms and face and the back of her neck, which was exposed by her high ponytail.

A black water snake cruised by, way too close, but not one bit interested in her. Her upper lip curled with distaste. Having grown up near the bayous, she knew nonpoisonous snakes from the baddies, a lesson she still remembered from her father. She wasn't afraid of them, but she didn't like the creatures.

"Watch out for snakes," René called out, laughing.

She turned and, without thinking, stuck out her tongue at him. It was an immature gesture that Valerie hadn't made since she was a child, probably at him. But, hey, the cumulative abuse from the rogue and his wacko friends merited the tongue, in her opinion.

He just laughed some more. "Is that lawyer sign language?"

"Yeah. You'll get my bill."

"Hey, if I'm gonna get charged for tongue, I want it in a different way. And I don't mean with ketchup."

She rolled her eyes.

He stood on the steps of the cabin, which was on stilts—a necessity when this close to an oft-flooding stream. Holding a drill in one hand, he wiped his forehead with the back of his other arm. He was building a rail up the steep stairs. "Wanna hear a lawyer joke?" he asked out of the blue, his dark eyes dancing with mischief.

"No."

"Did you hear about the new sushi bar that caters to lawyers?"

"No means no, buster. Besides, that one is as old as the hills."

"It's called Sosumi."

"Ha, ha, ha. Why don't you go drill a hole in something . . . like that hollow globe on top of your neck?"

"What's the difference between God and a lawyer?"

"I am not listening."

"God doesn't think he's a lawyer."

Her nap apparently over, Tante Lulu came out onto the porch, carrying a metal pail. "It's hotter 'n a June bride in a featherbed." Then she yelled out to her, "I'm goin' to pick huckleberries fer dessert since you ate all the beignets."

How nice of her to remind me.

"Wanna come with me?"

Hell, no! "No, thank you." The old witch would probably shove her in quicksand or into the jaws of an alligator to get rid of her, just so her stupid love spell, or thunderbolt, or whatever she called it, wouldn't take effect. Tante Lulu didn't consider her good enough for her nephew. *Hah!*

She did a shallow dive under water and swam. It was too dark to see much, but at least she'd shut out René's teasing chatter and the old lady's insanity.

When she emerged, she was about fifteen yards downstream and closer to the small island that caused a fork in the bayou. She decided to walk the rest of the way and explore a bit.

The island was small, about half the size of a football field. It might very well disappear the next time a big storm hit the Gulf. That was the bayou, constantly reinventing itself.

If she were a nature lover, she would probably be impressed by the stately live oaks with their dripping moss or the cypresses as old as God, but she was a city girl. All she saw were trees. Birdsong filled the air, which sounded raucous to her rather than melodic. The scent of magnolia blossoms and wild roses was cloying in its intensity.

There were probably alligators in residence in the vicinity, but she didn't see one. If she did, in her present mood, she would probably karate chop it, turn it inside out, and make it into a handbag.

Plopping down on the edge of the bank, she dangled her legs in the water. The weight of the past two days pressed down on her. If she were a crying kind of gal, now would be the time to let loose. But self-pity was not Valerie's thing, hadn't been for a long, long time. *Stop that whimpering, Valerie,* her mother's voice intruded again. *Your father's never coming back. Never, never, never!*

Bam! Bam! Bam!

René was pounding at the rail now, with a vengeance. Maybe he was frustrated by the cards fate had dealt him, too. She almost considered feeling sorry for him. Almost.

Bam! Bam! Bam!

Whatever possessed me to tell him I hadn't had sex in two years? My brain must be melting in all this heat.

Bam! Bam! Bam!

Valerie gritted her teeth as he continued his incessant pounding. Every damn bird in the bayou chimed in with protest.

Bam, bam. Squawk, squawk. Chirp, chirp. Eek, eek. Bam, bam . . . It was enough to drive a sane person crazy. Not that she felt particularly sane.

René reached in his toolbelt for more nails, and blessed silence reigned. But only for a second.

Bam! Bam! Bam!

Valerie had been a list maker from the time she was a little girl. Probably an inborn trait with the females of the Breaux family. They were businesswomen, Congress-women, jury consultants, Court TV anchors, chemists. In any case, the first step in solving a problem was under-standing the problem and that always began with a list.

Bam! Bam! Bam!

She decided to make a mental list now—of all the rea-sons she disliked René LeDeux.

No. 1: He made too much noise.

Bam! Bam! Bam!

No. 2: He wasted too much time on nonsense, like building a cabin, when he should be doing something bigger, like making gobs of money, or influencing society, or inventing a cure for cancer. Even lobbying to preserve the Louisiana environment, although even she knew that was a losing battle.

Bam! Bam! Bam!

No. 3: He should row that pirogue down the bayou and get help, even if it took three days. She would wait here for him, of course, sipping mint juleps and nibbling on bonbons. Lots of bonbons. There were probably bonbons hidden away in that Vermont-sized handbag Tante Lulu lugged around.

Bam! Bam! Bam!

No. 4: He should stop looking so damned tempting. Even with sweat rolling off him in buckets, even with that annoying smirk, even with way too many muscles, he was one prime specimen. Not her type at all, but prime nonetheless, she had to admit.

Bam! Bam! Bam!

Okay, so much for René. She had enough problems of her own.

When Elton Davis, TTN's "Daily Update" producer, had called her into his office two days ago, she'd been shocked to be handed a pink slip. Not so shocked when she learned that her replacement was Sonja Smith, a twenty-four-year-old former intern, who also happened to be Elton's girlfriend du jour. *Sonja, you are way too good to work your way up through the bedsheets.*

Valerie should have seen it coming. Five years of jury analyses alone should have given her all the clues. She was asleep at the wheel—uh, microphone—this time. She thought she knew how to swim with the sharks, but apparently she'd let her radar down.

For months, Elton had been hinting that she might want to consider plastic surgery to reduce a few wrinkles. *The nerve! I do not have wrinkles, even if Tante Lulu implied I have grumpy lines. Maybe a smile line or two. But definitely no wrinkles. I'm only thirty-five, for heaven's sake!*

Then there was the issue of her "coldness." Elton had actually tried to talk her into personality classes. She'd told him in no uncertain terms, "The only person in this room who's in need of a personality transplant has a penis. A small one, at that."

The final straw must have been when she'd refused to spice up her trial news analyses by doing more *National Enquirer*-style segments. The jerk had lined up, without her permission, actors to re-enact a so-called celebrity rape case, which was still wending its way through the justice system. She'd walked off the set that day, thinking she'd taken the high road. Little did she know it was the road to unemployment.

She could have stayed and fought for her job. But she decided, instead, to come back home and think. Years of law school and courtroom training had taught her never to act with haste. Cool down, plan, then take your opponent by surprise.

Hard to do when you're kidnapped, though.

I can still strategize.

The Trial TV bigwigs are probably looking for me already. Elton is no doubt in trouble. They'll be begging me to come back.

If they can find me.

Hmmmm. I need to think about what to ask for before I go back. No, if I go back.

Now where did that if *come from? Of course, I'll go back, with the right incentives. Won't I?*

Even if they beg me to come back, it's humiliating to be put in this position. Doubly humiliating when you consider I've been fired and kidnapped practically in the same day.

Somebody is going to pay. And not just the guy with the little penis.

But enough self-pity. Like that old lawyer joke—put a hundred lawyers in the basement and what have you got? A whine cellar. Valerie chuckled. *Things must be really bad if I'm telling myself lawyer jokes.*

And René doesn't think I have a sense of humor. Hah!

Alice in who?

"I feel like Alice in Wonderland after she fell down that rabbit hole," René said, propping his chin in one hand, the elbow braced on the table. "My world has certainly been turned into *chaos and nonsense.*"

About an hour ago, he had gone into the cabin where Tante Lulu's cooking had raised the impossibly hot temperature to scalding, which would make indoor dining torture. As a result, he, Tante Lulu, and Val were holding their very own version of the Mad Tea Party outside the cabin, their table being an old wooden door laid over two sawhorses. There was sweet tea, but, instead of the Queen of Heart's tarts, his aunt served them Cajun gumbo, crusty French bread, dandelion-vinegar salad, and some delicious concoction his aunt fancifully called Blueberry Huckle Buckle.

He sat on a high stump, and the two ladies sat on folding chairs. Their feast took place under a ridiculous tent-like structure of mosquito netting, which he'd erected at his aunt's insistence to keep away pesky mosquitoes and no-see-ums, those tiny gnats that plagued the bayou.

"Alex in Wonderland would be more like it," Val said with a soft smile, which she'd probably intended as a smirk. She had a really nice smile, René had to admit, when she wasn't sniping at him, which she did most of the time.

"Well, if you gets to be the main character, then I guess I gotta be the white rabbit," Tante Lulu remarked with a laugh as she patted her white curls. "Or mebbe the Cheshire Cat." She looked from him to Val in the oddest way, as if she knew something they didn't.

"Forget the Alice/Alex bit. I'm way more like the Mad Hatter." *Pure, one hundred proof, over-the-edge mental case. That's me.* René winked at Val to show he was just teasing.

She went suddenly still, and he wondered if the usually cold-as-ice Val could be affected by his wink. Some women were, René knew from past experience. Hmmm. A bit of information to store for future reference.

"Who you gonna be?" Tante Lulu asked Val.

"I cannot believe you guys are playing games while my life is falling apart. Crime scene charades. Jeesh!" She shrugged. "Okay, I can play, too. I guess I'm the Queen of Hearts."

I'd rather you be the Queen of Hearts tart, baby,

especially packing those "two years". No, no, no, I did not think that. It was just a mind blip.

"Well, iffen yer the Queen of Hearts, then René has to be the King of Hearts."

Holy shit!

"Why—?" Val started to ask.

"Don't ask," he interrupted.

Too late. Val finished, "—is that?"

"'Cause yer soul mates. Jeesh, ain't ya got the message yet, girlie?"

Val rolled her eyes. "We are not soul mates, but let's assume that absurd hypothesis and say that we are. I thought you didn't want me and René to get together."

"I don't, but sometimes ya jist gotta go with the flow."

"Which—?"

"Don't ask," he ordered again.

Too late again. She finished, "—flow would that be?"

"The thunderbolt. Bless yer heart, Val, but yer not too bright when it comes to love, are you?"

Val shook her head at the uselessness of arguing with René's aunt, something he and his brothers had learned long ago.

"Apparently not."

"Besides, it might not be too late. Mebbe if I stick around as a chaperon—"

"Whoa, whoa, whoa!" Val said. "Having a chaperon assumes there is something going on between me and René, which there is not. Not now, not ever."

I don't know about that. There was that one time. And nothing at all during those "two years". Man, oh man, why do I keep thinking about that? They oughta nominate me for the Dumb Men Hall of Fame.

Tante Lulu continued as if Val hadn't even spoken. "As a chaperon, I could mebbe steer the thunderbolt in some other direction. Remember that nice Cajun girl ya wuz engaged to at one time, René? Francine Pitre. Mebbe I should invite her to come out here. That would sure as shootin' bend the bolt, I betcha."

"Don't you dare." *What an idea! We could turn the Mad Hatters Tea Party into the Madder Hatters Tea Party. Ha, ha, ha.*

"You were engaged?" Val asked. Now she was the one with her chin propped on a cupped hand, her elbow on the table. She stared at him with incredulity.

What? A guy like me couldn't ever be engaged? "I wasn't engaged. I was . . . uh, engaged to be engaged."

"Same difference." Tante Lulu waved a hand in the air.

"And it was ten years ago, for God's sake."

Val continued to study him. "What happened?"

"We called it off." He could feel his face heat, which was a real feat in this already overheated atmosphere.

"*Pffff!* Frannie wanted to get married and have babies. René wanted to have hanky-panky. Thass what I think." Tante Lulu had an opinion on everything in the world, but she wasn't far off the mark with that one. At least that had been Francine's original plan . . . before she discovered something important about herself.

"What does this Francine do now? Is she married? With lots of babies?"

"Hell, no!" René said. "She's a Victoria's Secret model, never married, no kids."

Victoria's Secret? Val mouthed silently at him.

"I saw her last month in N'awlins, and she asked 'bout you. I think she still has a crush on you." Another of

Tante Lulu's opinions, this time so off the mark it boggled the mind.

Truth to tell, Francine was a lesbian and she lived with her longtime lover. She'd probably been bisexual at one point, when they'd been dating. But then she'd discovered her inner Ellen DeGeneres and it had been off to the races from then on. The female races, that is. *What a guy I am. Turn the ladies gay, that's what I do.* "A crush? Puhleeze, Auntie. Thirty-five-year-old women don't have crushes."

"Why not?" Val asked.

He gave her a look that he hoped conveyed that she not encourage his aunt.

"And, wow, thirty-five and a Victoria's Secret model. She must be something else."

"She is," René and Tante both said.

The most peculiar expression swept over Val's face. He understood it only when she glanced down at herself. In this regard at least, Val was like every other woman René had ever met. She thought her body was less than perfect.

Frankly, he thought her body was just right, not that he would ever say that aloud. His aunt had no such compunctions, however.

"Francine allus wuz too skinny. Yer jist right," Tante Lulu said, patting Val on the forearm.

"Hah! I'm always on a diet and never skinny enough."

Tante Lulu tried to be nice. "Everyone allus says people look ten pounds heavier on TV."

"Yeah, add that to the ten I need to lose off-camera, and you get the picture."

René smiled. He'd like to see where she was hiding those ten pounds.

"Stop smiling," Val said, noticing the direction of his stare, which homed in on the BITE ME slogan on her shirt. Talk about embarrassing!

Yep, there were a few parts of her body that looked good enough to eat . . . uh, bite, René thought.

He glanced over at the St. Jude statue sitting outside their tent. *Hey, big boy, I'm having impure thoughts here. Can't you do something about it?*

Like? a scoffing voice said in his head.

Like cleanse my mental palate.

You mean, a lust exorcism?

Oh, well, I don't know about that. Would there be green vomit involved?

Tsk-tsk-tsk. You watch too many movies.

So, you gonna help me?

No.

Why?

The Lord has a plan for you.

Uh-oh!

All he heard then was mental laughter, which was really weird, not that carrying on a telepathic chat with a plastic statue wasn't weird to begin with. Bonkers, that's where he was headed. He turned to face Val again. "Can we change the subject?"

"Please do," Val said.

"We need to discuss what we're going to do about our situation here."

"Do you mean the kidnapping situation?" she inquired sweetly.

Tante Lulu made a tongue-clucking sound of reproval as she began to gather up the dishes to take inside to wash. She got tangled in the mosquito netting, but finally managed to get free. Once inside the cabin, she must have turned on the radio because soft Cajun music drifted out to them.

"I care deeply about the bayou, Val, even though I'm not working for the Shrimpers Association anymore. And I understand the desperation that prompted J.B. and Maddie to bring you here, misguided as they were. You think it's a crime that they forced you to come here, which it probably is, but it's just as much a crime what's being done to the land in Southern Louisiana."

"But it's not *my* crime."

"I realize that."

"Then let me go."

"I can't."

"Why not?"

"Even though I wasn't involved to begin with, I am now. J.B. and Maddie are good friends. If I take you back now, in your present mood, you'll put them in jail. I can't allow that."

"Allow . . . allow . . . ?" she sputtered.

He nodded. "I might not have had anything to do with bringing you here, but I'm not doing squat to help you get back. Unless . . ."

She narrowed her eyes at him. "Unless what?"

"Unless you agree to forget this whole incident happened. No charges. No publicity. *Nada.*"

"Hah!"

He shrugged. "Then, welcome to Club Med Bayou, *chére.*"

She bared her teeth at him.

"I just don't understand you two," Tante Lulu said,

lifting the netting and coming back to the table for more dishes. "Where did all this hostility come from?"

"It goes way back," Val told her.

Please don't tell Tante Lulu about the incident. "Are you still fixating on the pantie incident?" he asked.

"What pantie incident?" Tante Lulu wanted to know.

"Your precious nephew talked me into showing him my Barbie panties." Val folded her arms over her chest and glared at him.

Not the *incident! Thank you, God!*

You could thank me, too, said St. Jude, or his overactive conscience. Whatever. At least he'd dodged another bullet.

"René!" Tante Lulu chided him.

"I was only seven years old," he said defensively. "And how about the time you told Sister Clothilde that I put itching powder on the toilet seats in the teachers' bathroom?"

"Well, you did."

"René!" his aunt said again, although a little smile quirked at her lips.

"But you didn't have to tell," he complained to Val. "I got ten smacks across the knuckles with Sister's ruler that day."

"Then there was the time you pinched my butt in the coat room," Val added to her list of grievances.

"You pinched me back. How about the time you told the other kids that I had cooties?"

"How about the time you mooned me?"

"I was mooning the whole Girl Scout troop, not just you."

"Lord-a-mercy!" Tante Lulu exclaimed.

"You were always teasing me."

"Mebbe he teased you 'cause he liked you," Tante Lulu said. "And maybe you retaliated because you liked him."

He and Val both ignored those remarks.

"You called me an asshole more than once," he reminded Val.

"Tsk-tsk!" Tante Lulu opined at his language.

"You were," Val contended.

"Was not."

"Enough!" Tante Lulu yelled out. They both looked at her. With fists propped on both of her tiny hips, she looked like an overaged, midget Rambo. "All that is old history."

"Obviously not," René said. *You don't know the whole of it, Auntie.*

"A snake doesn't change its spots," Val said.

"That's supposed to be a leopard, not a snake," he corrected her.

She stuck her tongue out at him.

"That's the second time today you've given me tongue, cupcake. Are you trying to send me a message?"

She snarled something under her breath that sounded a lot like "Asshole!"

"You wanna know what I think?" Tante Lulu asked.

"No!" he and Val said at the same time.

"I think you two been sniping at each other since you were youngins. I think it's past time you two . . ." She paused for dramatic effect.

René groaned.

Val, who could be such a fool sometimes, asked, "What?"

"Kiss and make up," his aunt declared, beaming.

"You've got to be kidding," he said.

"Not in this lifetime," Val said.

"I wouldn't bet on that," Tante Lulu said, glancing pointedly at the St. Jude statue.

René could swear the old guy grinned at them.

Chapter 4

Just girl talk . . .

"Whass that tickin' noise?"

"It must be some insect. Or a woodpecker."

"Oh. I thought it might be yer hormone clock tickin'. Ya are gettin' to that age, dearie."

Val gritted her teeth and restrained herself from strangling the old lady, who shared a bed with her. *Two years without sex, and what do I get? Me and Grandma Moses in the sack together! An AARP sleepover! Can life get any better than this?*

René was outside on a sleeping bag under the mosquito tent. *Smart guy! Putting some distance between himself and the Matchmaker from Hell. Or even worse, the Matchbreaker from Hell.*

Every mosquito and flying bug in Louisiana appeared to be here tonight, drawn by their exceedingly warm human blood. The temperature felt like 110, and sleep was proving impossible. Thus, Val's midnight chat with I-have-an-opinion-on-every-freakin'-thing-in-the-world Tante Lulu.

"Did it ever occur to you that not every woman yearns to be a baby machine?"

"Ya gots the hips fer it."

Valerie bristled. "Are you saying I'm fat?"

"No. Jist that some wimmen try to deny whass obvious."

"And that would be?"

"That they's made fer bein' mothers."

"What makes you think I would be a good mother . . . not that I have any inclinations in that direction?"

"Best ya be careful, girlie, or yer time clock's gonna explode in yer face one of these days."

"What the hell does that mean?"

"No need to be swearin'. St. Jude's in the house, you know."

Actually there were tacky St. Jude statues all over the place, inside and out. The old lady had a thing about decorating in a saintly style, and she imposed it on her nephews as well.

"What it means is that sometimes a body keeps sayin' they doan want somethin', over and over, almos' like they's tryin' to convince themselves. Then, when they finally wake up and realize they really did want it after all, it's too late."

"Is that your long-winded way of saying I don't know what I want?"

"Well, alls I'm sayin' is doan wait till yer hormones is rusty afore gettin' a lightbulb moment."

Rusty hormones? That is just super. Now I'll be picturing my body parts rusting out.

"Doan take it personal, though."

Oh, no. There's nothing personal about rusting femaleness. "Listen, I know you mean well"—*actually, I don't know that, but I can be diplomatic when I want to be*—"but I've just never had an inclination to clone myself, or cuddle babies, or provide an heir for some man. My goals lie in other directions."

"Like?"

"Like being the next Barbara Walters. Like having my own television show. Like being influential—the top of the heap."

"Ya sound jist like yer mother. I see her real estate ads on TV all the time. Betcha she could sell a house to a turtle."

"I am not like my mother," Valerie said icily. "Not at all."

Her tone must have seeped into the old biddy's thick head because she patted her on the belly. Tante Lulu had probably been aiming for her arm and missed. "I know yer not like Simone. I jist meant yer ambitious like she is. Those developments that she put in outside Houma musta raked in millions fer her. Bayou Paradise, she calls it."

Valerie felt herself blush. "I can imagine what René and his tree-hugging cohorts must think of that."

"They calls it Bayou Parasites."

Valerie cringed. She didn't have to be a rocket scientist or an environmentalist to know the effect those luxury homes with their swimming pools and man-made lagoons must be having on the bayou ecosystem. Not that her mother would care about that.

Hell, I don't care, either. Well, hardly. Okay, I do care, but I prefer not to think about it.

"What I meant when I said you and yer mama were alike is that yer both ambitious," Tante Lulu emphasized again.

"And that's a bad thing?"

"I din't say that. There's good ambition and bad ambition. Besides, who says wimmen cain't be ambitious *and* have a family? Even Barbara Walters had a *bébé,* dint she?"

"I think so, but if you can't give a hundred percent to something, whether it's a child or a career, you shouldn't do it."

"Hmmm. I wonder if you feel this way 'cause yer an only child. Betcha if you'd had a brother or a sister, you'd feel different."

"Hah! My mother and Joan Crawford were cut from the same mold. I shudder to think what she'd have done with more than one child."

Tante Lulu reached over to pat her again, and this time she didn't miss her forearm. "I heard stuff 'bout how she treated you a long time ago, but it hardly seemed true."

Oh, great! People had known about her abuse, or suspected it. That's all she needed. Pity. Maybe back then, it might have helped. No . . . no, it wouldn't have. It would have just angered her mother and made her take better care to hide her actions. Nothing would have changed, really.

"My mother never hit me," she said. "It was never really abuse." *I cannot believe I am defending the witch.*

"Hah!"

"What does that mean?"

"It means, iffen ya step in somethin' soft, ya cain't go callin' it pudding."

"That makes absolutely no sense." The scary thing was that it did make some kind of warped sense to her. "I don't want to talk about my mother anymore. And I don't want to talk about having babies, either."

"So what should we talk about?" Tante Lulu asked.

How about nothing?

"I know. We kin talk about sex."

"No thanks." *That's all I need. Sex advice from a Grandma Moses.*

"I know stuff."

I can't imagine what. "No thanks."

"Betcha doan know the best way to make a man get down on his knees and beg."

Oh—my—God!

Playing possum . . .

It was just past dawn when René saw Val walking toward him, a piece of toast in one hand, coffee in the other, and a wild glint in her dark eyes. Sharing a bed with Tante Lulu would do that to a person, he supposed.

Or more likely, the glint was for him. He braced himself for the onslaught.

The air was a little cooler this early in the morning, but the swirling clouds in a clear blue sky above and the steam rising on the water presaged another scorcher. The willows and cypresses that lined the banks provided little relief from the unrelenting sun. But the black and orange Monarch butterflies that flitted among the butterweed blossoms were having a field day.

He was sitting cross-legged near the bank, shirtless and shoeless, wearing the black boxers he'd slept in last night— a Christmas gift from his half sister Charmaine. They were imprinted with red lips, but in the dark the lips glowed and became tongues. A real kidder, that Charmaine was.

For a second, he wondered if his boxers were decent attire, then shrugged, deciding that they were no more indecent than his running shorts on Val's curvy body.

René had been up for an hour. It was his favorite time of the day, watching the jet-black night explode suddenly, bayou style, with the brightness of a new day. All the wading birds came out then—herons, egrets, ibises—leaving their roosts to find food for their young. Laid out on the grass next to him were a green trout and several sac-a-lait, or crappies, which Tante Lulu would put to good use.

"You're up early," he remarked, trying to be friendly.

"You would be, too, if you shared a bed with a senior citizen version of Dear Abby."

Uh-oh! He arched his eyebrows at her.

"She wants to tell me stuff about sex."

"Uh-oh!" he said aloud.

"Stuff that would, and I quote, 'make a man get down on his knees and beg'."

He had to smile at that image, him down on his knees begging Val the Ice Princess for God-only-knows-what. On the other hand, he had a really good imagination. *Two years*.

"It's not funny."

"I beg to differ."

"Nice undies," she said, eyeballing his shorts. "But I think I prefer your superhero ones."

"They don't fit anymore." *In more ways than one, baby*.

She made a snorting sound of disgust, then she jerked backward as she got a closer look at him. "*What* is that in your lap?" she demanded to know, scrunching up her nose with distaste as she sank down to the ground next to him.

Oh, good Lord, am I having a morning hard-on? Sonofabitch! I can't take me anywhere, he thought, his face heating with embarrassment. But then he realized that she referred to the baby possum all curled up and sleeping on his upper thigh.

"That has got to be the ugliest creature on the face of the earth. And, eeew, what a long tail! Is it a rat?"

"No, it's a possum. Chester has a broken hind leg— probably the reason his mother tossed him out of her pouch. Possums are only about the size of a bee when they're born. He's probably about two months old."

"Chester?"

"Remember that guy with a limp on those old *Gunsmoke* shows?"

She shook her head at his hopelessness. "Why are you holding it? Please don't tell me your aunt is going to cook it up for breakfast along with those fish." She glanced pointedly at his morning catch on his other side.

"We Cajuns do eat possum, but not baby possums," he remarked with a grin. "I'm considering whether to put a splint on Chester's leg and hope the mother takes him back. Or whether to just let him fend for himself."

"Which would mean that some alligator or snake or even a heron would gobble him up," she concluded.

He shrugged. "That's the way of nature. Only the strong survive."

"I'm beginning to see the dilemma here. The environmentalist in you doesn't want to interfere with the natural order of things. It would be breaking the code or something, right?"

He grinned at her. "Yeah, but sometimes rules are made to be broken." With those words, he tickled Chester behind the ears, then flipped him over on his back. The animal made a small squeaking noise and instinctively pretended to be dead, all four paws stuck comically up in the air, even the bent one. Sometimes possums, when cornered, pretend to be dead, as in "playing possum."

He reached over to get a broken piece of paint stick and tape. Once he got the leg straight and braced with the makeshift splint, he told her, "Wrap that tape around this, please." Chester was beginning to struggle and René couldn't hold him in place and tape at the same time.

Val got up on her knees and did as he asked . . . without hesitation, to his surprise. When she was done and they both examined their work, he suddenly became aware of her closeness. And she became aware of him, too, in that moment when their eyes connected. He had to remind himself that she was not his kind of woman. Not even close. *But two hot-damn years?*

There was an odd laughter in his head then. Maybe it was St. Jude getting his jollies over his sad attempts at self-delusion. Who was he kidding? He was attracted to Val, all right, and always had been.

She blinked rapidly several times, stunned by the sizzle that had sparked between them. He was stunned, too. Then she frowned, as if blaming him for pulling that sexual current out of thin air, all by himself. "Don't think you can catch me off guard and lure me in like one of your groupies."

"Groupies?" He hooted with laughter, the connection broken—thank you, God, or St. Jude, or whomever. He put Chester in the palm of his hand and stood.

"Yeah, I've heard that you play in a rock band, and that women swarm all over you." She stood, too, and dusted off her butt, which he was definitely not looking at. Definitely. Not. And he wasn't thinking about *two years,* either.

"The Swamp Rats are a far cry from a rock band. Frankly I can't remember the last time I was approached by a groupie, unless you count Wanda, the waitress at The Last Chance Saloon in Biloxi. And she only wanted change for the jukebox."

"You are such a liar. I can tell by the way you blinked. People don't realize that they give themselves away all the time by their body language. So don't think you can fool me. Ever."

He better make sure he didn't have any impure thoughts about her. Which of course caused him to immediately have impure thoughts about her. *I am so screwed!* "Come on. Let's see if Chester can find his way home."

They walked to the edge of the clearing and set the possum down, aiming him toward the wooded area where René had found him whimpering earlier. Chester stumbled a few times, going down on his chubby tummy, but then he limped off slowly, hopefully toward home.

He and Val smiled at each other, the first genuine smile they had exchanged in probably forever. His heart constricted in the oddest way.

Tante Lulu came out on the porch then and called out, "Breakfas' is ready. I gots grits 'n cane syrup, boudin 'n dippy eggs, beaten biscuits and white gravy. Come 'n get it."

"Holy crawfish! I'm the one gonna need Richard Simmons by the time she leaves," René said.

"Does she cook this much food all the time?" Val asked him.

"All the time. And if you don't eat, she acts as if you've put a spike through her heart."

"Back to your passion for the bayou. Let's make one thing perfectly clear. I am not going to help you. But I'll give you a bit of advice. You are not going to change people's minds about the Louisiana environment with some dull documentary on saving the snail darter."

"There are no snail darters in the bayou."

"Whatever! Smaller coastline. Missing plants. A disappearing animal no one has ever heard of. People just don't give a damn unless it hits them personally. Remember Bill Clinton's campaign for president? His advisers kept harping, 'It's the economy, stupid!' Well, I'm telling you that you've got to find an issue that screams, 'It's about you, stupid!' "

She made a good point. The problem was, he had no clue what that issue could be. *Unless . . . ?* He smiled as an idea came to him. "That's why I came home and gave up the fight. Even I know that plants are about as exciting as a lawnmower manual. But let me be the first to tell you, baby, there are going to be a whole lot of Cajun men, and their women, who are going to be unhappy campers come ten years or so down the line when they discover the Juju plant is no longer available."

She waited for him to elaborate, but he was no fool. He knew how to play her strings. Well, some of them. He held his silence, like a regular Cool Hand Luke.

"All right, I'll bite. What's a Juju plant?"

Yeeees! He gave himself a mental high five. "It's the

substance that gives Cajun men that extra zip, if you know what I mean."

"Puh-leeze."

"Really. When the oil fields were going gangbusters over in Texas, lots of Cajun men went over there to work. The Texas women went ballistic, practically jumping their bones, because they were such great lovers."

"Puh-leeze," she said again.

But that didn't deter him. She was listening, which he took as a good sign. "When the Texas men wanted to know what their secret was, the Cajun men told them that their mamas had been giving them Juju tea ever since they were old enough to get the notion."

Val was shaking her head from side to side, as if he were a really hopeless case. "I've heard that story before, except they usually credit the fat in crawfish as the secret to their supposed virility."

"Both of them work," he continued with a wink.

"Nice try, René."

He put up both hands. "Hey, I'm only reporting what they say. I'm not saying it's true or not."

She narrowed her eyes at him. "I think you made up this whole story just to distract me. You like to tease me, don't you?"

"I do."

"Why?"

He shrugged. "Because you're so teaseable."

"How immature!"

"That's me."

"Let's go eat. I'll probably gain twenty pounds before I emerge from this nightmare, for which you will be responsible."

"Is that a crime, too?" He laughed. "A fat felony?"
"If there isn't a charge for that, I'll create one."
"I know a real good exercise," he offered.
She sliced him with a glare.
"Or maybe not."

Chapter 5

Professor Dolittle, that's who he was. As in do little . . .

One day later, and Valerie was still sitting not-so-pretty in the middle of bayou hell.

It was only midafternoon but the skies were dark and a high wind was rising, which had prompted all the bayou animals to run for cover. Humidity was hovering around the hundreds, if the perspiration pouring off her body was any indication. Hopefully they would get some welcome rain soon to relieve the sweltering heat. If nothing else, Valerie was hoping the cistern would finally be filled so she could take a shower instead of bathing in the stream.

Sitting cross-legged on the floor before René's bookcase, she was trying to find something to read, but all she saw were nonfiction books, almost all of them dealing with the bayou, everything from simple swamp biology to Mike Tidwell's *Bayou Farewell: The Rich Life and Tragic Death of Louisiana's Cajun Coast*. Behind her, a humming Tante Lulu was cooking up another zillion-calorie Cajun feast for dinner, happily content to wait till someone in the freakin' world came looking for them.

René also appeared happy with so little, which amazed Valerie.

He was outside on the porch, where a Baton Rouge country-western station blared on the satellite radio. A Toby Keith marathon was apparently going on, and he sang along with each good-ol'-boy song: "How Do You Like Me Now?" "I Love This Bar." "Who's Your Daddy?" René had a really nice voice, she had to admit. She could see why the Swamp Rats, the musical group he played with on occasion, were so popular throughout Southern Louisiana. As he sanded the stair railing, he occasionally danced, too. Hands upraised. Fingers snapping. Hips rolling to the beat. Needless to say, he was a good dancer.

She wondered idly what else he did well.

No, I don't. Definitely not.

With a grunt of disgust, she picked up a notebook she'd found under the bottom shelf of the bookcase, rose to her feet, and went outside. Instead of being embarrassed at being caught singing and dancing by himself, René smiled at her and started to stretch out his arms and waggle his fingers in a beckoning fashion for her to join him in a dance. But then, his eyes latched onto her attire, and he stopped dead in his tracks. "Mercy!" he exclaimed.

She was wearing a red-and-white striped tube top of Tante Lulu's that was about two sizes too small with flame-red spandex shorts that were straining at the seams. Why the old lady would need or want such garments was beyond Valerie. "Hey, I'm here without any extra clothes, and you don't have any more clean shorts or shirts, and it's hotter than hell," she said defensively.

"Honey, you've been spouting legal charges ever since you got here, but I'm telling you now, it's a true-blue crime for you to go within a mile of any red-blooded male dressed like that. And right now, my blood is pumping crimson red. Whoo-eee!" He was looking at her as if she were naked. The lout!

She could feel her face heat up, but she wasn't about to tuck tail and run like an overly sensitive teenager. "Don't get any ideas," she warned.

"Hah! Ideas are popping up in my brain like erotic popcorn." He grinned at his analogy, then waggled his eyebrows at her.

"I've got more clothes on than you do," she countered. And that was the truth. René wore only a pair of cutoff jeans.

"Sweetheart, the only way we would be on equal footing in that department would be if I shucked my shorts." He put both hands to the waistband of his cutoffs and unsnapped the button.

She shrieked, "No!" He was probably just teasing, as usual, but she wasn't taking any chances.

He continued to grin and give her a head-to-toe scrutiny, over and over. Thankfully, he resnapped himself.

"Listen, Mister Lech, I want to talk to you about something." She waved the notebook in front of her and asked, "What is this?"

"My doctoral thesis."

"What do you mean, doctoral thesis? Don't tell me you hold a PhD."

"Not yet. Probably never. I haven't worked on it in two years."

That made sense. The notebook was full of penciled remarks in all the margins, indicative of a work-in-progress. "It reads like a futuristic novel," she remarked. "Even the title, 'Southern Louisiana 2075: Land of the Lost.'"

He shrugged. "That's what it is, a prediction of what's going to happen over the next seventy or so years. Southern Louisiana is eventually going to disappear into the sea, that's a fact, unless something drastic happens to change things."

She cocked her head at him. "I just can't imagine you in a college classroom."

"I'm insulted."

"No, you're not. You could care less what I think. Where did you get your master's?"

"Tulane."

"In what?"

"Biology."

She nodded. "What would you do with a doctorate?"

"I don't know. Teach at the college level. Maybe."

A college professor? Lordy, Lordy! Indiana Jones had nothing on him.

"Hell, Val, I was bored for a couple of years so I decided to go to school. Big deal!"

She wasn't buying that self-deprecating crap a bit. This man liked to portray himself as a simple fisherman and an accordion player in a low-down bar band. She had no trouble accepting his role as an environmental lobbyist, figuring his love of the bayou and a glib tongue had gotten him the job. It had never occurred to her that he had a college education—an *advanced* college education.

"Who *are* you?" she asked suddenly, kicking into jury analyst mode.

"Me, I am just a simple Cajun man." He gave her another head-to-toe onceover. "A simple Cajun man who is enjoying the view immensely."

As frustrating as he was, there was a small part of Valerie that delighted in her being able to turn on the bayou bad boy. *I can't believe I'm letting him get to me like this.* Holding the notebook up to her chest, she spun on her heels to walk into the house and get some kind of covering. "Stay right there till I come back," she ordered. "I have more questions to ask you."

"Like I can go anywhere."

Within minutes she was back outside, wearing one of René's dress shirts she'd found hanging in a closet. The shirt was open in front, but she was reasonably covered . . . though hotter than Hades.

René half-sat on the porch **rail,** with a longneck bottle of Dixie beer dangling from his fingertips, watching the rain begin to come down. The drops were light at first, like a fine mist, but the precipitation soon came down in blinding sheets, turning the parched earth into muddy pools. The stream would no doubt overflow if this kept up much longer, and the flooding might even reach the cabin. No reason for alarm, though, since the cabin was on stilts.

It was a moment out of time. The pelting rain, which had a unique, pure scent, created a cocoon around them—as if they were separate from the rest of the world. Just the two of them. Not even Tante Lulu, still inside, could intrude on this sense of intimacy.

She coughed to break the spell.

He turned and took a long swig from the bottle while staring at her. She watched his throat move as he drank and was amazed. Who knew a man's neck could be so sexy?

His gaze was hot and raw.

She felt naked, even with the shirt.

Those two years must be catching up with me. Sinking down into the Adirondack chair, she tapped the notebook in her lap and said, "Tell me about this."

Her voice betrayed her and came out in a choked whisper.

He smiled at her as if he understood. "Why? Are you suddenly converted to our cause? Sort of a Stockholm syndrome kind of thing?"

"You mean, where the prisoner falls in love with her captor?"

"Yeah." He smiled even wider. The jerk.

"Get real. The day I fall in love with you will be a cold day in the bayou. And, no, I am not converted to your cause. I don't even know what your cause is. But at least you're finally admitting that I'm a captive here."

"I had nothing to do—"

She waved a hand dismissively. "Enough with the excuses. Tell me about your research," she said, patting the notebook.

"In a way, I've been studying the bayou since I was a three-year-old toddling after Luc. He protected me and my younger brother Remy from our father most of the time, taking the majority of the lickings. The way he protected us was to take us down to the bayou for what he called a campout. It was his way of alleviating our fears."

"My childhood wasn't so hot, either," she confessed.

He raised his eyebrows skeptically.

"But I never became a bayou scientist as a result."

He shrugged. "From an early age I loved the bayou, but I recognized that some things were wrong. The biggest wake-up call came when my dad sold the family land, poor as it was, to an oil company. Almost immediately, the landscape changed. We could no longer drink the water. They dug canals. Pipes burst. Hell, our rusted-out trailer soon sat in a foot of water." He shrugged again. "But that was only one nail in the coffin. The biggest culprit by far is the levees."

"The levees?" She frowned with confusion. "Levees prevent massive flooding. Levees are a good thing, aren't they?"

"Not in Southern Louisiana. The annual flooding of the Mississippi over thousands of years is what put the rich alluvial deposits here that make up the bayous. The levees have straitjacketed that process. Taming the river has sparked a chain reaction of devastating proportions. Now mud deposited by flooding, which would normally have settled into swamps of Atchafalaya or Barataria Bay, is just carried out to the Gulf. Do you know that we are losing land the size of a football field every twenty minutes or so? In a year's time, we lose a landmass equal to Manhattan."

"No way!"

"Absolutely."

"Why isn't anybody doing anything about it?"

He laughed.

"Okay, I get it. That's what you've been trying to do as a lobbyist and getting knocked on your patoot at every turn."

"Yep."

"How can you just give up?"

He shrugged as color filled his face.

She realized something then. "You're not giving up, are you?"

"Of course not. How can I?" He looked at her and said, "Maybe I'm being overly pessimistic. There was a commission formed a few years ago and it came up with a proposal called 'Coast 2050: Toward a Sustainable Louisiana.' It's a coalition of eleven state and federal agencies that are going to try to rebuild the wetlands, but it would cost a whopping fourteen billion dollars."

"What will *you* do?"

"I'm not sure yet. That's why I came down the bayou, to think and regroup. I'll never give up, though. I'm kind of offended that you thought I would. That would be like knowing a family member is dying and doing nothing about it."

Just then, something happened that surprised them both. The radio announcer interrupted Toby Keith's "Whiskey Girl" and said, "We have a news bulletin regarding missing Trial TV analyst Valerie Breaux."

They looked at each other and froze.

René shoved away from the porch rail and went over to turn the volume up on the radio.

"Houma Realtor Simone Breaux, Valerie Breaux's mother, held a news conference today, along with her aunts, Congresswoman Inez Breaux, and herbal tea moguls Madeline and Margo Breaux, and her grandmother, oil lobbyist Dixie Breaux, along with FBI agents and local law enforcement officials, declaring Valerie Breaux a missing person."

Well, at least, they know I'm missing. And care.

"Oh, shit!" René said.

The FBI agent spoke up on the radio. "Ms. Breaux is officially missing under suspicious circumstances. Her car was discovered at the airport with her handbag and all her luggage. However, there has been no ransom note or other indication of a kidnapping. Not yet."

How about two days without contact? How about any woman leaving without her purse, you idiots?

"Oh, shit!" René said again.

"Please let my darling daughter come home," Simone Breaux said tearfully.

Darling daughter? That's a laugh. Her mother, and all the other relatives, would find a way to profit from this disaster.

"This is a friggin' nightmare!" René shouted.

She started to tell him that she had told him so, but decided he already knew that.

"Trial TV president, Amos Goodman, announced today that they are offering a hundred thousand dollar reward for information on Ms. Breaux's whereabouts that leads to her return."

"Now that is interesting," Valerie said. Mr. Goodman must have found out about her firing. The fact that he'd put up a reward must mean he wanted her back. She smiled with self-satisfaction. Some small-dick producer must be squirming big-time about now.

"But wait a minute, we have some breaking news here," the radio announcer continued. "The environmental organization Bayou Unite has just announced that Ms. Breaux is safe and in hiding as she prepares a TV documentary that will crack this state wide open once it airs.

Here is Joe Bob Doucet, a spokesman for that organization."

"I am going to kill him," René said.

"That's two of us," she agreed.

"Bayou Unite is proud to announce that Valerie Breaux, famous Houma lawyer and successful Trial TV analyst, will be doing a documentary about the destruction of the Southern Louisiana ecosystem."

"What!?" she screeched.

René just shook his head at the nerve of his good buddy.

"This documentary will be a wake-up call to all Americans," J.B. continued, "and a warning to oil companies, developers, and sport fishermen that their free ride is over. Further questions should be directed to our company headquarters in Baton Rouge."

"They have company headquarters in Baton Rouge?" she asked René.

"My garage," he said.

"You told me this was your only home."

"I lied."

She made a low growling sound of outrage—outrage at him and the nutcases who had kidnapped her, then used her for their own publicity purposes, the Trial TV bigwigs who would also make hay out of this debacle, and her mother and other relatives who no doubt saw dollar signs waving in the wind. Not one person worried about her safety or what she wanted.

Then another amazing thing happened.

Brrrrr-ing. A phone rang.

Inside the cabin it could clearly be heard.

She and René locked glances and simultaneously asked, voices shrill with surprise, "We have a phone?"

They both dove for the screen door.

A lady's purse: mirror to her soul . . .

Tante Lulu's pocketbook was ringing like crazy.

René was thoroughly disappointed in himself. They'd had a phone all along, and he hadn't even known it. He should have guessed Tante Lulu wouldn't stay here without some means of communicating with the outside world.

Val was leaning over, about to lunge for the purse, which he couldn't allow to happen. Not till they'd had a chance to decide who she would contact and what she would say. So he tackled her from behind, landing them both on the floor, barely having time to register how much that hurt, before wrestling her for the bag. In the course of their tussle, the phone stopped, and so did René.

He was staring, wide-eyed, at Val's breasts, which had come loose from her tube top. *Holy crawfish! Son of a gun! Lordy, Lordy! It's Christmas in friggin' July! Merry Christmas to me!* Turns out Valerie Breaux had two of the sweetest breasts he'd ever seen—full and uplifted and pink-tipped. Needless to say, he was imprinting them on his brain forever.

"You jerk!" she said, shoving him off her and pulling up her top.

"It was your fault for not handing over the purse."

"I want that damn phone." She advanced on him, claws raised.

He held the purse behind his back, and, man, was it heavy! What did his aunt carry in this thing—bricks? "Not yet. We have to talk first."

"I am all talked out. Listen, big boy, you might have had a chance up till now, because you hadn't actually been involved in my kidnapping. But from this moment forward, denying me that phone makes you an accessory to a felony."

Several things happened at once then. Val got up close and personal to his body as he tried to hold the phone out of reach; it rang again; toilet flushed; and water ran in the bathroom. Then Tante Lulu came out and exclaimed, "Oops!" as if she was hearing the phone for the first time.

"Oops? That's all you can say?" Val snarled at his aunt.

"Tante Lulu, you should have told us you had a phone." René chastised her with a little more finesse. The phone stopped ringing. The rain had stopped, too, which meant the heat would be rising again.

"What? I'm almos' eighty years old. I could have a heart attack any minute and fall over deader 'n a June bug. Ya thought I wouldn't want a phone to call Remy to take me to a hospital or morgue or somethin'? Jeesh! Talk about!"

"You are an accessory to a felony, too," Val told her. "I don't care if you're a hundred years old, you old biddy. You are going to the slammer."

Tante Lulu cocked her head to the side and seemed to be thinking on Val's threat. "Hmmm. Do you think one of those lifers will make me her bitch?" She shivered then, whether with fear or enthusiasm, it was hard to tell.

Val held out her hand to René for the phone.

Not a chance!

Instead he set Tante Lulu's bag on the table and began to empty it, item by item. A wallet that weighed about five pounds, stuffed to overflowing with cash, credit cards, and coupons. Several little Baggies that probably contained medicinal herbs for her *traiteur* practice; either that, or his aunt was smoking weed. Tissues. A see-through makeup case. Condoms, which made Val blush. KY Jelly, which made him blush. A blow-dryer. A box of Blonde Bomb hair dye. Three Richard Simmons CDs. Six parking and one speeding ticket, all overdue. A romance novel entitled *The Very Virile Viking*. A bag of rice and three Snickers bars. A bottle of My Sin perfume. A miniature vibrator, which he hoped was for some muscle problem. A *Star* magazine with a banner reading, "Headless Elvis Spotted in Bayou Swamp, Blue Suede Shoes Gave Him Away." An address book. A calendar. A palm-sized statue of St. Jude. A pair of shocking pink, velvet handcuffs, for chrissake. A bottle of Avon Skin-So-Soft bath oil, which was often used by hunters and fishermen as a mosquito repellant. And, finally, at the bottom, his phone.

He had to ask, "Tante Lulu, what are you doing with condoms, KY Jelly, and a vibrator?" He refused to mention the handcuffs.

"Took 'em away from Tee-John las' time he was at my house," she answered matter-of-factly. "Found 'em in his book bag."

Tee-John was his sixteen-year-old half brother and a wilder rascal there never was. Not even he and his two brothers could beat the boy with his antics at that age.

"You people are all nuts," Val opined.

"Join the club," he said.

"Doan tell me ya thought they was for me," Tante Lulu said, making *tsk*ing sounds at the two of them. "I din't even know that thingamajig was a vibrator. Looks like red lips to me. How do ya use that thing?" The last question she addressed to Val, who looked as if her flushed face might explode.

"Yeah, Val, how *do* you use that thingamajig?" he asked, batting his eyelashes with innocence.

"You stick it where the sun doesn't shine," she replied.

"Where is that?" Tante Lulu wanted to know.

Val very succinctly said, "Aaarrgh!"

René flipped open his phone and checked the queue. "Twenty-seven messages!" Talk about vibrations! His phone must have been set to vibrate underneath all the clutter in her handbag.

He was about to put the phone to his ear when Val said, "I want to hear the messages, too. They probably concern me."

He tapped the switch for speaker phone.

The first one was from Luc. "René, what the hell is going on? Remy was just here, and he told me that Tante Lulu said you kidnapped Valerie Breaux. Is this another one of your sexual fantasy weekend thingees? . . ."

René's jaw dropped open with shock. "I never engaged in a sexual fantasy weekend in all my life," he protested to a frowning Val and Tante Lulu.

". . . Like that time you and Celie LaBelle played cowboy and saloon girl for one whole weekend in that French Quarter motel? . . ."

I am going to kill my brother. "Except for that one

time," he told Val and Tante Lulu, who were frowning even more.

". . . Nah, I can't see you riding the ice princess. She always looked at you like you were soft stuff on the soles of her shoes . . ."

So he hadn't been the only one to notice Val's low opinion of him. It was Val's turn to be uncomfortable.

". . . Give me a call, little brother. I'm thinkin' you might need my legal advice. Oh, and Sylvie says to tell you to be nice to her cousin Valerie. I'm not precisely sure what she means by nice, but— Ouch! Why'd you pinch me, Sylvie?"

The next call was from Luc, too. "Holy shit, René! Those goofball friends of yours, J.B. and Maddie, were just here, babbling stuff about Val and a documentary and thong panties and your smoothness and Tante Lulu falling in love with Richard Simmons."

All of them blushed a little over that message.

Next up was J.B. himself. "Not to worry, René. We have all bases covered here. You do your job there, good buddy." In a lower voice, he added, "Did you get in her pants yet? I'm tellin' ya, smoothness is the key. When you lay on the LeDeux charm, you could get a nun to do the hula. Oops. Maddie's comin'." His message ended abruptly.

Val looked at him as if he were still soft stuff under the soles of her shoes—*surprise, surprise!* "You were going to try to seduce me into helping you?" she accused him.

"I . . . was . . . not. Never did I ever suggest or agree to such a thing." *The subject might have come up, though.*

"It wouldn't have worked anyhow, but I'll bet you thought I'd succumb when I told you I hadn't had sex in two years."

Oh, man! Did you have to say that? Don't you know that any Cajun man worth his salt has to rise to a challenge like that? And I do mean "rise."

"Two years?" Tante Lulu remarked. "Things mus' be mighty slow in the big city."

Val said something unladylike to his aunt.

His aunt just smiled sweetly, as if she didn't understand. "I had been thinkin' there was as much chance of you two hookin' up as gettin' cats to march in a parade, but now I ain't so sure."

Not in this lifetime, Auntie.

Remy called next. "You and Valerie Breaux alone together? Oh, that's right. Tante Lulu is there as a chaperon. Ha,ha,ha,ha,ha. Sorry. I'll call back later when I'm able to stop laughing."

René made a face at the phone.

The next caller was a surprise. "René, are you there?" It was Jack Reidell, his ex-boss from DC. "Just heard about the documentary. Great idea! Let's talk, my friend."

How could my life get so screwed up in such a short time?

"Hello. Is this the René LeDeux residence? This is Simone Breaux. Mr. LeDeux, do you know where my daughter is? If so, I recommend you call me immediately. If you don't, I will assume you are involved somehow in her disappearance and will take the appropriate legal actions. I know the police chief personally, and . . ."

So do I. And he's Cajun, Ms. Snooty. René fast-forwarded to the next call.

"She sounds just like you, Valerie," Tante Lulu observed.

Val glared at René's aunt as if she'd just said she resembled Attila the Hun.

"Or maybe not," Tante Lulu conceded, smiling sweetly again.

There were three requests from news media—the *Houma Courier*, the *New Orleans Times-Picayune* and the local TV station. They all wanted to interview him about the kidnapping and the documentary.

When gators fly!

Even his father had called, and Valcour LeDeux hardly ever contacted him. "René, you are in a heap of trouble if yer plannin' on stirring up those tree-hugger pals of yours. I'm warnin' ya, son. My friends at Cypress Oil are not gonna stand fer yer shenanigans again. Best you and that Breaux bitch watch yer backs."

You never change, do you, old man? If you could, you'd probably pull off your belt and try to beat me into compliance. Well, not anymore!

"Nice guy, your father," Val commented.

"Yeah, real nice," he agreed with equal sarcasm.

"Nice, huh? He's a bastard and allus has been," Tante Lulu said. She and his father were enemies from way back.

On and on the phone messages went till René just erased them all. The bottom line was he was involved in this fiasco now, even if he didn't want to be.

"I could use a drink," Val said, which pretty much reflected his own sentiments. "Is there any booze in this cabin?"

Tante Lulu's face lit up. "How 'bout dandelion wine?"

"Perfect," Val said.

Two hours later, they all sat at the kitchen/card table,

which Tante Lulu had covered with a lace tablecloth from his hope chest. The red beans and rice, along with the broiled trout and crappies he'd caught this morning, had all been consumed. Mosquitoes, out in full force due to the earlier rain, did kamikaze dives against the screens, but none of them cared.

All three of them were crocked.

And Val was back to wearing just her tube top, sans shirt.

And she was no longer looking at him as if he were soft stuff under her feet; instead, she kept licking her lips and staring at him as if he were covered with soft whipped cream that she wanted to lick off.

A bad idea, that.

Says who? his own brain countered.

This woman is going to be out of here soon enough. Why give her more ammunition to use against me?

Maybe I could charm her.

He was laughing inside his head now, at his own idiocy.

She is under the influence, just like that other time. No way would I take advantage of her.

Maybe I could sober her up a bit first. Not too much, just a little.

More mental laughter.

It would be a mistake. Me and Val are like oil and water, like pigs in a parlor, like the princess and the farmer, like . . .

Enough already! You are so hopeless, the voice in his head said. This time, he was pretty sure it was St. Jude and not his conscience, although they might be the same thing. *Face it, boy, you are more like a match to kindling.*

But he'd already called Remy, told him to fly his copter in tomorrow morning and get Val. Tante Lulu would leave, too. And then he'd be alone.

There is always tonight.

That was the wine speaking in his head. He knew that. But, frankly, he didn't give a damn.

On the other hand, he did give a damn. He was not going to get intimate with Valerie Breaux; that would be comparable to skipping through a mine field. It would hurt him and the whole bayou environmental cause. He needed to be the one to take the high road here. He had to be the chivalrous knight who forsakes the fair maiden for a greater cause.

How do I come up with this crap? I just wanna save my sorry ass.

With that decision made, he slammed his glass down on the card table, which caused Val and Tante Lulu to jerk upright with surprise, and said, "Good night."

Except he knew without a doubt it was not going to be a good night for him. *Chivalry sucks,* he decided, slamming the screen door behind him.

"What's wrong with him?" he heard Val ask Tante Lulu.

His aunt, bless her meddling heart, answered, "I 'spect it's the thunderbolt, honey."

"I didn't hear any thunderbolts," Val said, her voice a little slurred.

"Ah, but thass the best part. You only feel 'em."

Chapter 6

Sleepless in the bayou . . .

Two hours later René's wine buzz had worn off, but buzzing surrounded him nonetheless.

The mosquitoes, which abounded here in the swampland under any circumstances, were out in triple force after that soaking they'd had earlier. Inside his mosquito net tent on the porch, he lay sleepless on his sleeping bag, able to see by the light of the full moon the masses of the golf ball-size insects hanging onto the fabric.

It had taken him a long time to bank down his testosterone level. Thank God, he'd succeeded. Now that he was stone-cold sober, the implications of what he might have done with Val scared the crap out of him. He'd dodged a bullet big time.

But wait a minute.

The bullet—dressed in a white T-shirt of his that reached only midthigh—sashayed out onto the porch, down the steps, and headed toward the stream. *Mon Dieu!* Was she sleepwalking or what?

As quick as he could, he scrambled out of his net tent and called out to her, "Val! Wait a minute." But she was already dipping her bare feet in the stream, about to step in. "Are you crazy?" he yelled just as she hit the water.

She pulled off the T-shirt, then dunked herself under the thigh-high water and came up soaked all the way to the ponytail atop her head. She put the T-shirt back on, which molded to her wet body like a Frederick's of the Bayou piece of erotic lingerie.

"Did you say something?" she asked, reaching up to whisk back loose tendrils off her face. With that action, her breasts became more prominent and the indentation of her waist and flare of her hips were accentuated. With his excellent night vision, aided by the full moon, he took it all in. And his once-banked lust jump-started back to full-tilt boogie.

"Yes, I said something. You can't go traipsing out to the water in the middle of the night." *Especially looking like you do. Especially with me looking at you looking like you do.*

"Why not? It's blistering hot inside that cabin."

"Because you might bump into an alligator or a water moccasin." *Or me.*

"Oh."

"Oh? That's all you can say?" *Holy crawfish! I can practically see through that wet shirt.* "Are you still drunk?"

"No. Well, maybe a little."

More like a lot. Oh, great! Now I can't hit on her. Not that I would do that. Note to me: no hitting on Valerie Breaux. "A little bit drunk is like being a little bit pregnant," he muttered as he reached out a hand and helped her up the bank. Immediately, the mosquitoes started to attack.

"Oh my God! They're biting me all over, even with that Skin-So-Soft stuff of Tante Lulu's slathered all over me."

Why that slathering image turned him on, he had no idea. But it did. *Man, I am pitiful. Two weeks of celibacy will do that to a guy.* "Hurry. Get inside the mosquito netting."

They both ran for the steps. Unfortunately—or fortunately, considering his lust mode—Val thought he'd meant *his* mosquito netting, not the one where she slept with his aunt.

He stood outside the netting for only a bug-biting second before he scooted inside, too. It was a cramped space for the two of them.

"This is a bad idea, Val. A very bad idea." *But, man oh man, it sure feels like a good idea.*

"Why?" she asked, pulling his T-shirt over her head and using it to blot her hair and whisk over the itchy bites on her arms and tummy.

He stood glued to the spot.

Valerie Breaux was standing before him, bare-assed naked. Well, bare-breasted naked, considering the frontal view he was getting. And, yeah, he was viewing it, all right. Full breasts. Small waist. Long legs. And that enticing scrap of tiny fabric in between. *Mercy, mercy, mercy!*

"Will you dry my back?" She handed him his T-shirt and turned around.

You would think he would be disappointed to get only the back view now, but hot damn, Val had the sweetest upside-down-heart-shaped ass in the world.

"No," he said as emphatically as he could.

"Huh?" She started to turn around.

"No, no, no. Do not turn around again. Oh, jeez! Oh, hell! Okay, I'll dry your damn back." With those words of surrender, he began to dry her off with the T-shirt, but only as far as her waist. And he wasn't looking any lower, either. In fact, he threw the shirt down and faced away from her, giving her time to get decent.

"You are acting really weird."

"No, Val, weird is when a woman who hates me shucks down to practically nothing. That's really weird." He still refused to look at her.

"You're afraid of me," she accused.

Great! Now we're going to play "I dare you." He heard a rustling sound and assumed she was pulling the shirt back on. "Damn straight I am." He turned then and his eyes about bugged out. Val was lying on his sleeping bag, propped up on her elbows, still 99 4/10-percent pure naked. He couldn't have spoken then if he'd wanted. He put a hand to his mouth to make sure he wasn't panting or drooling. *I am in male fantasy heaven. So why do I feel like hell?*

"Why? You weren't afraid of me before."

What time before? Oh, that. "I was fifteen freakin' years old then. Now I know what could happen . . . all the repercussions." *Like coitus tooquickitus. Like lawsuititus. Like morningafteritus.* He tried but couldn't help staring at her. She was not super skinny, which seemed to be the trend for women today. Instead she was round in all the right places. *If I didn't know it before, I do now—I am a man who favors round.*

"I would be better this time."

Whoa, whoa, whoa! Every hair on his body was on an all-points red alert. "I beg your pardon."

She put both palms to her face for a second as if she were embarrassed . . . finally. "Actually, René, I don't recall much about that night, except that I threw up on you afterward."

She doesn't recall . . . does that mean? . . . Thank you, Jesus! He barely restrained himself from doing a little Snoopy victory dance in the cramped space.

"You might not have realized it but that was my first time . . ."

You might not have realized it, but it wasn't your first time

". . . and I don't even remember the details."

I repeat: Thank you, Jesus!

"I must have been awful, though, because you never called me or tried to see me again."

All these years I worried about what a bad performance I put on when she never even remembered it. Should I tell her? Yeah. Will I tell her? Nah. "Don't lay the blame on me. I never tried to see you because you avoided me after that night."

"I was afraid you were going to tell everyone how . . . uh, inept I was."

And I was afraid you were going to tell everyone how inept I was. "That's old history, Val," he said magnanimously. Meanwhile René was giving himself a mental high five.

"You don't strike me as the type of guy who stands around twiddling his thumbs when a reasonably attractive woman does everything but shout, 'Come and get me.' "

"Number one, I can't believe I am standing here carrying on a conversation with a mostly naked woman."

"So, take your pants off."

Un-be-freakin'-liev-able! "Val!" he said, sounding prissier than she ever had. "I am not taking my pants off." *I hope.* "Number two, 'reasonably attractive' doesn't begin to describe just how hot you are."

She smiled. "Really? No one has ever called me hot before. Thank you. Have I told you that I haven't had sex in two years?"

He groaned at the reminder. There wasn't a guy in the world who wouldn't consider that a challenge. "Number three, I am not standing around twiddling my thumbs." *Although there are a few body parts I wouldn't mind twiddling on you.*

"Are we really going to discuss this to death, René?"

"No, we aren't. You are going to get up, put the shirt back on, and go back to bed with Tante Lulu. Tomorrow you will wake up and thank the stars that you hadn't made the biggest mistake of your life." *I oughta get a medal for this.*

"Your aunt is snoring like a chain saw in there. Must be all the wine she drank. I'll never be able to sleep."

"Well, you can't sleep here." *Although I would really, really, really like you to sleep here.*

She smiled again, and he knew it wasn't sleep she had in mind. That made two of them.

"Listen, if you're thinking I'm an acceptable bed partner just because you've discovered I have a few college credits, forget about it."

"Well, yeah. There is that."

Snoots 'r' Us. At least you're honest about it. "I'm no more respectable than I was last week. I am a low-down, crude Cajun."

"I hope so," she said with another smile.

She is pushing my buttons today, big-time. If she keeps it up, I won't be able to resist. "So you're slumming?" *Like I really care!*

"I wouldn't use that word. Look, I'm going to be gone tomorrow. I haven't had sex in two years. You're suddenly not as repulsive as you've been in the past."

You are a piece of work, Ms. Breaux. "Should I be flattered or insulted?" he asked. She didn't even know or care enough to toss him a few scraps of false compliments, like "You are so irresistible, I've got to have you."

She shrugged, which really did interesting things to her breasts. "Guys do it all the time."

"Not me," he lied. In truth, he had had a few one-night stands over the years. At the skeptical arch of her eyebrows, he added, "Not anymore."

"Grown up, have you?"

"Yes, I have."

"Okay, how about a little cuddling then?"

He laughed. "You've gotta be kidding. I'm thirty-five years old. I do not cuddle with naked women." *I'd like to give it a shot, though. No, I wouldn't. Yes, I would. Hey, Jude, where are you?*

As silver is tried by the fire and gold by the hearth, thus the Lord trieth your heart . . . and libido, he heard in his head.

Is that from the Bible? he asked.

Dost thou honestly believe the word libido *is in the Bible?*

He was going freakin' nuts.

"What *do* you do with naked women?" Val inquired.

He could have wept then at the sheer naivete of her

question. With a sigh of surrender, he tossed the T-shirt at her. She cocked her head to the side, clearly surprised and a little embarrassed at what she presumed was a final rebuff.

"Just put the damn T-shirt on, and then, don't move."

"Why?"

"Because we're going to cuddle, dammit . . . sort of."

"Sort of?" She sat up and pulled the shirt on over her head, emerging with a grin on her face. "Is that a Cajun thing? Cuddling, Cajun style?"

"No, *chére*. Cuddling *my* style."

Start your engine, honey, we're off to the races . . .

What was she thinking?

She wasn't thinking was the answer, and for once in her life, it felt good.

Valerie had never acted so brazen, ever. And she wasn't drunk, or even slightly drunk, either. She was just so tired of doing the right thing. A childhood of conforming to her mother's view of what good girls did and did not do. An adulthood of following all the rules on her path to success. Image, image, image.

Well, enough!

For once Valerie wanted to act impulsively. Throw caution to the wind. Do what felt good. Truth to tell, she'd been attracted to René for a long time, despite how she'd tried to convince herself otherwise. What she'd hated was that he didn't reciprocate her feelings.

But now she was pretty sure he wanted her.

It had been two long years.

She was ready . . . more than ready.

Her motor was running.

It was only one night, after all.

Let the good times roll, as the Cajuns were wont to say.

But oh my God! What was that dangling from René's fingertips as he returned from the cabin? It was shocking pink and it sure as heck wasn't a condom.

He came back inside the net tent and twirled the velvet handcuff around a raised forefinger. Then he flashed her a wicked grin.

"I thought you went for condoms," she choked out.

"No need for condoms. We aren't going to have sex, exactly."

He knelt down beside her and secured a cuff around her wrist.

"What does that mean, *exactly*? Is this a Bill Clinton kind of terminology?"

He laughed. "You could say that. Are you game?"

"For what?"

"Near-sex?"

She laughed then, too. "*Is* this a game?" She was withholding her other wrist from the handcuff.

"For sure."

"Do you play this game often?"

"Never played before."

"You are such a liar."

He made a sign of the cross over his heart. "Never had the inclination or the need before. But you give me ideas, sweetheart."

Oooh, I like the sound of that. If he's thinking what I'm thinking . . . "What kind of ideas?"

"*Tsk-tsk-tsk.* Telling you would spoil the fun."

While she'd been talking, René had somehow managed to wrap the handcuffs around a porch post and back, clicking them onto her other wrist. She was still lying down, but now her arms were above her head. He rearranged the netting so there were no gaps at the floor.

He must have noticed the sudden fear in her eyes because he kissed her softly on the cheek and said, "Don't worry. I'll release you the instant you ask me to."

"Why did you tell me to put the shirt back on if you had these perverted games in mind?"

"Who says they're perverted?"

"It seems a little . . . um, childish."

"Hah! You are about to find out how the big boys play."

He lay down beside her then, propped up on his left side, on an elbow. Looking at her, he smiled slowly. "Are you as excited as I am?"

"No one could be as excited as I am," she admitted.

"Good."

He cupped her chin with his right hand and rasped a thumb over her lips. Back and forth. Several times.

"How do you feel about deep, wet kisses?" His voice was husky now, which made Valerie feel a bit less embarrassed about her brazen move on him and her ensuing overexcitement. Clearly, he was as turned on as she was.

"I'm not sure. Maybe I need a sample."

He chuckled and pressed his lips to hers. Softly at first—a gentle brushing back and forth as he sought the perfect fit. When he found the right alignment, he deepened the kiss.

"Open," he murmured against her mouth.

She did. And, oh my gracious, just that one-word request made her melt. And the kiss became something altogether different. Because her hands were restrained and could not touch him . . . because he touched her only lightly at the chin . . . all of her attention was focused on the kiss. For what seemed like forever, he caressed her with his mouth, he nibbled and nipped with his teeth, he licked and laved with his tongue until finally he plunged inside her mouth. By then, she was moaning for just that, and more.

He moaned, too. She could swear he did. And that made her melt even more.

When he raised his head after a really long time and gazed down at her, she saw that his lips were as swollen as hers, and his eyes were half-lidded with arousal. He leaned down and pressed his mouth against her ear, whispering, "I love kissing you." His breath against the sensitive whorls of her ears, as well as his words, were intensely erotic. Then he dipped the tip of his wet tongue into her ear, and she arched her hips off the floor in reaction. There appeared to be an invisible thread connecting her inner ear to her breasts and that center of her female folds. *Oh . . . my . . . goodness! Oh . . . my . . . goodness!* She wasn't sure if she moaned those words in her head or aloud.

"Uh-uh-uh," René cautioned, pressing a hand against her belly, pushing her back down. He was orchestrating this sex game, play by play. No coconducting.

"What do you want me to do now?" he asked.

"Touch me," she said without hesitation.

He smiled. "Where?"

"Everywhere."

"Oh, baby! Right answer." And he proceeded to do just that. Whisking his hand over her T-shirt, he traced a path over her breast, the curve of her waist, her flat stomach, the outside of her leg all the way to the ankle, then back up the other side. Carefully he avoided touching her where she most wanted to be touched.

"Lift my shirt," she said.

"Not yet."

"Release my hands, then. I want to touch you."

He made a low sound in his throat that was a combination laugh and gurgle. "Not yet."

"Why?"

"I'll explain later."

"There's an explanation for all this?"

"Mais, oui!"

He got up off his elbow, knelt astride her body, then sat back on his haunches. His eyes held hers, gauging her reactions as he began to fondle her breasts through the thin cotton of her shirt. He took her breasts in his large hands, kneading and shaping them, the hard points of her nipples pressing into his palms. He pinched and twisted the nipples, lightly, till they grew and ached.

Hot liquid pooled between her legs, which were held immobile by his weight. She could swear an actual throbbing began there; she became certain of that fact when he leaned forward and took one breast into his mouth, cloth and all, and suckled at her, the whole time playing with the other breast. She was feeling too many sensations all at once. The delicious torment of her breasts. His comfortable weight on her belly. The handcuffs. The white heat that tensed her inner muscles. With each rhythmic pull on her nipples, a throb beat out its own erotic response down below.

She was whimpering her pleasure by the time he switched breasts and continued teasing her, unmercifully. The only thing that saved her from weeping in utter humiliation was his raw sounds of masculine excitement as he ministered to her . . . not quite growls of triumph, not quite groans of surrender.

The worst part—or maybe the best, her mind beyond logical deduction at this point—was that she was prevented from showing the extent of her excitement. She couldn't arch off the floor, and she was prevented from taking control of this love play, which would be her norm. Not that anything about this was normal for her.

But wait, wait, wait. He was moving lower, over her shirt, pressing his cheeks to and fro over her belly, nuzzling her navel. Then he went even lower, past her groin area—*darn it!*—to her inner thighs where he began licking her, of all things. His fingertips tickled the back of her knees and then the soles of her feet. She didn't know whether to giggle or sigh with ecstasy. She settled for the latter.

Suddenly he sat up on his knees and looked at her. "How do you like cuddling so far, *chére*?"

She refused to answer.

"Speechless, eh? Ah, well, I have the cure for that." Swifter than she could say, "Whoo-ee," he inched her shirt up and over her head till it bunched at her bound wrists. She was fully exposed to him now, except for her thong.

Still kneeling between her legs, he studied her in a way that could only be described as hungry. His fists clenched as he tried to control himself, but Val could see the surrender in his hot eyes and parted lips. And she saw physical evidence of his arousal in the tenting of his shorts. Very physical evidence! She had never considered herself a sensual woman before, but she did now.

"You are so fucking sweet," he said in a voice husky with desire.

It was a crude thing to say, but Valerie was oddly flattered.

He kissed her, passionately. He caressed her now bare breasts to the point where she was mindless with need. "Please, please, please," she begged him.

"Shhhhh," he whispered and wet one nipple, then drew her deeply inside his mouth, where he alternately suckled then licked her with the tip of his tongue.

Finally, just from his making love to her breasts, she felt her inner muscles begin to spasm. She was going to come, just from foreplay. He would think she was really pathetic, so desperate after two years of celibacy that little attention would bring her to climax. She stiffened her body and fought the scorching waves that were already undulating out of her.

"Relax, sweetheart. Relax."

"Easy for you to say," she grumbled.

"Hah! Every time you twitch, I double twitch."

She had to smile at that description. "Okay, release me now."

"No way."

"You've proven that you can make me lose control during the previews. Now, let's move onto the main event."

"If you mean what I think you do about the main

event, forget about it. We are not going to have carnal knowledge of each other."

"It sure as hell feels like carnal knowledge."

"Naw. That was just semicarnal. But as for the main event, I can't do that, not tonight, but I do have another short feature in store for you."

She narrowed her eyes at him, then yelped with surprise when he lay down beside her again, rolled her onto her side, wrapped an arm around her waist, then rolled the two of them back so that he lay under her, both of them facing upward. He made a few adjustments, raising her arms higher, causing her breasts to arch. His erection nestled between her buttocks and her female folds. She could swear she felt the rapid beat of his heart against her back.

"This is crazy."

"You think so?" he said against her ear. *Ear sex again? Lordy, Lordy!* "Move your legs, sweetheart," he told her and helped her to spread them wide, bent at the knees, with her feet firmly planted on either side of his thighs.

Only then, when she was fully exposed, except for her thong, did he touch her there. She almost swooned. Immediately the heel of his palm ground against her most vulnerable part, causing it to ache in a most delicious way. And then . . . and then . . . and THEN, his expert fingers plied their arts in the most incredible, sexual way just where she wanted, just the way she needed. How did he know all that? Why didn't all men know that?

Even though his left hand pressed against her tummy, she was able to arch up, up, up when her orgasm hit her in nerve-splintering waves. The whole time, he whispered wicked, graphic things in her ears, all encouraging her to let loose. Which she did. And she couldn't even be embarrassed about that. Not even her scream of ecstasy in the end, which could have awakened the dead, or Tante Lulu, which it thankfully did not.

As her racing heart returned to normal and drowsiness overcame her, she felt her restraints come loose and René cuddled her in his arms, crooning soft words to soothe her. She felt his erection pressing against her side, and she murmured, "You didn't come yet."

"Next time, *chére*. Next time, guaranteed."

"But it's not fair . . . that I got all the pleasure."

"That's where you're wrong. I got pleasure, too. It was the best—"

"Puh-leeze," she interrupted. "Don't try to tell me it was the best sex you ever had. I'm not buyin' that line."

"*Tsk-tsk-tsk!*" He chuckled and nipped her bottom lip with his teeth. "It was the best *near-sex* I ever had."

She couldn't argue with that.

Chapter 7

Two years . . . and counting

He couldn't avoid Val any longer.

It was probably delusional of him, but he wanted to remember last night as a good experience. If Val was like most women, she would pull a Jekyll-and-Hyde on him now and turn the whole thing into one of those morning-after regrets. *It's not you, René. It's me. Yada, yada, yada.*

Although it was barely 9 A.M., Remy had just landed his copter in the bayou on its water buoys, thus scaring the bejesus out of every animal within five miles. Tante Lulu was inside the cabin doing some last-minute packing; she was probably also making him meals for the next few days, unable to believe he could cope on his own. Val was inside the cabin, too, doing God only knew what. For sure, she was avoiding him, just as he was her.

They had to talk before she left. But he refused to ask her what she was going to do about the "kidnapping" once she was back in Houma. And he sure as hell didn't want to discuss their near-sex episode. *Maybe I should just shake her hand and say, "Thanks for a great time, sugar. See ya."* Oh, yeah, that would go over great. What I'd really like to say is, "Wow! You and I made magic, Val. I would really like to get to know you better. And I don't just mean sex. Can I call you sometime?" Oh, yeah, that would go over great, too. She would think I just wanted another chance to pick up where we left off. I do, but . . . aaarrgh!

Remy crawled out of the copter followed by their half-brother, sixteen-year-old Tee-John, who'd presumably come along for the ride. Both of them worked to tie the vehicle's rigging to a tree stump. Then, grinning from ear to ear, they waded through the water toward him.

"Hey, René," Remy said, still grinning.

"Hey, René," Tee-John said, also continuing to grin.

"'Bout time you got here," he complained, which was a really ridiculous thing for him to say.

"I don't see any blood or bruises," Remy remarked as he came up on the bank. His boots and khaki pants were wet up to the knees.

He didn't bother to answer, recognizing the mischievous glint in his brother's eyes.

"I mean, I figure four days with you and Valerie 'Ice' Breaux together, she should have done some major damage to you by now. At the least you should have freezer burn on some important body parts," Remy explained, pretending to examine his body for frostbite.

"There is that mark on his neck," Tee-John pointed out, also coming up to stand in front of him. He wore only a tank top, swimming trunks, and athletic shoes sans socks. He probably considered himself some kind of Teenage Hunk of the Month. He probably was.

"I suppose it could be a bruise from her trying to strangle him to death," Remy said to Tee-John.

"Or it could be a hickey," Tee-John offered back.

"Or teeth marks," Remy observed. "Yep, that's what I think it is."

Uh-oh. Before he could catch himself, René slapped a hand to the suspicious spot, thus confirming his brothers' suspicions.

Laughing openly now, his brothers were slapping each other on the back with glee. At his expense.

"Did you run into a door, bro?" Tee-John asked then.

"No. Why?" *Sometimes I don't have the sense God gave a goose. I should know better than to encourage my brothers.*

"I could swear your lips are all puffylike."

"I'll give you *puffylike.*" René reached out an arm to punch his brother, but he feinted left, then right, and put some distance between them.

"You are in deep shit," Remy remarked then, just a mite serious, although his lips still twitched with mirth. "And I don't mean for fooling around with Val."

"Tell me about it." And he didn't mean that as encouragement for Remy to actually tell him something.

Tee-John walked past him, up the steps, and into the cabin. They could hear him teasing Tante Lulu, who loved the scamp. She would probably be feeding him before they left, figuring he might die of hunger if he didn't get any of her good Cajun food in his belly.

"J.B. and Maddie took their shrimp boat out to the Gulf for a few days of fishing," Remy told him, sitting down on the steps. "Luc ordered them to stay out of sight till you talked with them."

"Good."

"They think you walk on water, Bro."

"The last time I tried, I was three sheets to the wind and I got a bucket of water up my nose."

Remy grinned at him. "But, man, forget about your fan club. Everyone else in the world is gonna be on your tail. It's a good thing you're not coming back today."

René joined his brother on the porch and let his silence be a question.

"Val's mother is on the rampage. Threatening lawsuits. Claiming *her* daughter would never get involved with any of those wacky environmentalists or any of those wacky LeDeuxs."

The two brothers smiled at each other, not at all concerned about the LeDeux reputation. In fact, they'd both done plenty to fuel it over the years.

"Did she forget that her niece Sylvie is married to a LeDeux?" René asked Remy.

"Convenient memory lapse. Anyhow, she has riled up her clan of Breaux bitches and they in turn have riled some politicians and news media."

He shrugged. No big deal. He wasn't afraid of Simone Breaux or the politicians. Val, on the other hand . . .

"I don't think it's just legal action you have to fear," Remy said, as if reading his mind.

Like I didn't know that! "What else?"

"J.B. and Maddie mentioned a highfalutin documentary, which if it does any good, could affect some of their pocketbooks. People fight dirty when money is involved. You might be in danger."

He waved a hand dismissively. "Dad already called to issue one of his usual threats."

"Like?"

"He's gonna beat the crap out of me if I don't toe the line—*his* line that is. He's not big enough to do it himself anymore; so, he'll probably hire someone to do the dirty work."

Remy shook his head hopelessly. That about said it all when it came to their father. The bastard!

"Besides, there isn't going to be a documentary. It was all a fabrication J.B. and Maddie dreamed up in hopes of stirring the hornets' nest."

"They did that, for sure."

"You don't convince someone to do you a favor by kidnapping her. Talk about!" *Nor do you have near-sex with her and expect her not to be suspicious of your motives . . . even if it was her idea.* "I can't fault J.B. and Maddie, though. Their hearts are in the right place."

"Their hearts, and other innards, may very well be in prison by the time Val is done with them. What about Val, by the way? Luc stands ready, if you need him. What's she gonna say, or do, when she returns?"

"I don't have a clue. She's made lots of threats, but my gut instinct says . . . I don't know."

Just then, Tee-John came out with a catfish sandwich in one hand and a can of RC Cola in the other. Setting the soda on the porch rail, he took a bite of his sandwich, then said, "What is *that*?" Tee-John went down the porch steps and picked something up off the ground by the tent. It was pink but, oh my God, it was not a flower.

Flashing a "gotcha" smirk, Tee-John held it up high and asked, "Been playin' cops and robbers, have you, big brother?"

René felt his face heat up as he stomped down the steps and walked over to grab the freakin' handcuffs, which they must have forgotten last night. Tee-John danced away, still holding the cuffs out of reach. "Tee-John" was the Cajun diminutive for Little-John, which became a misnomer the more he grew; the boy was as tall as he was. That didn't mean he couldn't whup him good if he didn't behave himself.

"What is it?" Remy asked, coming up to stand by René.

"Handcuffs," René said. "I got 'em from Tante Lulu, who got them from guess who?" He looked pointedly at Tee-John.

"Tee-John!" Remy said with a laugh. "I'm surprised at you."

Hah! No one was surprised at anything Tee-John did.

Then Remy looked at him and grinned. "René! I'm surprised at you, too."

Yeah, right.

"They're not mine," Tee-John said.

"They's from Charmaine," Tante Lulu said, coming through the screen door, lugging a wheeled overnight case behind her that was bulging at the sides, as well as her humongous purse, which was also bulging at the sides. "She got them fer me as a souvenir from the Lucky Duck Motel."

The three of them just gaped at their aunt.

"It was jist the condoms 'n' Vaseline stuff and vibratin' lips that I got from Tee-John. Jeesh! Doesn't anyone ever listen to what I sez? What're those red lips fer anyways, Tee-John?"

"It's a cigarette holder," Tee-John said . . . with a straight face yet.

René and Remy stared, open-jawed, at their brother. You had to be impressed with a kid who could come up with such impromptu crap.

"Din't I tell you not to be smokin' those coffin nails?" Tante Lulu said, wagging a forefinger at Tee-John.

"I won't anymore." Tee-John ducked his head with exaggerated shame. The boy was a real piece of work.

Remy and Tee-John helped Tante Lulu carry her bags to the copter. Before he left, Tee-John stuffed the handcuffs in René's back pocket with a little pat on his ass for good measure.

Val came out then. And whoo-boy! This was the Val he used to know, not the one he'd gotten to know the night before. This was the model for the intimidating Ice Breaux. She wore the silver-gray business suit she'd arrived in with high heels. Her hair was brushed back and wetted down off her face into a knot at her neck. She wore a little bit of makeup, thanks no doubt to Tante Lulu. She looked good, but she looked as far removed from René LeDeux as caviar from crawfish. She was uptown Creole; he was low-down swamp Cajun. He'd forgotten that for a few blips the night before.

"René . . ."

"Val . . ." he started to say at the same time.

"You go first," she said.

"I'm sorry."

There was a sudden wounded look in her eyes at his words.

"Not about last night. I'm not sorry about that. I mean, I'm sorry about this whole mess. I know you don't believe me when I say I wasn't involved. Still, I probably could have gotten you back sooner." *Like the first day.*

"Yeah, I figured that." She studied him for a moment, then said, "I'm not sorry about last night, either. Oh, don't go getting all worried. I'm not going to latch onto you now and make you feel obligated to see me again."

I dodged a big one there. "I never thought that."

She waved his protests aside. "I suspect I owe you thanks for not taking things further."

Oh, no, we are going to discuss this thing to death. Just leave it be. When will women learn?

"But I'd rather just leave it be."

Surprise, surprise! "What are you going to do?"

She cocked her head to the side, wondering what he meant. He could have meant any number of things. Was she going back to Trial TV? Was she going to file charges against them? Was there a remote chance she might help them? Was she going to see him again, ever? Was she now planning on ending her two-year celibacy?

"I don't know," she said then. "I just don't know."

That's exactly what he had told Remy.

"At least my two-year bout of celibacy is over."

What? What? "Uh, I don't think so. I hate to break it to you, darlin', but last night did not end your celibacy. Next time is when your celibacy ends. Part A goes into part B, that's when celibacy ends." *I should cut off my tongue and feed it to that passing gator over there. Why don't I just give her a sex education lecture?*

"Is that a fact?" She put a fist on one hitched hip in challenge.

Practically a fact. "Definitely a fact." *Or maybe I should put a little Cajun lightning on it and eat it myself.*

Yep. Tabasco Tongue. I can't wait to hear what I say next. Talk about!

"*Next time,* huh? And what makes you think there's gonna be a next time. What makes you think I would let *you* be the one?"

"The thunderbolt." *I cannot freakin' believe I said that.*

Val laughed. "You've been hangin' around your aunt too long."

For sure. But he laughed, too. At himself.

"Anyhow . . . good-bye." She held out a hand for him to shake.

He looked at her hand. He looked up at her still kiss-swollen lips. He shook his head and grinned slowly. Then he yanked her forward and kissed her soundly on the lips. In the background, he could hear Tante Lulu telling Remy and Tee-John, "It's the thunderbolt. Bless his heart, he caint help hisself." When he was done with his world-class kiss—and, yes, it was world-class, if he did say so himself—he said against her ear, "That's the way we Cajuns say good-bye, *chére.* And remember, *next time,* guar-an-teed!" *They oughta pickle my tongue and put it in the Ripley's Believe It or Not museum.*

She didn't say anything, just stared at him, speechless. But not for long.

Val reached around him.

He thought she was going to smack him on the butt. But, nope, leave it to Val to get the last word in, so to speak. She pulled the pink handcuffs out of his back pocket and waved them in his face before stuffing them in the waistband of her skirt.

He arched his brows at her. "Souvenir?"

She laughed. "Evidence."

Welcome home, baby . . . not!

The copter landed at the far end of the private airport, but still a crowd awaited Val outside the small terminal as she prepared to disembark.

"You must be really popular," Tee-John, René's too-cute-to-live younger brother, remarked.

"Hardly," she answered. "It's just my mother and a few dozen of her closest friends. You know, politicians, police, oil execs, and sundry other people under her thumb."

"Betcha that Valcour is out there," Tante Lulu said. "Betcha he's gonna open his trap and say sumpin dumb. Betcha he'll try to give me the evil eye. Betcha I could smack him silly and not break a sweat. He's so thick with the oil people he smells like the back end of a diesel engine." She looked to Tee-John and added, "No offense meant ta you, sweetie. He may be yer daddy, but he and I go way back."

Tee-John squeezed Tante Lulu's shoulder. "I'm on your side."

The copter's passenger door was opened by an airport attendant and they all stood.

"Hey, Val, did you give René a hickey?" Tee-John threw that question at her out of the blue, then batted his sinfully long eyelashes at her with mock innocence.

"I refuse to answer that question on the grounds that it may be incriminating."

"Good answer, counselor," Remy said, smiling at her.

Remy was an extremely good-looking man, but on one side of his face only. Apparently he'd been injured in

Desert Storm. Funny how easy it was after the initial shock to overlook his disfigurement.

"Do I need to call Luc? They're not gonna arrest us, are they?" Remy asked. He was serious, although he didn't appear too concerned.

"Not unless you do something stupid. Like open your mouth." Before Remy had a chance to be offended by her brusque remark or in fact do something stupid, Valerie morphed into a role she knew how to play expertly. Back straight, lawyer nonexpression on her face, attack-mode ready.

Tante Lulu took in all the people and exclaimed, "I see the buzzards has come to feed."

How true!

"You kin allus stay at my cottage iffen ya doan wanna go home jist yet," Tante Lulu offered, surprising her. Then the old lady surprised her even more by giving her a warm hug. "Jist call me iffen ya feel the need."

Valerie couldn't say why, but the old bird's kindness touched her immensely. Walking away from the copter, Valerie headed directly toward the waiting crowd, instead of attempting to avoid them by going to the other side of the terminal.

"Shelley," she said, reaching out to shake hands with the local TV reporter. She and Shelly Thornton had attended Our Lady of the Bayou School together; she was married to Ronnie Eichenlaub, the station owner. "How are you? Let's do lunch."

Her warmth and invitation seemed to throw Shelley off guard, but only for a second. "Valerie, is it true that you were kidnapped? Can we step over to the side and conduct an interview?" She motioned toward her cameraman whose film was already rolling.

"Oh, not right now, hon. I feel so sweaty after being in the bayou without air-conditioning for four days." She blew upward at the wisps of hair on her forehead. Before Shelley had a chance to protest, she said, "How about tomorrow at one P.M.? Shall I come to the station?"

"Uh . . . yes . . . sure," Shelley said, pleased to be handed an interview opportunity.

"Hey, how about us?" It was a reporter from the Houma newspaper. The man next to him was holding up a copy of today's *Times Picayune* from New Orleans, where she assumed he was a reporter.

"Call me," she said to both of them. "I promise to tell all, but not today, boys. I am beat." *Well, I managed to sidestep the kidnapping question . . . for now. Let's see who's next. Uh-oh!*

Simone Breaux broke through the rope barrier and rushed forward, arms outstretched. Her mother was fifty-five, but could pass for forty-something with all her plastic surgery, the same sleek upswept hairdo she'd worn for twenty years, trim figure, which she worked hard to maintain—not Richard Simmons, but some private trainer who kept her on a veggie diet and a five thousand dollar walking machine—and a silk pantsuit that had probably cost more than René's cabin. The TV camera and newspaper photographers were taking it all in. Never miss a photo op, that was her mother's slogan.

"Darling, I've been so worried," her mother wailed just before she put a hand on each of her daughter's shoulders and gave her air kisses on either side of her face. How different from Tante Lulu's sincere expression of comfort.

Against her ear, her mother said, "Your suit is wrinkled, and you need more makeup." She actually sniffed her then and crinkled her nose, as if she could smell the bayou—or God forbid—sex on her. *Not that I actually had sex, as René had so aptly pointed out an hour ago. Just near-sex. Jeesh, my brain is melting in this heat.*

"Stand straight and let me do the talking," her mother said through her plastered-on smile.

"No way!" she said, stepping out of her mother's pseudo embrace.

"I've arranged a press conference in one of the lounges of the airport," her mother said, hastening to catch up with her. "We should present a united front. Your aunt Inez will give the opening introduction. Your aunts Madeline and Margo will be in the audience for support, and your grandmother Breaux, too."

Valerie stopped suddenly and looked at her mother. "Don't you want to know if I'm okay?"

"Huh? Of course."

"You haven't asked."

"Don't be pert with me, young lady."

"I'm thirty-five years old, Mother. Hardly a young lady."

"This is not the time or place for you to have a breakdown," her mother said in a hushed tone.

"When would be a good time?"

Her mother didn't answer. Instead her attention was diverted to the area near the terminal where the LeDeux gang had gone. Tante Lulu was talking animatedly to someone while she pointed at Val. Val headed that way. Hopefully her rental car was still in the parking lot.

"What is *he* doing here?" her mother asked, glaring at the latest addition to the LeDeux party.

Now that they were closer, Valerie recognized Lucien LeDeux, a well-known Houma lawyer. You'd never know it by his attire, though. He wore a red, green, and white Hawaiian shirt over black shorts with sandals.

"Hello, Auntie Simone," Luc said. Luc was only related to them by marriage, but he delighted in reminding her mother of the relationship.

Her mother growled and muttered something about "ambulance chaser."

Luc turned to Valerie then and winked. "Hey, Cuz. I hear the thunderbolt has struck." He glanced at her, then Tante Lulu, then back again.

"It did not," she protested. She hardly knew Luc, even though he was married to her cousin Sylvie, whom she hadn't seen in years. She recognized that Luc was just trying to needle them both. The fact that he expected her to turn her nose up the same as her mother rankled a bit.

"What thunderbolt?" her mother wanted to know.

"The love thunderbolt," Tante Lulu informed her. "Dontcha know nuthin'? Val and my René is prob'ly in love by now."

Valerie's mother bared her teeth at Tante Lulu, who just smiled innocently. "Over my dead body," Simone said. Then she looked pointedly at Valerie and said, "I'll see you at home." She spun on her heels and walked away.

"Is my rental car still in the lot?" she asked Remy.

Remy nodded. "Tee-John went to get it for you. He'll

be pulling up any minute now. He just got his driver's permit and any excuse to drive is—"

A black BMW pulled to a screeching stop just outside the chain-link fence. How he started the car without her keys, she didn't want to know. Country music blared from the radio through the open windows and sunroof. Shania Twain was bemoaning the fact that it only hurt when she breathed.

Yep. A perfect commentary on her life.

Chapter 8

Home not-so-sweet home

Val was back home in Houma.

Here in her bedroom in the historic minimansion, the walls seemed to crowd her. Her mother's family had lived here for 150 years or more. She wondered how she had managed to live here for eighteen or so years.

The room was decorated the same as it had been when she was a toddler, the same as it probably had been before the Civil War. Red and black Aubusson carpet on the floor, dark mahogany four-poster bed with heavy gold brocade bedspread matching the tasseled drapes that hung about the narrow floor-to-ceiling windows. Carved plaster moldings around the ceiling with an ornate center medallion. Priceless antique furniture passed through generations of Creole families, mostly in the federal style using native cypress stained to resemble the satinwoods so popular in the nineteenth century. On the walls were original signed Audubon prints of bayou birds and a massive oil painting of a Southern belle having her fortune told by a black mammy.

Formal and dark, that's how she would describe it.

Definitely not the warm, cozy room that a toddler would feel comfortable in. Not a teenager, either. And God forbid that she put a crayon mark on the museum-quality wallpaper or get a glass stain on the Hepplewhite nesting tables. Her eyes darted quickly to the closet, then away just as quickly, not wanting to be reminded of what happened when little girls were bad.

Hard to believe that only twenty-four hours had passed since she'd been deep in the bayou. Even harder to believe that she actually wished she were back there. She was drowning in all the distasteful memories this showcase of a room brought back to her, not to mention the crap awaiting her this day.

She had three appointments with the news media scheduled over the next few hours. But first, she had to face her mother, who wasn't speaking to her after their shouting match the night before. It hadn't been shouting per se; her mother had civilized shouting down to an art form. Also gathered below, ready to pounce, were her grandmother, Dixie Breaux, her aunts Madeline, Margo, and Inez Breaux, and the longtime family lawyer, Armand Cuvier. Her mother, it turned out, had drawn up a plan—a typed-up plan—of specific things Valerie was expected to do about her recent "kidnapping." It had infuriated her mother that she wouldn't even read the damn thing or fall in with her strategy for milking her recent adventure for all it was worth. She was talking money, jail time, political benefits, personal gain. In essence, according to her mother, Valerie had the wherewithal to bury the entire LeDeux clan and the bayou environmentalists along with them. Her mother had wanted to have the police and FBI present, but Valerie had put her foot down then. "No police. No FBI. If and when there are charges to be filed, I will contact authorities. No one else."

If that wasn't enough, she'd found several interesting messages on her answering machine.

Elton Davis, of the small penis, had called three times. Most of his messages were pretty much like the first. "Hey, babe! How ya doin'? You didn't really think I fired you, did you? Ha, ha, ha! I've got a great idea for you. Call me."

Hmmm. There must be something in it for dear old Elton. Either his tail was in the vice for firing her, or he had some sleazy idea that only she could do and thus make him look good.

Amos Goodman, head of Trial TV and boss of Elton Davis, had called, too. "You and I need to talk, Ms. Breaux. Call me when you can. I'd like to have a meeting, face to face."

Hmmm. She'd only met the head honcho on a few occasions the past three years, and then strictly in group settings, such as a company cocktail party. It must be important.

One of the cameramen she worked with a few years ago, Justin Dugas, had called, too. "Hey, Val, if the rumors are true that you're considering a bayou documentary, count me in. I do freelance work now, and I would love to tackle that job. I'm from Chauvin, in case you didn't know. My maw-maw and paw-paw were shrimp fishermen here before God was a baby. I'm part Houma Indian. Anyhow. Here's my number." Justin was a twenty-something young man who'd covered a notorious child slavery trial with her two years ago. He had black hair that hung down his back, an athlete's body from years of running track, and a real talent for videography and photography. In fact he'd won a Pulitzer for some photos he'd taken in Afghanistan two years ago.

Hmmm. She was intrigued that Justin called her . . . and that he believed she'd consider such a nonprofit, low-profile kind of project.

Missing from her phone queue were any calls at all from the LeDeuxs . . . in particular, René. She really had thought he would have called her to see how she'd fared. Or just to talk.

On the one hand, she wanted to discuss her out-of-character proposition and why he hadn't taken it to its natural conclusion—and what he thought of her now.

On the other hand, she was mortified by her behavior. She'd never been the aggressor in sex before, but she'd practically jumped René's bones without invitation. Maybe it was best just to drop it. Pretend it had never happened.

Furthermore, she thought his family would have tried to pressure her not to file charges.

Nothing. They were leaving it up to her.

She didn't know whether to be impressed or pissed. Whatever. Right now, she had to go face the big guns—her family—and after that, the lesser guns—the news media. She walked over to a free-standing mirror in an antique oval frame and checked herself over one last time: a tailored black silk blouse, open at the neck, its collar folded neatly over the lapels of a crisp white linen suit, great-grandmother Gisette's pearl drop earrings, black designer pumps, more than enough makeup to accommodate the cameras, and not a hair out of place to accommodate her mother. If nothing else, Valerie did professional woman to a tee.

She walked down the wide central staircase and through the double-wide corridor to the back veranda, not once glancing at her surroundings, not even the paintings of family members in ornate frames who watched her progress. This was the house that *Architectural Digest* had once declared "a masterpiece of Southern charm" and whose meticulous landscaping was deemed "an ode to antebellum Louisiana and its history" by *Southern Living* magazine just last year. That old cliche "a house is not a home" popped into her mind just then.

The Breaux posse was seated around a large, round, white wrought-iron table, along with their attorney. They were all fortifying themselves with mint juleps, a specialty of Ada Rose Johnson, their longtime housekeeper.

Ada Rose, whose plump body was stuffed into a traditional maid's uniform and orthopedic shoes, winked at her from behind the gang and raised a mint julep from the tray she was carrying as a silent question to her. Valerie shook her head. No liquor today. She wanted her brain clear and alert.

She noticed her mother giving her a once-over to see if her attire was appropriate. Since she said nothing, Valerie assumed she was presentable.

After saying hello to all the other ladies present, whom she'd already greeted the night before when they dropped by the house, she leaned down and gave the lawyer a kiss on the cheek. His snow-white hair, goatee, and mustache were precisely cut and groomed, as always. His white Palm Beach suit epitomized the Southern gentleman of old.

"How are you doing, Armand?"

"Jus' fine, darlin'. I heah ya'll had a mite of trouble."

"Just a mite," she said, and sat down in the empty chair next to him.

"What are you plannin' on doin' 'bout it?"

"Nothing," she said.

A communal gasp sounded from her family members.

"For now," she added.

Her mother narrowed her eyes at her. If they were alone, she probably would have slapped her face . . . or tried to. She was too big to shove in a closet.

Her aunts exchanged meaningful glances as if they expected no less of her. Growing up, she had always been the perfect one, but in recent years her mother claimed that she'd been yankee-ized, a sin in the South. It came from too much living up North.

"Precisely what did happen, m'dear?" Armand asked her.

"Environmentalists want to do a documentary on Southern Louisiana and the bayou. For some reason, they thought I would be a good person to do it."

"Which environmentalists?" her grandmother asked sharply. "René LeDeux?" Her grandmother had been a lobbyist for the oil companies for years till her retirement last year at the age of seventy-five. She still acted as a consultant for Cypress Oil. Dixie Breaux was not and never had been the poster girl for warm, cuddly grandma.

Valerie nodded. "Among others."

"You oughta sue his pants off. The nerve of those LeDeuxs. Scum, all of them!" It was Inez Breaux speaking now. Inez was a U.S. congresswoman and the mother of Valerie's cousin Sylvie, who'd embarrassed her mother mightily a few years back by marrying Lucien LeDeux. "That René had the nerve to come by my office last year and try to get me to vote against oil subsidies. *Pfff!*"

"Why you?" Aunt Madeline asked Valerie.

Precisely what I asked, though it sounds a bit offensive coming from you, Auntie. "I went to school with René. He knew that I was involved in television and assumed, incorrectly, that I would be the right person to do a documentary."

Her aunts Madeline and Margo owned a mail-order tea company, which had been on the opposite side of the courtroom from Lucien LeDeux on one occasion. He'd made them look foolish, to say the least. There was no love lost.

"Did he kidnap you?" Armand asked, point blank.

"Actually, René had nothing to do with my going to his place." *Oh, you owe me big-time for that one, René.* "It was all the idea of his friends Joe Bob and Maddie Doucet from the Shrimpers Association." *Well, that was a good job of evading the question.*

"Don't play games with us, Valerie," her mother said. "I am not buying this story of yours. You would not have left your luggage and handbag in a rental car at the airport. You would have called to let me know where you were going and for how long. And, by the way, when were you going to let me know you got fired?"

Valerie felt her face heat up with embarrassment. Did her mother have to bring that up in front of everyone? Actually, by the nodding heads, she could only assume that they'd already discussed her "failure" in the workplace prior to her arrival.

Before she had a chance to defend herself, Armand squeezed her hand and said, "You always have a place at my law firm."

"Thank you," she said sincerely, "but that won't be necessary. Besides, I'm not sure I am fired." She saw the aunts about to question her and raised a hand to halt them. "My job prospects are not the issue here."

"You're right, Valerie," her grandmother said. "Your work performance is not at issue here. Family is. And, frankly, your attitude is not helping this family. Not at all."

Valerie stiffened with affront.

"My business is being attacked by those environmental psychos," her mother said. "People are afraid to buy real estate in my new development because of the unfounded concerns these people have raised. Plus, they don't like having to drive through picket lines to get to their homes. It would be just like those psychos to try to get at me through my daughter. Imagine how I felt when the press said you might be working with them. A knife in the back, that's what it was."

Why does everything always come back to you, Mother?

"And those LeDeuxs," Aunt Margo practically sputtered. "Someone ought to put the whole lot in jail."

"There could be political ramifications if people get stirred up about pollution again," Aunt Inez added. "And a massive voter registration drive based on the so-called green agenda could very well spell disaster to my career."

"Are you saying you're in favor of pollution, Aunt Inez?" she asked with exaggerated shock.

"Of course not. Don't be insulting. What I do favor is jobs over some measly tree-huggers' latest complaint."

"I don't see why René can't be more sensible, like his father. Now there's a man who knows which side his bread is buttered on," her grandmother said, then chuckled. "The oily side."

"Grandma!" Valerie exclaimed, knowing full well even before her grandmother bristled that she hated being called that. She preferred to be called Dixie. "That Valcour LeDeux is an alcoholic son of a bitch."

"Valerie Breaux!" her mother said in her sternest Joan Crawford voice.

"Well, it's true. Everyone in Houma knows what he is, how he treated his kids when they were young, how he sold out his family lands to the oil company . . . how—"

"Might I remind you, young lady," her grandmother interrupted, "that your family is aligned with the oil interests. Me, in particular."

"My Cypress Oil stocks helped fund your very expensive college education," her mother pointed out.

"I beg to differ. I had a trust fund left to me by great-grandmother Breaux that should have more than covered my education. Last time I checked, there were no oil stocks in my portfolio," she argued, which was a pointless exercise. Her mother never listened to her.

Armand put his face in his hands, then threw his hands up in dismay in a very theatrical manner. "Ladies, ladies, ladies! Why am I here? If we are not going to discuss a lawsuit against Bayou Unite and its separate parties, I may as well go to my club for lunch."

"I am not filing a lawsuit, Armand," Valerie said in as

firm a tone as she could manage. "Maybe later, but not right now."

"Why?" her two aunts asked at the same time.

"Because I need more facts."

"About what?" Her grandmother appeared genuinely interested and puzzled.

"Everything. The project Bayou Unite has in mind. Why they targeted me. Whether I do in fact have a job at Trial TV. What my legal alternatives are. Everything."

"You haven't decided anything for sure then?" her grandmother asked, hopefully.

"No."

Her mother narrowed her eyes at her again. "That old hag Louise Rivard implied that there's something going on between you and René LeDeux. Please tell me that isn't true."

"Define 'something going on.'" Almost immediately, she realized her mistake. It never paid to give her mother any opening.

"I swear, Valerie, you are going to be the ruin of me."

Once again, why is it always about you, Mother?

"She means," Aunt Margo interpreted for her mother, "have you fallen in love with that trailer park stud?"

Valerie laughed and reminded herself to repeat that back to René when—*if*—she saw him again. "I can say without question that René LeDeux is not in love with me. And I am not in love with him." *In lust, maybe, but not love.*

She felt a tight constriction in her chest, just thinking about René LeDeux being in love with her. Not that it would ever happen. But what if? And then the oddest thing happened. She could swear she heard a voice in her head say, *You must give love to receive it.* What did that mean? Her conscience, or some celestial being was telling her to love René?

Before she had a chance to bite her tongue, Valerie informed them all, "I need to get myself a St. Jude statue."

Five jaws dropped in union.

And the voice in her head gave a joyous, *Yeeeessss!*

Those low-down Cajun blues

He was lonesome.

How pitiful was that?

Next he would be listening to old Hank Williams songs on the radio and crying in his beer. Not that he had any beer left. Or that he was actually crying.

René was a man who relished his privacy. He could spend weeks in the bayou wilds without seeing another human being and be happy. Too much time spent in the city and he was climbing the walls. He liked people, but he didn't mind being alone.

Until now.

The worst part was, now that he was all alone, all he thought about was sex and Valerie Breaux. *Two years* had become like a blinkin' neon sign in his mind. He wanted—no, *needed* to be the guy who broke her fast.

Why he'd come to all these conclusions now, and not while she was still here, he had no idea. Probably a cruel jest of St. Jude's, who kept tsk-tsk-tsking in his head.

Valerie Breaux was screwing up his friggin' life, big-time.

Something needed to be done.

He picked up his satellite phone, hit automatic dial, and said, "Remy, get your ass out here today. I need to raise some major hell in Houma."

Don't go home again: what Thomas Wolfe shoulda said

Three days back home with her mother and Valerie was ready to strangle someone.

It had been a mistake to come back here to Houma, even before her "kidnapping," she realized now. If she'd been hoping for a haven where she could rest and reflect on her life after the firing, forget about it. There were some problems that did not go away with time . . . like her relationship with her mother.

Years ago, after law school, Valerie had spent some time in therapy trying to resolve her bitter feelings about her childhood. The result had been that the psychiatrist had recommended she just put the past behind her and move on. Easier said than done.

The news media was as bad as her family. They were chomping at the bit to run some kind of exposé. Thus far, she'd been able to fudge, giving them no definitive story on her brief foray into the bayou. Why she didn't just tell all, she wasn't sure. Fish or cut bait, one exasperated journalist had advised when she'd evaded yet another question of his. "Soon," she'd promised.

Today was Friday. Tomorrow afternoon she would be flying back to New York for a Monday morning meeting with Mr. Goodman. That was another area where she couldn't seem to make a decision. Returning to Trial TV in her old capacity as an analyst on their popular show *Trial of the Week* seemed untenable now. How could she work with a prick like Elton after what he'd done, no matter how he tried his revisionist history of claiming she'd misunderstood her firing? Yeah, right. "Don't let the door slam after you, Valerie." Hard to misunderstand that.

Another area of concern for her was René LeDeux. She couldn't stop thinking about the rogue. While she'd been with him, he'd been nothing but an annoyance to her, except for that last night when aliens had taken over her brain. But now . . . Lordy, Lordy, he was on her mind constantly. She wanted to make love with him, really make love with him. She wanted it so bad that she dreamed about it. One hot, wild night of sex, that's all she wanted. What a ridiculous fantasy! Good thing he wasn't around for her to act on it.

So now she was strolling the streets of Houma, biding her time till she could leave tomorrow. Probably for good. Probably for the best.

Houma, the parish seat of Terrebonne Parish and the de facto capital of deep bayou country, was a rather small town with a population under fifty thousand, but very unique. It was thirty-five miles north of the seacoast and laced with bayous. In fact, it was called the "Venice of America." There were antebellum mansions built with sugarcane money, next door to modern mansions built with oil money. A mixture of old and new.

She decided to go into a bookstore and browse, as much to look over the books as to escape the continuing heat wave that had hit Southern Louisiana this summer. It was always hot in the South, but this year was the hottest in history. If you didn't wear a hat, even your scalp got sunburned.

To her surprise she found herself drawn to a section on Louisiana bayous. She picked up the Tidwell book on the dying wetlands and a trade paperback copy of *Coast 2050: Toward a Sustainable Louisiana,* the 1999 proposal for reclaiming the bayou ecosystem that René had mentioned. Added to her pile were *Shantyboat on the Bayou,* a couple of Kate Chopin novels, and several coffee-table picture books on the bayou. When she was standing at the checkout, she ran into Sylvie Breaux, who had an armload of children's books.

They hugged warmly, and after they'd both paid for their purchases, stood outside in the sweltering heat.

"Have you had lunch?" Sylvie asked.

She shook her head, and they both headed next door to a small restaurant. She ordered an oyster po'boy, dressed, which meant all the trimmings—she was going on a strict diet once she returned to Manhattan—and Sylvie opted for crawfish etouffee with warm French bread. Both of them ordered iced sweet tea.

Sylvie was several years older than she and had three children, but she looked wonderful. She practically glowed with happiness. Other than the happy glow, they probably resembled each other; both had the dark Creole hair and eyes, the straight Breaux nose, and average figures. Neither of them could pass for anorexic.

"You seem very happy, Sylv."

"I am. You have no idea—" She seemed choked up, but then she continued. "I love Luc and our life together. I never dreamed I could be this happy."

"With a LeDeux yet?" She grinned at Sylvie.

"Ahhh! The family has been talking."

"Nonstop."

"You used to be so shy. It is hard to picture you with a guy with Luc's reputation."

"I would be offended if I didn't know how well-earned that reputation was. You wouldn't believe what he did to me yesterday. We were at the furniture outlet in Lafayette looking for a new bedroom set. He told the clerk we were looking for a bed with stirrups so he could land in the saddle a lot quicker. I thought the saleslady was going to swallow her teeth."

Valerie laughed, picturing the scene. "It isn't hard to imagine Luc doing that. But shy Sylvie Breaux? I would imagine you running out of the store in tears."

"I've changed. I told the clerk I preferred one that vibrates."

"Well, of course," she said, tongue firmly in place, "a woman and her best friend, a vibrator."

"How about you, Val? Are you happy?"

She shrugged. "I'm in a state of limbo these days. I'm going back to the city tomorrow. After that, things should be more clear."

"Are you going to file charges?" Sylvie didn't beat around the bush. "Everyone is surprised it hasn't happened already. Luc has already contacted a bail bondsman."

"I don't know if I'll go to the police or the feds, since it was a kidnapping. Probably not, since I've delayed this long."

"You do know that Tante Lulu is planning a wedding?"

"Nooooo." She shouldn't ask, but she did. "For whom?"

Sylvie just grinned.

"Is she nuts?"

"Probably."

"How is René?" she blurted out. She'd promised herself not to ask.

"He's okay. Kind of quiet since he got back yesterday. He's staying in Remy's houseboat while he's in town."

Unbidden, she saw an image of herself and René engaging in wild monkey sex on a houseboat. *I am absolutely pathetic.*

"He and his old band, The Swamp Rats, are playing at Swampy's Tavern tonight. Luc and I are going, along with Remy and Rachel, and Charmaine and Rusty. Why don't you join us?"

"Oh, I don't think so. As I said, I'm leaving tomorrow for New York, and I have lots of packing to do."

Sylvie cocked her head to the side and folded her arms over her chest. She wasn't buying her excuses, not one bit. "Are you afraid to see him?"

"Of course not." *Petrified!*

"Will you think about it?"

"I'll think about it." *That's all I'll think about now. Darn it!*

Chapter 9

Dumb men talking dumb

René had been raising hell for two days, ever since he'd arrived back in Houma—drinking, jamming, playing all night bourre, a Cajun card game, but he was still practically climbing the walls with frustration. Because, in all his hell-raising, women were significantly and oddly missing.

"You should just go get laid," his brother Luc advised him backstage at Swampy's Tavern where he was preparing to perform a second set. The bar was overflowing, even more than the usual Friday night crowd.

Has he heard about the two years? Nah, he couldn't have. He's just reading my pathetic mind. "That's your sage advice? Get my ashes hauled and everything will be just fine and dandy." *Not a bad idea, actually. Too bad the only one I'd want handling my ash is verboten right now.*

"It always worked for me. Still does." Luc waggled his eyebrows at him. "If you ask me—"

Thirty-five years old, and I still need help from my big brother? I . . . don't . . . think . . . so. "Butt out, big brother."

"Tante Lulu is embroidering pillow cases."

"Shit!" He knew without asking what Luc was going to say next.

"The letters R and V enclosed in pretty little hearts."

"It ain't gonna happen."

Luc just smiled. They all knew how persistent their aunt could be.

"She hasn't had sex in two years," he blurted out. *Holy hell, why would I reveal something so private to my brother?*

"Who? Tante Lulu? Man, I would have thought it was a lot longer than that."

"Eeew! I do not want to picture Tante Lulu having sex, even with Richard Simmons."

"Richard Simmons? The exercise nut?"

"Yep. She's hoping someone will bring him to her eightieth birthday party. She thinks he's really hot."

Luc's eyes went wide. Tante Lulu had a tendency to do that to people. "So, who was it then who hasn't had sex in two years?"

He thought about declining to answer, but then decided, *What the hell!* "Val."

Luc smiled even wider than before. "How do you know?"

"She told me, and if you repeat it to anyone, I swear I'll cut off your tongue and feed it to Remy's pet alligator."

Luc pretended not to hear his warning. "Well, that cinches it then."

"Cinches what?"

"A man's gotta do what a man's gotta do. Val would

not have told you that unless she wanted you to do something about it."

"You think?" *I swear, there must be a "dumb man" gene in my family.*

"Absolutely. It's sort of like throwing down the gauntlet . . . except that you, dumb schmuck, didn't act on the challenge."

"I did, sort of."

Luc put his face in his hands and counted loudly to five. When he looked up, he said, "There is no such thing as 'sort of sex'."

"Yes, there definitely is, and, no, I am not going to explain."

Luc shook his head and grinned at him. Then he changed the subject. *Thank God!* "Are you going back to work on your cabin after the weekend?"

"No. I might start working with Project 2050 as a field consultant. And I might finish up my doctoral thesis."

"Well, sonofagun! A doctor in the family!" Luc said, clapping him on the back with congratulations. "When were you going to tell me about it?"

"When I got a chance to get a word in edgewise." He grinned at his brother. "You were too busy spewing sex advice."

"What brought on possibly working with Project 2050? I thought you'd given up on the bayou work."

"Nah. I just got sick of the games they play in DC. I'll die kicking and screaming in some polluted bayou stream, up to my eyeballs in oil slick, before I give up totally."

"Just a different venue for fighting then?"

"You could say that. The next couple years are going

to be critical. The bayou either sinks or survives depending on drastic measures taken now. Ten years from now will be too late."

Luc put up his hands in surrender. "Hey, you're preachin' to the choir."

"I know that. I'm like a windup toy. Get me started and I can't stop."

"Just be careful. There are a lot of special interests who are determined not to let you succeed. And they're deadly serious."

"Like our father?"

"Oh, yeah! Not that I think dear ol' Dad would have the nerve to harm you himself, but he might have a leg or two of yours broken by one of his thugs."

He shrugged.

"Can I assume Val isn't going to be doing your TV documentary?"

"Hah! Val was never doing a bayou TV documentary, and it was never *my* idea to begin with."

"At least she didn't report J.B. and Maddie to the police or the feds."

"I don't know about that. I guess we would have heard something by now. But it could still happen." *I wish she would decide one way or another, for sure. Then I could put some moves on her, and it wouldn't be interpreted as influencing the witness, or whatever they called it. I can't hit on her now, though. I just can't. Even a telephone call would be out of line.*

"Don't tell me you haven't called her."

"Of course not."

"You are so not my brother. Didn't I teach you all the right moves? Jeesh! Why haven't you called her?"

"Why should I call her?" That question sounded stupid even to his own ears. And he wasn't about to get involved in a lengthy explanation of why Val needed to make a decision first.

Luc arched his eyebrows meaningfully.

"You've gotta be kidding. I should call Val to get laid? No dates. No courting. No mushy stuff. Get right to the main meal without all the appetizers."

"Works for me," Luc said, laughing.

"I can picture it now. 'Hey, Val, I'm a little horny here. How 'bout a nooner? Or better yet, an all-nighter?' And her response would be, 'Drop dead!' Or 'Drop dead, asshole!' "

"*Tsk-tsk-tsk!* You are so crude. That's not what I meant."

"Liar!"

"I meant, why not call her and just ask what she's planning to do about the so-called kidnapping?"

"No subtlety in that."

"Well, Mr. Subtle, it's better than sitting on your hands, waiting for something to happen."

One of his guitar players yelled into the room. "You about ready to go on, René?"

"In a sec," he replied, picking up his *frottir,* a washboard-type musical instrument.

"It's been nice chatting," Luc said, teasing as usual. "I've got to get back to our table before Sylvie gets picked up by some cowboy. I'll see you in a little while." Luc was just about to leave when he stopped in the doorway. "I forgot. Sylvie said to tell you she might have a surprise for you tonight."

He groaned. "Not another stripper riding up on a

Harley with birthday cupcakes on her boobs. And I was actually expected to blow out her lighted candles. Talk about!"

"Remy and I did that, not Sylvie. Besides, your birthday isn't for three more months."

"Oh, God! Not another fix-up! I don't think I could survive another of her matchmaking efforts. Please tell her that I can meet new women on my own. Honest, I'm not shy."

Luc was practically rolling over with laughter, tears brimming his dark eyes. When he was finally able to talk, he said, "I can definitely say there are no new women on your horizon. None tossed your way by Sylvie, anyway."

Once he left, René heard Sylvie come up to Luc out in the hall and say, "You didn't tell him, did you?"

"Nope."

Both of them laughed all the way down the hall.

All René could think was, *Uh-oh!*

A walk on the wild side

Valerie walked tentatively up the wide wooden steps of Swampy's Tavern. It was late, almost eleven o'clock; it had taken her this long to get up enough nerve to come.

Wild Cajun music blasted from the open doorway, a mixture of traditional French ballad and bouncy Zydeco coming from a jukebox or sound system. A few people—two girls and a guy—came out, laughing, and Val was relieved to see that her attire was okay. She'd found an old pair of jeans in her bedroom drawer, left over from high school days. They were tighter on her now but suitable for this atmosphere. On top, in deference to the continuing sweltering heat, she wore a sheer white formfitting blouse with embroidery over the breast area—long sleeved but low-cut, also a high school leftover. Back then, she'd thought she looked sexy in it; now, at thirty-five, she felt a little bit silly. On her feet were white sandals.

She eased her way into the crowded tavern and immediately was hit with a wave of even greater warmth. Despite the air-conditioning, there was just too much body heat to keep the room cool. No one seemed to mind, though. In fact, some people were dancing with abandon up front on the small dance floor. Mostly a Cajun two-step with an occasional rebel yell thrown in.

Worming her way through the crowd to the bar, she watched a giant of a man, bald-headed with one hoop earring and a Popeye physique, handle drink orders like a real pro. Behind him was a sign that read, BEER: HELPING WHITE BOYS LEARN TO DANCE SINCE 1837. Another sign read: BEAUTY IS IN THE EYE OF THE BEER HOLDER. This was not a touristy New Orleans-type crowd who ordered Hurricanes and other exotic drinks. This was a beer-and-shots clientele.

"What'll it be, pretty lady?" he asked, when he finally worked his way down the bar to her.

She figured the "pretty lady" tag was routine for him. Still, it made her feel welcome. "A diet soda, please. Lots of ice."

He raised his bushy eyebrows at her, eyeing her see-through blouse, probably thinking the outfit went more with hard liquor. But he quickly prepared her drink and slid it over to her.

"I thought The Swamp Rats were supposed to perform tonight."

"They are. Any minute now. You lookin' for anyone in particular?"

"René LeDeux," she said, without thinking.

The bartender chuckled and said, "That figures." Then, he added, "You sure you don't want a set of oyster shooters?"

"No. Why?"

"That's standard fare for the LeDeux women . . . before they bite the bullet."

That made absolutely no sense to her. But it didn't matter. She scanned the room and noticed the table near the front where Sylvie and Luc LeDeux were sitting. Also there was Remy LeDeux; she assumed that the woman sitting next to him was his wife, Rachel. She also noticed Charmaine LeDeux . . . well, Charmaine Lanier, now that she was back with her first husband, Raoul. Charmaine had big hair and a movie-star body; in fact, she had been Miss Louisiana at one time. But it was her husband who drew everyone's attention. Raoul Lanier was a drop-dead gorgeous cowboy. Women passing by their table did double takes when they saw him, not that the other men at the table were too shabby. To his credit, he seemed to have eyes only for his wife.

The canned music stopped abruptly and a man—presumably the tavern owner—stepped out onto the small stage. "Ladies and gentleman, are you ready for *real* Cajun music?"

"Yeah!" everyone yelled.

"I can't hear you," the owner said, smiling widely.

"Yeah!" the crowd roared, accompanied by catcalls, whistles, and clapping.

"I give you The Swamp Rats." The owner stepped back and the band ran onto the stage with as much joie de vivre as if they were playing to a sold-out crowd at the Meadows. Immediately, they began playing an old classic, "*Jolé Blon.*" They sang it in a twangy Cajunized French, both poignant and melodic. Some members of the audience sang along with them.

And there stood René. After all her wicked thoughts about him the past few days, there he stood. Grinning, singing, having a merry old good time. While she'd been miserable. The louse!

He wore faded, tight jeans, a black T-shirt with a leather vest, worn cowboy boots and the *frottir* over his shoulders. He was tall, at least six-foot-two, so there was a lot of lean body covered by those tight jeans. His black hair was longish, covering his neck. His dark eyes danced merrily as he sang and gave little waves to people he recognized on the dance floor or at the tables.

He was Cajun sex on the hoof. And he knew it.

"Aren't they good?" a waitress asked next to her, as she waited for her order to be filled.

"Yes. Yes, they are," Valerie replied honestly. Even though she'd grown up in Cajun country, she'd never been a real fan of the music, but she had to appreciate it here tonight, both for its quality and as a cultural treasure.

"They were offered a record deal a few years back, but they turned it down."

"Really?" Valerie gave the chatty waitress her full attention now. Meanwhile the band segued into a rowdy version of "Diggy Liggy Lo."

"Yep. These guys all have other jobs and they dint wanna give 'em up."

"Really?" Valerie repeated. She would hope so since they were all in their early to midthirties.

"Uh-huh. One's a baby doctor over in Lafayette. 'Nother is a biologist or sumpin'." Valerie figured that one would be René. "One guy owns a car dealership. One's a famous rodeo rider—well, famous 'mongst rodeo folks. And the last one writes vampire novels, I think." She tried to pick out who was who, which was impossible. If she hadn't known better, she would have bet René was the rodeo rider when it was probably the short, half-bald guy playing the keyboard.

"Amazing!" Valerie said, not realizing she'd spoken aloud till the waitress responded, "That's for sure," and left with her tray of drinks.

The band played two more songs. Valerie thought about making her way to Sylvie's table, but it would be difficult, and she imagined making herself conspicuous in the process . . . something she did not want to do. She was out of place. Putting on a pair of jeans didn't make her fit in. It was a bad idea coming here, she concluded finally. She should just go home.

At that exact same moment, René saw her. She saw surprise, then pleasure light up his face. He whispered something to the guitarist near him and the next song became the old Willie Nelson hit "Always On My Mind." Yep, that about said it all. René *was* always on her mind lately. Did he know how she'd been obsessing over him? Was this his cruel way of teasing her? *Oh, God, I have to get out of here.* Tears welled in her eyes, probably due to the smoke and humidity, and she spun on her heels—

Only to hit a brick wall in the form of the huge bartender. "Goin' somewhere, pretty lady?" he inquired sweetly, with a scowl on his face. "Without paying?"

"Oh, I forgot." She fumbled in her jeans' pocket and pulled out a five-dollar bill. "Here. Keep the change."

The bartender raised both bushy eyebrows at her but pocketed the money. He moved aside.

And there stood René.

"Hey, Gator," he said to the bartender, who jabbed him in the forearms with some hidden message and walked away.

"Hey, *chére,*" he drawled to her. "Goin' somewhere?"

"Yes. I'm going home."

"I don't think so."

"I beg your pardon."

"No need to beg, sugar, not for my pardon anyhow," he said suggestively, taking her by the elbow and backing her up against the wall. He stood in front of her, one hand braced over her head. Meanwhile his band continued to play some instrumental Cajun songs, and people danced up front. René's absence was barely noticed. "You came to see me. Why rush off now?"

"I didn't come to see you," she lied. "I came to meet Sylvie for a drink."

"Ahhh. So that's what my surprise is. You. Remind me to send Sylvie a dozen roses tomorrow. Maybe two dozen." He winked at her.

Valerie felt the wink all the way down to her curling toes. A part of her body that a lady never mentioned came to attention and practically hollered, "Yahoo!" Not that she would ever say any of this out loud. "I'm beginning to think I've been set up."

"Me, too." Smiling with unconcern, he twirled a strand of her hair on his forefinger, then tugged, letting it come out in a long ringlet. She'd worn her hair down tonight, and the high humidity turned it to frizz. She hated it. He seemed to like it. A lot. He repeated the twirling exercise over and over.

Who knew that twirling hair around a forefinger could be so erotic?

"Did you like my song?"

She refused to answer.

"I sang it for you."

"Which song?"

He laughed because he knew very well that she was playing coy with him. Since coyness had never been a trait to be desired in her book, Valerie sighed deeply and admitted, "Yes, I liked your song."

He leaned down closer to hear her words, and Valerie could smell piney soap and aftershave. He was so close, if she turned her head just so, they would be kissing.

Awareness of the chemistry sizzling between them was in his eyes and husky voice as he revealed, "It's true . . . what I sang. You have been on my mind. Way too much."

Lordy, Lordy! I am in way over my head here. I need to play it cool. Isn't that what teenagers always say? What made me think I could come here, say howdy, and go home unsinged? "You've been on my mind, too. Way too much." *Well, you idiot, so much for playing it cool!*

"What are we going to do about it, babe?"

"Nothing." *But, ooh, I'm thinking stuff.*

"I don't think I can accept that."

"I'm going back to New York in the morning." *Thank God! No telling what I might do.*

His face fell before he masked over his disappointment. "For good?"

"Probably."

"Don't go."

"Huh?"

"I didn't mean to say that. It just slipped out."

"I have to go back. I have appointments with my employer there."

"Don't you mean your former employer?"

"Maybe not."

"Look, let's get one important matter out of the way first. Are you going to file a complaint against J.B. and Maddie? Or Tante Lulu? Or me?"

Disillusionment washed over her. *Is that all he cares about? Covering his . . . their asses?* "No. I've decided not to make a criminal complaint. Not that I couldn't, not that it wouldn't stick."

He should have been ecstatic over her news, but instead he was pensive. "Why?"

She didn't need to ask what he referred to. "It might not be my cause, but I recognize a noble cause when it hits me in the face. All of your intentions, though misguided, were good."

"I had nothing to do with—"

"Enough already."

"Do you know why I didn't have intercourse with you the other night?"

Valerie felt her face heat up. Talk about blunt questions! "Because you knew your legal liabilities would go through the roof if you did. Sex with a captive—that's a biggie."

He smiled at her use of the word "captive," probably because of its sexual connotations. "Not even close, sugar. It was because, if I did, you'd think that the only reason I made love with you was a sort of bribe. I screw you; in return, you won't screw me."

"I wouldn't have thought that." *It's the first thing I thought of.*

"Maybe not right away, but later you would have. Morning after wisdom."

"You've had a lot of experience with that, have you?"

"Mais, oui!" He tweaked her under the chin, then gave her a quick butterfly kiss across her mouth. "The reason I quit before the gospel, so to speak, and the reason why I haven't called you, or climbed into your bedroom window one night—and, yes, don't look so shocked, I did consider that. Well, the reason is that when we do make love, I don't want there to be any questions why."

I shouldn't ask. I really shouldn't, but I can't help my-self. "Why?"

"Because, darlin', I want to be inside you so bad I can't stand it anymore. I'm tired of just thinking about you. I'm tired of waking up with you on my mind and getting no work done because you're on my mind. I'm tired of thinking about those two damn years of yours and worrying that someone else will be the Mickey to your Minnie. I'm a walking hard-on, and it's all your fault. I want to make you laugh and cry and scream out loud when I'm inside you. Any questions?"

Are you kidding?

"Okay, then, let's dance."

Chapter 10

Getting down and dirty, Cajun style

René LeDeux was a born womanizer.

No use denying the fact. He was thirty-five years old. He'd been around the block and then some. Hell, he'd been around a city of blocks.

He loved women. He loved pursuing them, he loved making love to them, he loved the triumph of their inevitable surrender. Despite one sexual fiasco long ago, he knew what he was doing.

From his years of scoping out females, he recognized that he had a small window of opportunity with Val. Fifteen minutes max, he figured, before her brain kicked in with logical questions, like, What the hell am I thinking? Sex with the bad boy of the bayou? I don't think so. Nope, he had to strike while the iron—um, Valerie—was hot . . . while her hormones were still racing with this sexual chemistry that sizzled between them, while her brain was lodged about three feet lower, just like his was.

He followed her to the dance floor, staring at her transparent blouse and her nice tight jeans. He pressed his lips together to make sure he didn't speak his observations aloud. Horniness did that to a guy—turned him inside-out, down-and-dirty crude. Like sex itself. He couldn't wait. Besides, Val probably thought her attire was librarian tame. Hah! He had news for her. Every man in the place would take one look at her and think, *Saddle up, cowboy!*

She stopped suddenly and peered back over her shoulder. "Are you staring at my butt?"

Who? Me? "Absolutely."

"Well, don't."

Yeah, right.

She walked out onto the crowded dance floor, turned around, and tapped her foot with impatience. Not a good sign. Yep, fifteen minutes and time's a-wastin'. The lady thought she didn't want to dance with him, but she did.

He made a short hand signal to his band to play a slow song next. What did they do? Played a fast song, of course, grinning the whole time. As they wailed to "Big Mamou," Val began to sway her hips from side to side in her dignified version of boogie.

Once again, he thought, *Yeah, right.* Grabbing her by the hips, he yanked her flush against his body, which caused her to yelp. *Call me Mr. Smooth. Not!* Then he wrapped her arms around his shoulders, and he locked his hands around her waist. If she hadn't known what he had in mind before, she did now.

"Jeesh, René, you're embarrassing me."

He assumed she was referring to his erection pressing against her belly. "Not half as much as I'm embarrassing myself." Actually, he wasn't all that embarrassed.

She arched her head back to tell him, "This isn't a slow dance."

"It is for us." A little annoyed at himself now, he shoved her face into his neck, then locked his hands around her waist, as before. Surprisingly, she nestled in his arms and sighed against his neck.

He pulled her even closer and closed his eyes. Her hair smelled like lily of the valley. He moved himself against one of her valleys. She felt soft and supple and very desirable. They swayed from side to side for a while, not speaking . . . not with words, anyhow.

"Are you trying to seduce me?" she asked, her warm lips moving against his neck.

"Yes. Do you mind?" *I wonder if she'd like to go outside and hop in the back seat of my car with me. Probably not. Calm down, big boy. You're gonna scare her away. Hell, I'm scarin' myself.*

She paused for a long, telling second. "No."

"Good. I wasn't going to stop anyway." *That back seat's lookin' better and better.*

She laughed, and the soft flutter of her breath against his ear felt like fingertips . . . somewhere else.

Suddenly, inordinately happy, he stepped away from Val and twirled her under his arm twice in an old jitterbug move, then dipped her low in his arms, her back bent, hair hanging almost to the floor. While she was in that vulnerable position, he kissed her. As far as kisses went, it wasn't anything special. Still, Val gasped and stared at him, wide-eyed, when he drew her upright and back into his arms.

He heard clapping and hooting encouragement from behind him and guessed it must be his family. He could care less if he was making a spectacle of himself. He felt too friggin' good.

Val stepped back from his embrace and smiled. "You think you're such hot stuff, don't you?"

He shrugged and smiled back at her. *Define hot. Do I think I could make you burn? Mais, oui.*

"You think you can pull my strings and I'll do anything you want?"

Oops! Guess I'm a little too obvious. But she was still smiling.

"Guess again, big boy!"

Oops again!

Val did something then that proved to him what he should have known all along: Val was not like any other woman. She began to dance in front of him. She shimmied down into a bent knee position, then shimmied back up. The embroidered swans on the front of her see-through shirt danced, too. Snapping the fingers of her widespread arms, she beckoned him forward. When he stepped forward, the contrary witch moved seductively to the side. Now she danced around him, rolling her hips, swaying her shoulders, making a flirty moue of her mouth, brushing him as she passed by . . . a breast against his arm, a hip over his butt, her fingertips grazing his jaw, which hung open with incredulity.

He laughed with appreciation of her provocative show. But if she thought to challenge him by dancing, she had another think coming. René was a good dancer, most Cajun men were. It was in the blood. Next time she moved in front of him, he stepped in behind her. Putting a hand on each hip, he undulated behind her. Catching the beat, he met Val rhythm for rhythm. He was better than Patrick Swayze any day of the week. Into her ear, he whispered, "We Cajuns invented dirty dancing, *chére.*"

She put her hands over his, still on her hips, and moved against him. He saw stars, he swore he did. "We Creoles know a thing or two, as well, *cher.*"

"For sure," he choked out.

They danced their hearts out with the next two fast songs—"Sugar Bee" and "Louisiana Man"—all of it foreplay of the best possible kind. Both of them laughed and smiled at each other as they teased and raised their mutual arousal a notch or two.

When the band started a slow song, he pulled her back into his embrace and hugged her warmly. Sweat rolled off both of them in the steamy heat they created. At first, they just danced in silence. Well, silence, except for the panting from physical exertion . . . or something else. He kissed the side of her head.

"Are you crazy?" she said.

He wasn't sure if she referred to his blatant seduction, his dancing, or his general state of mind. It didn't matter. "A little bit," he admitted, then added, "over you." And that was the God's truth. He might kid himself that he was in control of this seduction, but his attraction to Val was way out of his scope of expertise. He was flying without a net here.

He thought she would call him on the cheesy remark, accuse him of giving her a line. But, no, Val fooled him again. "Me, too," she whispered.

This caused his already feverish testosterone level to go ballistic, like one of those hammer and bell games at a carnival. But then he realized something truly embarrassing. The band had stopped playing to take a break, and he and Val were dancing alone to no music.

"Oh, shit!" he murmured and steered a seemingly

dazed Val toward his family's table where everyone was grinning from ear to ear. Normally he would have been pleased at Val's dazed condition. Hell, he would have been clapping himself on the back with self-congratulations. Now he pinched her arm to wake her to the reality of the teasing that was sure to come.

"Oh, my God!" she said when she realized what she'd . . . they'd . . . done. "What are you doing to me?"

What am I doing to myself?

Introductions were made all around to the six grinning people sitting at the table. Val sat down next to her cousin Sylvie, and he sat on Val's other side. Charmaine, his half sister, sat next to him. She sported big Texas hair and lots of makeup. From her ears dangled glow-in-the-dark dangly earrings. Good God, what kind of shirt was that she was wearing? She was the owner of several hair salons, but a skintight T-shirt that proclaimed in glittery letters, EXPERT BLOW JOBS? Talk about! The fact that smaller print read HOUMA HAIR SPA was beside the point. What was she thinking? What was her husband thinking, to let her go out in public like this? Hell, what was he thinking, to suppose anyone could tell Charmaine what to do?

Charmaine just grinned at him, as if reading his mind, daring him to say something negative. If he did, she would cut him off at the knees with some outrageous remark. He knew she would—probably something to do with his badass reputation.

"So, Val," Luc said, mischief glimmering in his eyes, "I hear you haven't had sex in two years."

René gave Luc a dirty look for blabbing. Sometimes his brother had a warped sense of humor.

Sylvie elbowed Luc for his insensitive remark and

whispered something in his ear. Immediately, Luc reached over Sylvie to take Val's hand and squeeze. "Hey, Val, I'm sorry. Me, I'm just a crude Cajun boy who doan know no better." Luc was playing the dumb Cajun role to the extreme.

Val turned to René in horror. "You told him?"

"I didn't tell him," he lied. "He guessed."

"How could he guess such a thing?" She slapped him on the arm, real hard.

He winced. "Luc is really talented that way. Psychic. Sort of."

"Bullshit!" Remy said.

Everyone laughed.

"Hey, Val, nothing to be ashamed about," Charmaine said. "I was a born-again virgin recently."

Everyone turned to stare at Charmaine, who had been married and divorced four times—virginity on her was like a wart on Cinderella. At least it took the attention away from him and Val.

"Darlin', be honest with these folks," Rusty told her. "Your born-again crap didn't last very long."

"Long enough," she said, elbowing him.

"How long?" Remy asked. His wife, Rachel, elbowed him.

René moved away slightly from Val in case she decided to join in on the elbowing.

"A few weeks," Charmaine said. "And it was rather nice. Sexual tension out the kazoo, if you know what I mean. So I admire you for taking a stand, Val. Good for you!"

Rachel and Sylvie concurred.

Val groaned and put her face in her hands for a moment.

No, no, no! Two years of celibacy is not good. Do not encourage Val.

"Could we talk about something else?" Val urged.

The subject changed, thank God, to Tante Lulu's up-coming birthday bash.

"We rented the Veterans Club meeting hall down the bayou, with all its picnic grounds," Charmaine told them. "The reception hall at Our Lady of the Bayou church isn't big enough. Plus, they don't allow liquor there, and I can't imagine any Cajun party without beer."

The men all nodded.

"Just how big is this party going to be?" René asked.

"Three hundred or so," Charmaine said.

"Three hundred?" Val was surprised. None of the rest of them were, though. Tante Lulu had touched a lot of lives over the years.

"Will The Swamp Rats play?" Rachel asked him.

He nodded. "Wouldn't miss it."

"Will you be contacting Richard Simmons about com-ing?" Charmaine asked Val.

"Huh?" Val appeared as stunned about being singled out as by the question.

"Tante Lulu told us that Val knows him," Charmaine informed the rest of the table. "God knows where or how Tante Lulu developed this fascination for the guy, but she did, and it would be the biggest thrill for her if he could come."

Everyone turned their attention to Val, who looked as if she'd been poleaxed. "I . . . I . . . I" she sputtered at first. "I don't know Richard Simmons. I just said I had met his manager a few years ago and—"

Luc waved a hand airily. "Three degrees of separation. Good enough."

"I . . . I . . ." Val continued to sputter. His family had that effect on people sometimes.

"She'll try," René offered for Val. Then to her, in an undertone, he said, "Just pretend you're gonna try. They'll forget about it eventually."

"I'm thinking about having a belly dance troupe come in for entertainment, too. The Scheherazades," Charmaine said.

My family ought to form its own carnival. Where do they come up with this shit?

"Why belly dancers?" Rachel wanted to know.

"Yeah, Chippendale dancers would be more appropriate for our dear ol' aunt," Luc said, chortling. Sylvie elbowed him again.

"Because Tante Lulu and I took belly dancing lessons at one time under the Scheherazades. We even entered a competition, and she won," Charmaine explained, beaming.

That picture boggled the minds of them all. Not the picture of Charmaine, but Tante Lulu. "At her advanced age, the image of Tante's Lulu's wrinkled skin in a revealing harem outfit is not pretty," René mused aloud.

"I've seen her in a belly dancer outfit," Rusty said, his eyes twinkling merrily. "Actually, she looked kind of cute."

Charmaine kissed her husband on the cheek. "You are so sweet."

Rusty gave the guys a look that pretty much said, "You all could learn a thing or two from me."

"I've always wanted to learn belly dancing," Sylvie said.

Luc grinned at her.

"Me, too," Rachel said.

Remy grinned at her.

"You really should," Charmaine advised. "You do know that belly dancers have much better orgasms, don't you?"

A pronounced silence fell over the table. Then everyone burst out laughing.

"Well, it's true," Charmaine said, also laughing.

"It is," Rusty agreed. And Charmaine elbowed him.

René glanced at Val, whose face was red as a beet. He would apologize for his family's tendency to discuss intimate things, but then he thought, *Nah. She'll get used to it. If she sticks around that long. Hmmm. Will she stick around that long?*

"Well, it's been nice, everyone, but I have to go," Val said, standing abruptly.

That answers my question about her sticking around.

"I have an early morning flight to catch," she elaborated.

After a brief spurt of conversation all around, he stood next to her and said, "I'll walk you to your car."

"You don't have to do that."

"Yes, darlin'," he said, "I definitely do."

A walk on the wild side

Valerie and René walked across the parking lot toward her car, which was parked near the end since she'd arrived late.

"I would drive you home, but I have to perform the last set with my band," he said.

"Why do you keep making assumptions like that?"

"Like what?"

"That you would drive me home, simply because you chose to, as if I would have no say in the matter."

He looked down at her and grinned.

"You have a nice family, René. You're lucky."

"I've grown attached to them, but I'm surprised that you don't think we're a kooky bunch."

"I never said you weren't kooky. But I learned a lot about people when training to be a jury consultant. You have to look beneath the surface. For example, you see a guy with sunglasses on a dreary day and the first reaction is he's a shady character with something to hide, or he thinks sunglasses make him look macho. But there could be other reasons."

"Like?"

"He has an eye disease. He is shy and hiding behind the dark lenses. He does in fact have something to hide. It was sunny earlier, and he forgot to take them off. Lots of reasons."

"And how does this apply to my family?"

"Take Charmaine. She gives the impression of being a brainless bimbo. Her attire. Her manner of speaking. Her outrageousness. But if you listen carefully, you hear some intelligent words tossed in. You understand that she built two highly successful businesses, not just from being able to wield a curling iron, but having real business talent. I wonder what she is trying to camouflage with this persona she's created for herself."

"That's amazing. Tell me more."

"Well, Luc delights in portraying himself as a hick lawyer. Hawaiian shirts, being unshaven even in the courtroom, taking on outrageous cases. My aunts Margo and Madeline hate him for the time he represented that rusted-out trailer park against them in court. He actually convinced a jury that it was a historic treasure. Bottom line, he's a shrewd lawyer who takes on the underdog, not a badass good-for-nothing."

He laughed at what she assumed was an accurate portrayal of his brother. "How about me?"

"Aaaah," she said. "You're a harder nut to crack."

"Dark and mysterious, huh?" He waggled his eyebrows at her.

"You could say that. I can't believe that you let people think you are a shiftless coonass. You aren't offended by that word, are you?"

"Hell, no, coonass is a term of endearment amongst us Cajuns. Go on."

"I still haven't totally figured you out yet. Like I said a minute ago, things aren't always what they appear on the surface. Do you deliberately hide your intellect, your college degrees, and your true work because you are modest?"

He snorted his opinion.

"Or because you are involved in secret, dangerous missions?"

"James Bond. That's me, baby."

She smiled. "Maybe it's sort of a slap in the face at people who misjudged you early on when you put a true face forth. You know that saying about you might as well play the game if you've got the name."

"Living up to my bad reputation?"

"Precisely. Then again, it could be because you are insecure at heart. You really don't think you are worth much. I suspect that living with Valcour LeDeux wouldn't have done much for a kid's self-esteem. Small-minded people might have made you feel like trash."

René said nothing to that, which made her think she had hit too close to the quick. She hadn't intended to hurt him; so she decided to change the subject. "I can't believe I have to get up in a couple of hours to get to the airport."

They arrived at her car. She turned and pressed her back against the driver's door. He stood in front of her, fingering the lapels of her blouse.

"Will you be coming back?"

"Some day, I'm sure."

He shook his head. "Soon?"

"I don't know. It all depends on the outcome of my meetings on Monday."

"Come back," he said in a voice that was raw with masculine need. The unspoken words were "to me."

And suddenly, she really did want to see him again. Well, not so suddenly. She'd been drawn to him ever since her return to Louisiana. "Do you think your aunt put a spell on us?"

He smiled, understanding. "Either that, or it was St. Jude. They're a powerful combination."

"I rather doubt a saint would plant such impure thoughts in my head."

"I don't know about that. St. Jude has been known to use underhanded methods to gain his ends." He thought for a second, then added, "You have impure thoughts about me?"

She just nodded, staring fixedly at his mouth, which

was full and parted and oh so tempting. "Kiss me," she murmured, surprising not just him, but herself.

"I want to make love with you sooo bad, but I want our first time together to be memorable, not against a car in a tavern parking lot. If I kiss you, I won't be able to stop."

Valerie sighed. This man was potent with a capital P. But something he said niggled at her brain. "It wouldn't be our first time."

She could swear his face got red then, though the lighting was dim at this end of the lot.

"I have a little itty bitty confession to make," he said.

Her suspicious nature went on red alert. She didn't have to be an expert in studying people to know something was up.

"Actually, it *will* be our first time. You see, that other time, we didn't really do anything." He launched into a bumbling convoluted explanation dealing with premature ejaculations, lifelong embarrassment, and pink vomit. Finally, understanding seeped into her brain.

She slapped him on the arm, the second time that night. When did violence come so easy to her? When René LeDeux re-entered her life, that's when. "You lied to me."

"Did not," he asserted. "I just failed to tell you that little itty bitty detail."

"You louse! I'll give you itty bitty." She began pounding his chest. "All these years you let me believe—"

"No, no, no!" He pulled her into a tight bear hug so that her arms were restrained. "I only found out a few days ago when you disclosed that you had no memory of that night."

"And you failed to tell me then . . . why?"

"I was embarrassed, and whew! What a relief to find out that you were never aware of my lack of finesse. But now you know."

"Let me go," she said against his chest.

"Are you going to hit me again?"

She hesitated. "No."

When he released her, she said, "I despise dishonesty."

"I wasn't dishonest . . . precisely."

"Don't play games with me, René."

"I'm sorry. My only excuse . . . well, it's a guy thing."

She folded her arms over her chest, exasperated. "You were only fifteen years old."

"Yeah, and believe you me, it was a big deal at the time. Having the rocket go off before all engines are firing is not a feat a guy wants to claim."

She had to smile.

"Every day I went to school I expected to hear that you had finally told everyone of my failure."

"And every day I went to school expecting to hear that you had bragged about your conquest and my failure. Girls aren't supposed to vomit the first time, I don't think."

"We're even then?" he asked hopefully.

"Not even close," she said.

"You're gonna make me pay, aren't you?"

"In spades. I have to go now."

"I had big plans for tonight."

"I could tell."

"Will you hit me if I try to kiss you good night?"

"You said you wouldn't be able to stop if you kissed me."

"I've cooled down since then."

I haven't.

He moved in closer and arranged her arms around his neck. Then he moved in even closer, pressing against her lower belly.

"I thought you said you cooled off."

"That's cool for me," he said with a short laugh. "I should forewarn you, I am an expert kisser."

I know. "If you don't mind saying so yourself?"

"The best kisses are carefully arranged. For example, all other body parts should be perfectly aligned."

"Huh? What do you mean?"

He lifted her slightly by the butt so she was on tiptoe and rode the cleft of her jeans, just right. Somehow, her legs had become spread and he was between them—surprise surprise—just right.

"Oh," she said, answering her own question.

While her tush half-sat against the car door and her arms were still loosely looped around his neck, he put both of his hands on her breasts and used his thumbs to bring the nipples to hard peaks. Realizing that she wore no bra, he made a low guttural sound, then slipped his hands under the hem and up till he caressed the naked flesh.

Every part of Valerie's body throbbed then. Her lips ached for his kiss; her breasts ached for rougher treatment from his hands; her female parts ached for all of his hard length pressed against her.

"Oh, baby," he said against her mouth as he finally took her in a kiss that was at once tender and devouring. His tongue stroked her mouth, in and out, simulating the sexual rhythm taking place below. Her tongue did the same to his mouth. It was hard to tell who was kissing whom, where he ended and she began. She felt her body coiling with tension and knew she had to stop before it went too far. Jerking her mouth away from his, she gasped, "No, René. I don't want to come like this. Not again."

Still holding her, he arched his neck back, eyes closed, and inhaled and exhaled deeply, fighting for control. Finally he released her and stepped back. He was deeply aroused, she could tell without looking down. His eyes were half-lidded. His lower lip drooped in a sultry fashion. He wanted her as much as she wanted him.

"Your wish is my command, princess," he said, finally. With regret he turned to go, brushing his fingertips across her swollen mouth. At the last second, he turned and looked her in the eyes and said, "Come back when you can, *chére*. Wild horses won't be able to stop me then. Next time we will make magic, I guar-an-tee."

That night, Valerie had dreams of magic.

Chapter 11

Giving a new meaning to "Give me a buzz, baby"

René called Val at four-thirty that morning.

It was a really stupid thing to do. He'd played another set with his band after Val left. He'd sat around chewing the fat with his family for another hour after that. He'd gone back to Remy's houseboat where he'd tried to read a book. And all that time he kept thinking about Val. Maybe she'd been right when she'd wondered if a spell had been put on them.

And now, pathetic soul that he'd become, he was risking a Simone Breaux rage by calling her home in the middle of the night. Luckily Val picked up on the second ring.

"Hello," she said sleepily.

"Hi."

"René?"

"Uh-huh."

"What time is it?"

"Four-thirty. What time do you have to get up?"

"Five."

"See how thoughtful I am. Your very own wake-up call."

He heard soft laughter at the other end and a rustling noise. She was probably sitting up in bed.

He leaned over to turn out the bedside lamp; somehow it seemed more intimate talking to her in the dark. "Are you going to come back, Val?"

"You already asked me that."

Does the word pathetic *ring a bell?* "I wasn't satisfied with your answer."

"I can't make promises. There are so many extenuating circumstances that may affect my decision."

"You sound like a lawyer."

"That's what I am."

"We have unfinished business, babe." *Like, two years and counting.*

She hesitated before saying, "I know. But sometimes it's best to leave certain things unfinished."

"Bullshit! I want you to come back. If you want to, you can come back. It's as simple as that."

"I'll try."

He decided that was a good enough concession for now. Time to pull in the heavy-duty ammunition. "What are you wearing?" *Yeah, what does someone who's been celibate for two years wear? A chastity belt?*

Soft laughter again. He loved her soft laughter.

"Are we going to have phone sex?" she inquired innocently.

God bless innocent women! "Was that an invitation?" *It couldn't possibly be.*

Silence.

Holy shit! He'd only been kidding, but she must be interested. Otherwise she would have told him that he was a crude ass, or something similar. *Whooee! I am better than I thought. Amazing!* "Val?" he prodded for an answer.

"I've never had phone sex before," she said.

"Neither have I," he lied, "but I'm game if you are. Besides, we've already had near-sex. How different could it be?" *Game? Hah! More like chomping at the bit. Honey, I want to end that two-year vigil soooo bad.*

"I don't know about this. . . ."

No, no, no. You are not going to back out now. You don't toss a hungry dog a bone, then say, "Oops, give it back." And I am definitely a hungry dog. "What are you wearing?"

"A nightgown."

"Take it off, darlin'."

"Why?"

Questions, questions, question! Why do women always have to question everything? "Take the damn thing off, Val."

There was a short silence, after which she said, "I did it."

Oh my God! Babe, you would not believe the images I have right now. Triple X-rated! "How does it feel?"

"Wicked."

"Wicked is good."

She chuckled and said, "Now you. What are you wearing?"

"Jockey shorts."

"Take them off."

"Say that again."

"Why?"

Aaarrgh! Another question! "Because it turns me on, dammit. Stop asking why."

"Why are you getting irritated?"

"I'm not getting irritated. I'm impatient." *Actually, I'm so excited . . . overexcited. Slow down, cowboy.*

"René?"

"Yeah."

"Take them off. Please."

He smiled to himself. After a moment or two, he said, "I did it."

"Liar. You did not."

Oops! "How do you know that?"

"I'm a jury analyst. I study people . . . their appearance, their gestures, their *voices*. I could tell by the tone of your voice."

Man, oh, man! I better be careful. "I did it now," he told her after shrugging out of his underwear. "Do you want to go first, or should I?"

"Are you kidding? I wouldn't know where or how to start."

I do. "I'm touching your face," he said, "running my fingertips over your lips. Remember how it felt when we kissed earlier?"

"Remember? I'll never forget. You were right. You *are* a good kisser."

I cannot believe Valerie "Ice" Breaux just told me I am a good kisser. He smiled. "I can remember your taste."

She laughed. "What? Diet Coke? Or breath mint?"

"Neither. You have your own distinct taste. It's sexy."

"That's good, René. *You* are good."

That's what I keep telling you. "Thank you, ma'am. Your turn."

"I'm lying here naked in my bed, imagining you are here, too. You aren't touching me—"

"Why not? If I was there, I would definitely be touching you." *And proving why you should end your two-year saga.*

"Tsk-tsk! This is my fantasy, René. Where was I? Oh, yeah, we are both naked in my bed. Not touching. But you are looking at me. And you know what? You make me feel attractive when you look at me, even when I have clothes on."

"Of course, you're attractive."

"That's not what I mean. When you look at me, I feel desirable, womanly."

"Okaaay." *Okaaay!*

"So, you're looking at me, head to toe, slowly. And it turns me on."

"It turns me on that I can turn you on." *And that's the God's honest truth.*

"What next?"

"Well, sweetie, it just depends on how daring you are."

Turns out she was very daring. Turns out he was, too. By the time her alarm clock went off a half-hour later, they were both depleted and splayed out flat on their backs on their respective beds.

After they said their soft good-byes, René clicked off his phone and smiled into the dark. *She'll be back.*

The Big Apple didn't seem so rosy

Valerie had been back in Manhattan for more than a day now, and nothing seemed the same.

Her small apartment with its tasteful furniture and lack of clutter seemed cold to her. The Bayou Black landscape painting on the wall that she'd inherited from a great-great-grandmother was a pale imitation of the real thing. The much-prized view of the Hudson River from her living room window was nothing compared to a bayou stream in the middle of nowhere.

She should have been preparing for her upcoming meeting with Elton and then Mr. Goodman. Instead she continued to read the fascinating material she'd picked up in the Houma bookstore on the demise of the bayou. Especially Mr. Tidwell's book, which read like a nonfiction novel and gave a poignant but alarming view of what was happening to her very own homeland.

And wasn't it surprising that she had suddenly developed an attachment to her native Southern Louisiana? Perhaps the love she'd had at one time for that primitive land, when her father used to take her on bayou expeditions, had lain dormant all this time. Perhaps she'd purposely tried to hate the very thing she loved . . . because he had left. Certainly something to think about.

Just before she was about to go out the door, the phone rang. Her heart skipped a beat. Could it be René?

No such luck.

"Hello, is this Val?" a thick Cajun female voice asked.

"Tante Lulu? Is something wrong? Oh my God! Did something happen to René?" *The idiot could have staple-gunned his hand, or been attacked by an alligator, or been gunned down by some fanatic oil company hired gun.*

The old lady chuckled. "I knew you cared about the

boy." Thirty-five years old, and she still considered René a boy.

"Why did you call?"

"Oh, I was jist wonderin' iffen ya had a chance to talk to Richard Simmons yet."

Is she crazy? "No, I haven't, and I don't expect to anytime soon. I'm off to a business meeting right now."

Instead of arguing with her or apologizing for interrupting her busy day, Tante Lulu went off on a tangent. "Do ya s'pose ya could pick me up sumpin' afore ya come back home to the bayou?"

"I'm not sure I'll be coming back. Anytime soon," she added to avoid her asking about that issue.

Not to worry. Tante Lulu skipped right over that important fact. "Charmaine bought me some panties at that Saxy Fifth Avenue store a few years back. They wuz really comfortable, dint ride up in the crack or nuthin'. Me, I cain't find them anywheres 'round here. White cotton. Sexy Lady label. Size two. And, by the by, René sure is missin' you."

How the old lady moved from one subject to another was unbelievable. Sort of a stream of consciousness-type of one-way conversation. But who cared about that? *René misses me.* She smiled widely.

"He started to go out on job interviews today. Wore a suit and everythin'. Even his red chili pepper tie. Whooee, he looked handsome, that boy did. Probably be the last day he hasta wear a suit, or so he sez. He ain't lookin' fer suit jobs. You shoulda seen him, though. I'm almos' done with yer bride quilt. You ended that two-year sex fast of yers yet? Prob'ly not, René doan have that look about him . . . ya know, the silly grin men wears when they'd had their way with a woman. When ya think you'll be comin' back? Best you get here fer my birthday party."

Whoa, whoa, whoa! "Tante Lulu, there is not going to be a wedding. So, please, no bride quilt."

"We could have my eightieth birthday celebration and yer wedding the same day. Save lots of money that way. Do ya think ya could be ready by September? I have René's mama's weddin' gown, iffen yer interested. But, no, that would be bad luck seein' as how she wed up with that rat Valcour in that dress. Mighty purty, it was, though."

Aaarrgh! It's like talking to a wall. "Tante Lulu, I have to go now."

"Okey dokey. Should I give René yer love?"

"Don't you dare." *If I ever decide to give René my love, it's going to be in person.*

"Toodle-oo!"

As Valerie stared at the dead receiver in her hand, she thought, *Who in the world says "toodle-oo" today?* But then, a more important thought came to her. *René misses me.*

It was in that pensive, but not unhappy, mood that she entered Elton Davis's plush office an hour later. The carpet was so thick her high heels sank into its depths. The walnut furniture was high-end and lavish. An elaborate stereo sytem and a wet bar graced one wall. On another side was a spectacular view of Madison Avenue. Elton treated himself well.

"Val! It's so good to see you," Elton gushed, coming out from behind his gargantuan desk, which was better suited to the Jolly Green Giant than his at best five-foot-ten frame. His arms were spread in greeting.

Surely the jerk didn't expect that she would allow him to hug her. No way! Val stretched out her right hand for a shake, which caused Elton to pause momentarily with surprise, then take her hand and pump it. Even that brief skin contact felt smarmy.

"This is great, Val," he said, indicating a chair for her while he scurried behind his desk, like the rat he was. "Ready to get back to work?"

Huh? She deliberately widened her eyes and cocked her head to the side.

His face flushed with the realization that she wasn't going to play nicey-nice with him.

"Let's cut to the chase, Elton. What's up?"

"I'm hurt by your attitude." He flashed her a puppy dog expression of dismay that he foolishly thought would melt her heart. As if! He looked like Goofy with a cinder in his eye.

"Listen, Elton, I don't have time for your games. You asked to see me? What's the deal? Did someone call you on the carpet for firing me?"

"Now see, there's the thing. I never really fired you. You misunderstood what I said and left before we had a chance to hash things out."

"Bullshit! You can feed that line to whomever will listen, but I'm not buying it. Tell me what you want."

She saw the anger that he hid under a controlled smile. "I have a new assignment for you. Wait till you hear about it. How about if we give you carte blanche and a prime-time slot to cover . . ." He paused in a ta-da fashion. ". . . your own trial."

"I beg your pardon."

"You file kidnapping charges against those redneck weirdos who kidnapped you, and then you cover the trial. Isn't that great?"

Even Elton managed to shock her this time. "That is just super. But have you considered the conflict of interest in my covering a case in which I am the plaintiff?"

He waved a hand dismissively. "We can get around that. I've already checked with legal." He beamed his toothy smile at her, as if he'd just handed her the moon. "Of course, there would be a sizeable pay raise with the job."

Unbelievable! He actually thought she would bend her standards for the sake of money and a promotion. And that word "redneck," did he make that assumption because the people in question were from Louisiana or the bayou? And he'd referred to them as weirdos. Well, J.B. and Maddie *were* weirdos, but he didn't know that. He was assuming that environmentalist equaled short of a brain fuse.

"I haven't filed a complaint, Elton, and I probably won't. Kidnapping charges are not going to be filed. So, no trial."

She waited for him to digest that information. And, frankly, she was angry now. The guy fired her and then tried to use her, all in one breath.

"Well, I'm sure we can find some other place for you at Trial TV." The lack of enthusiasm in his voice resonated in the air between them.

Valerie stood then and said something she'd wanted to say for a long, long time. "Elton, you turd . . ." she paused. "Take your job and shove it."

As she walked proudly out the door and down the hall-way, she felt surprisingly light and cheerful, as if a weight had been lifted from her back.

She had two hours to kill, then it was time for her to meet with Mr. Goodman. He was in the same building but three floors up. She spent the interval taking a walk in Central Park. Then, cool, calm, and collected, she entered Mr. Goodman's domain exactly on time.

Unlike Elton's office, which was embarrassingly opu-lent, Mr. Goodman's was almost austere. True, it was a corner office with a magnificent view, but the furniture was spare and almost Shakerlike in appearance. Stand-ing, the sixtyish gentleman of the old school, with dark pin-striped suit and black wing-tip toes, gave her a warm smile. "Good afternoon, Ms. Breaux. I'm so pleased to see you again. Come, sit over here." He motioned toward a small sitting area with two upholstered chairs and a round glass coffee table.

After they were both seated and she'd declined his offer of coffee, he got right to the point. "I understand you declined Elton Davis's offer."

"I did."

"Probably a wise decision."

She arched her brows in question.

"He's an ass."

"Agreed."

"Here's the thing, trash TV is hot. Everything from Jerry Springer-style talk shows to reality shows that shock to x-rated sex on regular TV. It's a fact of life we have to deal with right now."

"Can't we try to do better?"

"Of course we can, and we do. In fact, I believe you

have added a touch of taste to our programming . . . even when it was a bit trashy."

"Tasteful trash, huh?" She had to laugh, if that was what her life amounted to the last few years.

"I like the ring to that. Mind if I use it sometime?"

"Feel free," she said, waving a hand magnanimously. Valerie was "reading" Mr. Goodman as they talked, and she deemed him an honest man.

"As you know, Ms. Breaux, Goodman Enterprises owns Trial TV. Also the Nature channel, the Home Design channel, Crime Solvers, and soon a new channel called Investigative Reports, or IRC. The latter will broadcast all kinds of things; we don't even have guidelines at this point. Do you get my drift?"

"Loud and clear," she replied with a smile. He must have heard the rumors that she was considering a bayou documentary. "Are you saying that, if I come up with a formal proposal for something called, let's say, 'Bayou Uncovered,' you would be willing to consider it?"

"Absolutely. But keep one thing in mind, my dear. I've been in this business a long time. The public doesn't want cut-and-dry propaganda, no matter how important. It has to affect them personally. And there has to be an angle to draw them in."

"Like Elton's shock 'n' rock brand of programming?"

"Not necessarily. Find a hook to draw people in to watch, then you can preach to them all you want."

Hmmm. I wonder if . . . no, that would be too far fetched . . . but, hell, it wouldn't hurt to try. "Did you know there is a bayou plant, the Juju plant, which is responsible for the renowned virility of Cajun men? And if the pollution and coastal erosion continues at its present pace, the plant will be lost forever?"

"Bingo!" Mr. Goodman said, with a laugh. "I don't suppose you know some especially virile Cajun man who could be the narrator for this *potential* documentary."

"Bingo!" Val said then. "The Juju Man."

Suddenly her life looked a little brighter.

The only problem would be convincing a certain Cajun man to go public with his prowess. *Piece a cake!*

She could swear she heard laughing in her head.

When you're hot, you're hot

"No! Absolutely not!" René exclaimed into the telephone.

He couldn't believe that Val actually believed he would allow himself to become the poster boy for Cajun virility. *As if I could! As if I would! Talk about! I would never willingly expose myself to the ridicule I would get. I can just imagine what my brothers would do with that information.*

"Can't you trust me that it would be done tastefully?"

"No."

"My boss, my former boss, said I bring taste to everything I do."

"No."

"You said you wanted me to come back."

"I do, but not so I can take off my clothes and run buck naked through the swamps in front of some TV camera."

"I never suggested any such thing."

"Are you going to be in this thing, too? You know,

wearing some fur thingee, probably muskrat skins, like a female Daniel Boone with cleavage." He was laughing at the image and all the possibilities. Wasn't there a cult that espoused fur sex? Fuzzies, or Furries, or some such thing. Lordy, Lordy! Fur sex with a woman who hadn't had sex in two years. They would burn the lens off the TV camera.

"Now you're being silly."

"No, I'm not. Tit for tat, baby."

"I'm being serious, René. I've been doing a lot of reading, and I believe I could do a good job in portraying the massive problems affecting the bayou. But we need a hook."

"Well, your hook is going to be planted someplace else, other than my private parts." *I cringe just making that joke.*

"What do you think J.B. and Maddie and the Bayou Unite folks would think of my idea?"

"You are not going to mention this to them. That is an order." *I am not going to have those two flakes attached to me like barnacles, begging me to do it.*

She laughed, as if him giving her an order was laughable. Which it was, of course. "Tante Lulu told me that you're looking for a new job."

"I am. When did you talk to my aunt?"

"Today. She called me to see if I could buy her some panties at Saks Fifth Avenue."

"Oh my God! At least it wasn't Victoria's Secret."

"She told me that you looked really hot in a business suit."

"I always look hot, darlin'." *Don't I?*

"Modesty is not one of your strong points. There was one more thing she happened to mention."

Uh-oh! "If she said that I got drunk Sunday night, it was a lie." *Buzzed, yes. Drunk, no.*

"She said that you were missing me."

He heard the shakiness in her voice, and he paused to get his voice calm. "That is the truth, *chére.*" After several moments of silence, he asked, "How about you? Have you been missing me?"

"I've been really busy with meetings and everything and . . . oh, hell! I'm missing you like crazy."

He smiled. "Come home to the bayou."

Instead of answering him directly, she asked, "Where are you living now? At your place in Baton Rouge, or in Remy's houseboat?"

"In Baton Rouge most of the time. And I hate it, being away from the bayou. I'm gonna sell it." He gave her an address but was afraid to ask if she was writing it down.

"Where would you live then?"

Wherever you are, sweetheart. Oh, shit! I hope I didn't say that out loud.

"You couldn't work from your cabin, could you?"

"Probably not . . . maybe . . . I don't know yet. Depends on the kind of field work I do eventually."

"We'll talk about the documentary when I see you," she said.

"We're gonna do a lot more than talk."

"Is that a fact."

Practically a fact. "I told you what will happen next time we meet."

"Two years is a long time, René. Are you sure you can handle that?" He heard the tease in her voice.

He just chuckled. Answer enough.

"My plane gets in tomorrow night," she said.

"Do you want me to meet you at the airport?"

"No. I'll see you when I see you."

He wanted to say something special to her then, but he couldn't think what. It was too early to say those three words women loved to draw out of men, and the right time might never come. But he should be able to say something.

"I care about you, Val." *How pitiful is that? The King of Smooth is more like the King of Unsmooth.*

"I care, too, René. I don't know why. I just do."

That was good enough for now.

Chapter 12

There is virility . . . and then there is VIRILITY

Valerie's taxi didn't arrive at René's town house till eleven o'clock, due to several plane delays and extreme security precautions in the airports.

She wore a swirly gauze skirt down to her calves in varying shades of green—everything from pale celery to dark jade. A formfitting, short-sleeved mint-green shirt hugged her breasts and abdomen and was tucked into her waistband. She'd had her hair done at her favorite Fifth Avenue salon to achieve its mussed look. A manicure and pedicure had produced the bright red lacquer that she now sported. She'd shaved her legs . . . twice. And she'd had a bikini wax, even though she hadn't worn a bikini in more than ten years.

She was ready.

And so was René, if how he stood in the open doorway waiting for her was any indication. He wore a white Toby Keith concert shirt that read WHO'S YOUR DADDY? and black jogging pants. Barefooted, he came down the steps slowly, paid the cab driver, and took her luggage in each of his hands. He motioned with his head for her to preceed him up the steps.

But she dug in her heels. "Aren't you even going to say hi, or give me a kiss hello?"

"Hell, no," he said, looking directly at her for the first time. She saw the smoldering heat in his eyes, and it almost scared her. Almost. "If I kiss you now, we'll end up having sex on my front steps, and I'll explode way too soon. I have a history of that, as you know."

God, he's still fixating over what happened nineteen years ago. How sweet! Satisfied that he was happy to see her, even without the words and actions, she walked up the steps in front of him, making sure she swished her hips from side to side.

"You are going to pay for that," she thought she heard him mutter. Then he asked, presumably staring at her swishing behind, "Are you wearing a thong?"

She smiled to herself and peered at him over her shoulder, then winked. "No."

It took him several moments to register that she meant that she wore nothing. His jaw dropped open and he said, "Jesus, Mary, and Joseph!"

What happened next was so quick, her brain spun. She stepped into the hallway and was about to comment on his collection of expressionist watercolors when the door slammed behind her, René dropped her luggage to the floor, and she was pinned up against the wall with her skirt up to her waist. René was running his hands over her backside . . . her panty-clad backside. "You fibbed," he said, nipping at her mouth with his teeth.

"Did you honestly think I would go through airport security with no underwear? They would probably have insisted on a cavity search."

"I could do that," he offered. But then he dropped

down to his knees in front of her. Pressing his face against her belly, he held her with arms around her thighs. The silence in the hallway was deafening.

"René? What's wrong?"

"Nothing's wrong. Everything is right, finally, and it took my breath away."

"Oh, René," she said softly, and sank down to her knees, too. Taking his face in her hands, she kissed him gently. "Let's just take this slow. We don't have anything to prove here."

"Hah! You might not, but I do."

"Forget about *that*. Now, do you want to give me a tour of your home?"

"No. I'd much rather do a body tour . . . or two . . . or twelve."

He kissed her then. Hungry, hungry kisses that went on forever. His mouth was wet and hot on her, his tongue driving, his hands everywhere at once. Somehow they found themselves on the floor, with him lying on top of her.

"Oh, shit, we're going to have sex on the hallway floor, aren't we?"

"I hope so." She shrugged out of her panties the best she could with him on top of her. Reaching a hand inside the stretch waistband of his pants, she took the hard length of him in her hand.

"Jeeeeeeeesh!" he shouted, shoving her hand aside. "Don't do that. Not yet. Holy-holy-holy-holy-hell! What are you doing to me? Let me get up. We'll go to my bedroom."

"No! Now! I want you now," she said, arching her hips

up against his rampant erection. "I want you freakin' *now*."

"What? Okay. No. I need to go get a condom."

"Don't worry. I'm on the pill."

"Two years of celibacy and you're on the pill. Why?"

"Uh, René, can we discuss this later?"

"Oh. Yeah." Panting for breath, he pushed his pants down, while she drew her skirt up, and within seconds he was poised at her entrance. Then, oh my God, he thrust himself into her, all the way to forever. Her inner muscles clasped and unclasped around him in an instantaneous orgasm that about blew her lid off and melted her red nail lacquer.

When she had a chance to catch her breath, she looked at René. Eyes closed, he was braced on his forearms. His neck arched back, the cords standing out with tension. And he was still hard inside her, God bless him. Why was he holding back? Oh. That old premature ejaculation fixation of his. "Move, dammit."

He opened his eyes and stared at her, dazed. "I want to fuck you so bad I can taste it."

"Then do it."

"It's too soon."

"No. It's way too late, baby. Come on. Please. Come on."

He smiled then and slowly, ever so slowly eased out of her almost all the way, then just as slowly back again. The friction was sweet torture.

"Wider," he said in a voice husky with arousal. Pushing her knees up and out, he demonstrated what he meant.

And she felt him ease in another unbelievable inch or

more. And his pubic bone touched her in just the right spot. And red stars danced in front of her open eyes.

"You feel . . . so good . . . in me," she gasped out.

"I feel so good being in you," he said, also gasping.

Then began the long, long strokes, in and out, over and over till Valerie thought she would go mad. She moaned continuously. She wrapped her legs around his hips. She grasped his buttocks and kneaded them. For a guy who worried about popping off too quick, René was taking an awfully long time to climax.

In fact, he stopped. Deeply imbedded in her, he reached down and separated her more so the most sensitive part of her was more exposed. Then he said, "Look at us, darlin'."

Her dark hair was mixed with his dark hair there. It was impossible to tell where she ended or he began, or vice versa.

"Sweet, huh?" His voice was husky and low.

"Sweet," she agreed.

Then he began the hard, fast strokes she'd been yearning for. Everything was happening so fast now. Sensations hit her in every part of her body. Where they were joined. Inside. Her breasts. All of her skin.

And the noise. The slick, wet sounds of sex. The moans, from both of them.

He arched his back, bared his teeth and groaned, "Yessss!"

She would have yelled "Yessss!" too, except she was concentrating on not having her eyes roll back in her head. But she went with him on that wave of ecstasy, hard ripples of released tension emanating from their joining to all parts of both their bodies.

Laughing, René raised himself up on his elbows and brushed several stray curls off her forehead. So much for her hundred-dollar hairdo! "Cryin' catfish, Val. I haven't made love with my pants around my ankles since I was a teenager."

"And I've never made love inside the front door on the floor. But we were good, weren't we?"

René looked at Val, who looked so incredibly hot with her sex-mussed hair and her flushed face that his heart constricted. He wanted to say so many things to her. Instead, all he said was, "Damn good."

He eased himself out of her in painful pleasure, then stood, pulled up his sweat pants and jockeys all at once. For a second, he just stared at her, taking in the picture of her with her lower body exposed up to her waist. Moisture glistened on the tight curls between her legs, and didn't that make him feel all studly and full of himself? He'd come through just fine, double entendre intended.

But, whoa, suddenly he was turned on again. They had the whole night before them . . . hell, they might even have a lifetime. He had to pace himself.

Reaching down, he took her hand and pulled her to her feet and into his arms. He just hugged her for a moment, and murmured "thank you" into her ear.

She leaned her head back and said, "Hey, thank you."

I could love her.

Where that thought came from, he had no idea, but sonofagun that was dangerous territory this early in the game . . . even late in the game. Still, the voice in his head repeated, *I could love her.* It was probably that pesty St. Jude planting insidious ideas in his brain. That had to be it.

"It's not every day a girl gets to end her two-year drought in such spectacular fashion. Let's hope my next lengthy period of self-denial has a guy like you at the end of it."

The prospect of her going celibate again bothered him a lot. Even more bothersome was the prospect of her with another man. It was not going to happen, he decided then and there, neither of those things. But he wasn't going to think about the implications of his resolution.

He gave her a tour of the house, which didn't take all that long. There were only two bedrooms, one of which he used as an office. It was a basic man's place with minimal furniture, though what he had was good handcrafted stuff. On the hardwood floors were Cajun woven carpets in bright colors. Of course, he did have the odd accessory—though not so odd for his family—of an assortment of St. Jude statues in every room. There was even a St. Jude refrigerator magnet. And there was an accordion on top of the fridge.

The town house's biggest drawback now was that it was in the middle of the capital city—an asset when he worked as a lobbyist. But it was not near the bayous he loved. That would change now.

"Are you hungry?" he asked. "I bought Chinese."

"Chinese for a Cajun? Isn't that a sacrilege or something?"

He grinned. "It probably has okra or crawfish in it somewhere. You can't totally get away from Cajun anywhere in Southern Loo-zee-anna."

"I am hungry," she said, "but let's wait. I'm still too excited to eat."

René about swallowed his tongue at that casually dropped bombshell. *She is still excited. Thank you, God!*

God has nothing to do with it, the voice in his head said.

"Do you have any wine?"

"I do. And it's chilled, too."

They both sipped at the chilled sauvignon. Then René walked over to the stereo and flipped a switch. A soft Cajun instrumental came on. "Will you take off your shirt?" he asked abruptly as he turned back to her. She stood framed in the kitchen archway.

Her eyes went wide with surprise.

"I want to see you." When she didn't immediately do as he asked, probably due to shyness, he set his glass down and pulled his own shirt over his head, dropping it to the floor. "You can see mine first."

She gave a short hoot of a laugh. Like the trade would be anywhere equal. But she did put her drink on the kitchen table, then tugged the hem of her shirt out of the skirt. Ever so slowly, like a born temptress, she drew it over her head.

He studied her for a moment. "Man oh man, I didn't think anything could be better than your heart-shaped ass. I was wrong, your champagne breasts are a tie, at least." *Valerie Breaux is a hottie. Whooee!*

"Heart-shaped . . . ?" she started to sputter, then smiled. "Champagne and hearts, huh? I like that."

"Not nearly as much as I do, darlin'." *What a lucky guy I am!*

"What now?" she asked with a flushed face as he continued to stare at her. "I'm kind of rusty at this. Actually, I never was very good."

"Don't underestimate yourself, baby. You're good, all right." He held his arms out for her. "Let's dance."

He could tell his request surprised her. *Always best to keep the ladies guessing.* She'd probably thought he was going to skip all the foreplay and just jump her bones again. *Hah! I am getting my smoothness back by leaps and bounds.*

Flicking off her sandals, she came toward him, wearing only her gauzy skirt. Fair exchange. He only had sweats on and no shoes, as well. He took her in his arms and danced. He loved to dance. He especially loved dancing with Val with her breasts nestled in his chest hairs. He shifted himself from side to side several times to abrade her nipples to hard peaks. Her small gasp of pleasure was his reward.

He moved expertly to the rhythm, and Val followed him perfectly. They were a good match.

He ran the flats of his hands down her bare back. She did the same to him, then daringly slid her hands inside his pants and cupped his buttocks.

He about lost it then. It took all his self-control to set her away from him, still devouring her with his eyes. Her breasts were pink-tipped and hard as pebbles. He touched them with his fingertips, and she inhaled sharply with pleasure, then arched her back slightly so he would touch her more. But, no, he had other things in mind. Undoing the waistband of her skirt, he let it slide to the floor in a frothy puddle. This was his first full-fledged look at her body, and she was beautiful. All white pearly skin that curved in all the right places. No fashionably skinny frame like other women yearned to have. More the softness that most men preferred.

Lifting her by the waist, he sat her on the back of his couch, her feet on the seat. Since it was freestanding, not against a wall, she had to hold on with her hands to avoid falling backward. "Open for me, babe," he urged.

Her face flooded with color and she started to balk. "I don't like this, René."

"For me, *chére*. Do it for me. I want to know all of you."

Slowly, she parted her legs, but not very far.

He arched his brows at her. "Surely you're not afraid. I didn't think you were afraid of anything. Not snakes, or smarmy producers, or wiley Cajuns."

At that challenge, she raised her chin high and parted her knees wide. She was fully and completely exposed to him.

He shimmied out of his pants, the whole time looking at her there. Then he glanced down at the erection he was sporting, then back to her face. "This is what you do to me. This is how much I enjoy looking at you." He touched himself briefly, running a loose fist from his balls to his tip, and became even bigger. She gasped with shock at his gesture. "Men like to watch women touching themselves. Do you enjoy watching me?" he asked.

Her face got even redder. "I don't know. It's new to me. Maybe."

He fisted himself again, but only briefly. He didn't want to come this way. "*This* is a reflection of how attractive you are to me. That's all I'm trying to show you."

"Let's make love then. No more of me on display."

"We will make love, darlin'. More than once. But first, we do it my way. Okay?" *Please, please, please.*

She hesitated, but then she nodded.

I think I'll say a novena of thanks tomorrow . . . or next week . . . or I'll ask Tante Lulu to say one for me. No, I can't do that. She would ask me what I'm thankful for.

He knelt on the floor in front of the couch and used the fingertips of both hands to part her folds more. Her nether lips were pink and slick with moisture.

"You are beautiful there. Did you know that?"

She shook her head slightly, which was charming, really.

"I'm going to taste you now. Hold on tight." He leaned forward and ran the tip of his tongue up one side and down the other.

She shivered and made a small whimpering sound.

He repeated the same journey several more times with his tongue and his fingertips, sometimes alternating with fluttery vibrations. But always he avoided the one place he knew she wanted to be touched. Finally, he tongued her there, light butterfly sweeps at first, then fast, fast, fast. She was keening continuously then.

But he had more in store for her. Much more.

Inserting a long middle finger inside of her, he massaged her inside and used a rhythmic pumping of the heel of his hand on the outside so he was coming at her from both sides.

She screamed, she actually screamed as wave after wave of convulsions shook her. It was the most erotic thing he'd ever heard.

She wilted then and would have collapsed backward, except he caught her in his arms, and in one deft move, he was lying on his back lengthwise on the couch with her on top of him.

"Are you ready to make love now, darlin'?" he inquired.

She started to laugh with incredulity at his question. But she soon stopped laughing when he raised her up so she was sitting on him, her legs folded on either side of his hips. He arched his body upward, and within seconds, she was impaled on him.

At first, she just blinked at him, too shocked at the position she was in. But then, he felt her inner folds accommodated his width and length. And she smiled.

Smiling is good. Smiling means I'm doing something right.

"That's nice," she said.

"Nice?" he exclaimed. "Nice is a sweet kiss on the cheek. Nice is a grandma word for good girls. Nice is a sweet praline. This is definitely not nice. This is spectacular." And it was. He'd never felt this virile before in his life. Maybe he was so good because she was so good.

"René?"

"Hmmmm?" He was trying to focus his attention on nonrelevant things to delay his orgasm. After all this effort, he didn't want to come too soon. *Tante Lulu doing a belly dance. Me catching a five-pound catfish. The time I helped a lady have a baby in the back of her station wagon. Okra.*

"I don't think I can do this again."

"Huh?" *Oh, no, no, no. You are not going to pull a "This was a mistake" on me now. No, no, no.* "Am I hurting you?"

"No, you're not hurting me," she said, grinding her hips around *it* in a circular fashion to demonstrate.

It felt that little bit of friction like manna from heaven, and René closed his eyes for a second, just in case they'd crossed.

"I just meant that I don't think I can come again so soon. And I don't think I have the energy—"

Oh. Is that all? "I'm gonna give you energy all right. And I promise you, baby, you *can* come again."

She laughed, whether in disbelief or in reaction to the vehemence of his response, he didn't know . . . or care.

Valerie was in fact laughing out of sheer joy. She had never felt such freedom before. No inhibitions. No worries about how she looked or whether her actions were normal. René made her feel as if anything she did would give him pleasure. She loved him for that. *In fact, I could love this man.* For a moment, Valerie froze. She had no idea where that mind blip had come from. Probably she was having a delayed reaction to having thrown her career away, at least the career she had thought she always wanted. But there were surprisingly no regrets. And in the midst of all these liberating feelings was this man. Later, she might think he was a pig, but for now he was gorgeous and thoughtful and playful . . . and oh my gracious what was that he was doing now? *Ay yi yi!*

Most men by now would have done the in-and-out dance a few times and the program would be over. Not René, bless his heart. Nope, he was half sitting up, taking her left breast in his hand, raising it upward with the nipple pointing outward, and then . . . and THEN . . . he took the whole breast into his hot, wet mouth. He stopped briefly and asked way too sweetly, "Do you like that, darlin'?" Without waiting for an answer, he resumed his delicious torture.

"Yikes!" she yelled.

To which he smiled against her breast.

Intense sensations ricocheted throughout her body from the nipple he was assaulting with his flicking tongue and nipping teeth. She would have jumped right off of him, but his other hand was behind her nape, holding her in place.

She heard him chuckle before switching hands and breasts. *Hah! I'll show him.* Focusing her attention to that place where they were joined, she clenched and unclenched her inner muscles a half dozen times in quick succession.

"Aaaaahhh!!" he hollered, falling backward and raising his hips and her right up off the couch.

"Do you like that, darlin'?" she repeated his question, just as sweetly.

"Witch!" he said, swatting her on the behind when he was able to catch his breath. "I take it you have your energy back."

"In spades. They oughta bottle you, like one of those adrenaline rush drinks."

He smiled. "Who moves first?"

She wanted to say something smart and witty and teasing but couldn't think of a thing. "I'm really not very good at this."

"You could have fooled me. Just do what feels good to you. Believe me, I am not particular."

She leaned forward, bracing her hands on either side of his head and lifted her butt slowly, higher and higher, to the tippy top, then sank just as slowly back down again. The fact that he closed his eyes and made a sort of whoofing sound with his mouth told her she'd probably done it right. So, she repeated herself. And it felt so good that she closed her eyes and made the same whoofing sound, like a woman in labor, except this was labor of the best sort. When she did it a third time, René jackknifed up, flipping her on her back at the other end of the couch. Now he was on top.

"Enough sweet torture," he choked out, then began to assault her body with long hard strokes that stoked the heat inside her. She wanted to reach up and kiss him or caress his body, but she needed to concentrate on her center where all the action was taking place. "Come, *chére*, come. Come. Come," he kept urging her. "I can't come till you do."

"Why not?" she asked.

"Hush!" he gasped out with a laugh. She supposed this was not the time for conversation as he continued to pound into her. "Just frickin' come!" he begged.

And she did.

And he did.

And both their worlds rocked.

Chapter 13

Male Fantasies 'r' Us

They were sitting in his kitchen, eating Chinese food, buck naked. Was this a guy dream-come-true or what?

René could tell that Val was a little embarrassed to be nude in this bright light, but she would never admit to such a weakness as feminine insecurity about her body. So, she went along with him. *Am I a lucky duck or what?*

"Stop grinning like that," she snapped.

Note to self: quit grinning.

It was fun watching Val eat. She ate, like she engaged in sex—with relish. She'd scarfed down two egg rolls and half a carton each of lemon chicken, fried rice, and lo mein, all followed with several healthy slugs of white wine.

He couldn't blame Val for having a voracious appetite and thirst after all their mutual exertions. His was the same.

Her fortune cookie read: "You need more exercise," which pleased him mightily. His read: "Life is good." And man, that was the truth. But then he opened another one and it said, "Beware of thunderbolts," which alarmed them both. Shades of Tante Lulu. A real woo-woo moment.

It wasn't any better when Val cracked open the last one: "The saints are watching over you."

"St. Jude?" he wondered, glancing at the refrigerator magnet, which seemed to wink at him.

She laughed and said, "Goodness, I hope the saints haven't been watching us."

"I'm happy," he said, propping his chin in his cupped hand with his elbow on the table. *Actually, happy doesn't begin to describe how I feel, baby.*

"And stop staring at me."

Uh-oh, the lady is a little testy. Someone needs a hug. "Why? I like staring at you. Besides, you can look at me all you want."

She laughed. "I need to take a shower," she said.

More sex. He brightened at that prospect.

But then she added, "Do you have a shower cap?"

"Why do you need a shower cap?"

"I paid a hundred dollars for this hairstyle, buddy."

"You're kidding. I know a barber in Houma who could style you for ten bucks, fifteen max."

She gave him one of those looks that pretty much said, "Men! They don't have a clue."

"I know what you were thinking," she said, shaking her head from side to side.

He decided to go for cool. "What?" he asked with as much innocence as a man carrying two thousand pounds of testosterone could manage.

"You're thinking you're going to do me again just because I mentioned the shower. Well, forget about it. You did me twice already. Now it's my turn to do you."

"And you thought I would argue with that?"

So it was that he ended up in his glass-enclosed

shower with Val *doing him.* He was a modern guy. He knew when to bend. Yep, he didn't mind one bit letting her "do him."

Her hundred-dollar hairdo didn't stand a chance.

The lull before the storm

By the time they entered René's bedroom an hour later, both of them were more than ready to sleep.

Wearing a knee-length, spaghetti-strapped, nylon nightgown she'd pulled from her suitcase, Valerie combed her wet hair. René was lying on the bed, his arms folded behind his head, watching her. He wore a smile. That's all. *What a guy.*

She noticed the store folds in the sheets and was touched. He must have gone out and bought new bed linens. And the towels in the bathroom had been new, too. For her? And he had lit candles arranged all around the bedroom. *How endearing!*

"At some point, we need to talk about the documentary," she said, sitting on the edge of the bed.

"Not now." He was trailing a fingertip along her thigh, raising the gown higher.

She swatted his hand away. "Tomorrow?" *You better agree. Justin is coming in the afternoon to brainstorm.*

He nodded. "I'm not promising anything, though."

You'll do it. "I understand."

He yawned loudly, open-mouthed. "Come here, darlin'," he urged, opening his arms for her.

She turned off the bedside lamp. The room was still

illuminated by the candles. She slid into the bed and his arms, resting her face on his chest.

"Do you want to make love again?" he asked. Valerie couldn't fail to hear the lack of enthusiasm in his voice.

"You are so full of it. As if you could rise to the occasion again so soon."

"Hah! You'd be surprised—"

"Shhh," she said, putting a fingertip to his lips. "Later."

Almost immediately, he fell sound asleep. Just before she fell asleep herself, she thought, as she had earlier, *I could love this man.*

No more than an hour later—candles still burning—he awakened her to make love. Unlike the frenzied, hungry sex they'd engaged in thus far, this was a soft, slow study of each other's bodies. A silent expression of feelings too new to be spoken aloud.

After that, they slept in each other's arms until daylight. Not that it was the sun streaming through the window that awakened them. No. It was the pounding on the front door downstairs.

She blinked drowsily at René, and he blinked back at her. They both said, "Uh-oh!" at the same time.

The pounding continued, louder now.

They quickly got out of bed and rushed to the window.

"Oh my God!" she exclaimed.

René looked as if he was in shock.

A pink Thunderbird was parked out front with a bumper sticker that read, NOT SO CLOSE, I'M NOT THAT KIND OF CAR.

It was Tante Lulu.

And a cop.

There are whirlwinds . . . and then there are whirlwinds

René pulled on his sweatpants and Valerie wore his Toby Keith T-shirt, which ended about knee-high. When he opened the front door, midpound, they were both presentable, but just barely.

Tante Lulu pushed past them into the hallway huffing with outrage. She wore black kiddie-sized spandex tights and a black T-shirt, also kiddie-sized, which pronounced in neon pink letters, EXERCISE THAT! Her curly hair was pink today to match the letters and her pink athletic shoes. The shoes had a logo on them that appeared to be Barbie. Yep, she'd been shopping in the kid's department at Wal-Mart again. And, yep, she must still be on her Richard Simmons kick.

"You kin talk to my lawyer." Tante Lulu had stopped midway down the hall to point at Val before she continued on her way.

Val, who in her skimpy attire looked like no lawyer the cop had ever met said, "No, no, no! I am definitely not that ding—that woman's lawyer."

The cop's jaw dropped for a nanosecond as his eyes swept over Val from head to red-painted toes. In an instant, his face went blank again.

"What did my aunt do?" *Knowing her, it could be anything. I remember the time she was arrested for prostitution . . . at age seventy-five. Not that she was doing anything. Lord knows! But she was dressed like a hooker—thanks to some fashion advice from Charmaine—and walking through a red-light district. Said she was just looking for an old friend.*

"Seventy in a fifty-mile per hour zone."

Whew! Is that all? "Did you give her a ticket?"

He nodded. Clearly he was more upset than René. Tante Lulu had a way of affecting people that way. "I'm more concerned about getting her off the highway. At her age, I wonder if she shouldn't have her license revoked. Can't you do something to make her give it up voluntarily?"

Why don't you just ask me to give myself a vasectomy with a butter knife? "I'll try," he said.

"When I motioned for her to pull over, she gave me the finger."

Good for you, Auntie. No, I don't mean that. What a childish thing to think. "Are you sure? Maybe she was waving to you." He fought the smile that twitched at his lips.

"I know when I've been flipped the bird."

"Did you give her a ticket for that, too? Is there a crime for that, Val? Felonious Finger or something?"

Val didn't answer. She was looking as if she'd just landed in the middle of Wonderland.

"You might think this is funny," the cop said, "but I'm not amused." He slapped the ticket into René's hand and turned toward the steps to his car, which had its bubblegum siren lights blinking. Even at this early hour, various neighbors were peering outside to see what the problem was. They probably thought René was being arrested. He hadn't always been the best neighbor. Think loud music and rowdy friends.

After he closed the door, he and Val walked to the kitchen where Tante Lulu was already examining the contents of his refrigerator and obviously finding it lacking, if her *tsk*ing noises were any indication. She took out one of the cartons of Chinese food, opened and sniffed, then put it back.

"Ain't you got any of that boudin I gave you las' month?" She had her back to them and wasn't that a sight—her nonexistent backside to them as she bent over.

"It's in the freezer," he said.

"Good. I'll make us a good breakfas'." She turned and gave them her full attention. "Good golly! Guess I doan hafta ask if yer two years is up, Val. You both look like you been put through a meat grinder. And, Lordy, Lordy, who's doin' yer hair now, Val? Ya gotta go see Charmaine."

It was the first time this morning he'd gotten a good look at Val, too. His eyes widened at the sight she presented. Her hair, which was wet when they went to sleep, had dried in about fifty different directions. Her cheeks were whisker burned. Her mouth was a swollen vision of male sexual fantasy. And was that—? yes, it was—a bite mark on her inner thigh.

Val looked as if she wanted to sink through the floor.

Then Tante Lulu turned her attention to him. "Ya better do the right thing, boy. Ya wuz raised right. I still think y'all could have yer weddin' and my birthday bash on the same day."

He put his face in his hands.

Val made a soft gurgling sound that he would have found cute under normal circumstances, but not when they'd been invaded by the Cajun Godmother.

"What are you doing here?" he asked his aunt.

"I heard Val wuz gonna do the TV story on the bayou, and I figgered ya'll would need my help."

"Where did you hear that?" Val demanded to know.

"I got sources," Tante Lulu replied. "You wanna do some exercises with me this morning, Val? I brought my 'Sweatin' to the Oldies' tape."

"I get plenty of exercise, thank you very much," Val made the mistake of saying indignantly.

Tante Lulu, of course, took her cue. "Thass obvious."

Val's face reddened at her mistake.

"Go get yerselves dressed," his aunt ordered both of them then. She'd already pulled out eggs, milk, onion and a pigload of other stuff he didn't even know he had. "I'll make us a big Cajun breakfas'. Then we kin start plannin'."

"She is not going to plan my documentary," Val hissed as they walked up the stairs. "And where did she hear that I was going to be involved in this documentary?"

He shrugged. "The bayou grapevine, I suppose. And, hey, I have a bigger beef than you do. I never even agreed to be involved in this documentary."

She flashed him a look that said he would be involved all right . . . or suffer the consequences. *Maybe I should ask her what those consequences would be. Then again, maybe not.*

Tante Lulu came out of the kitchen and yelled up the stairs, "And no hanky-panky. I ain't havin' any brides with big bellies in this fam'ly."

Val gasped, but he grabbed a hold of her upper arm and pulled her along.

Once they were inside the bedroom, Val turned on

him. He was leaning with his back to the door. "How do you put up with that old woman?"

He shrugged. "I love her."

She lifted her chin, angry, he could tell. "Just how long do you think it will take her to prepare this monster breakfast?"

"About a half hour, I suppose."

"And how long for a bout of hanky-panky?"

He smiled then. "Long enough."

With his hands behind his back, he locked the door. He supposed she was going to make love with him as an act of rebellion against his aunt.

Like I care why. I'm getting morning sex, and I didn't even have to beg.

Work, work, work . . . then play

René had made a joke one time when they were back in the bayou about Alice in Wonderland. Well, by early that afternoon, that's exactly where Valerie felt she had landed.

Justin arrived first, looking all single guy studly in dark ponytail and tight jeans. After he'd told her that he was part Houma Indian, Valerie could have kicked herself—being a jury analyst and all—for not recognizing his heritage from his high cheekbones and coloring.

He was a handsome man—another thing she had failed to note before—and René disliked him on sight. Valerie took a warped delight in his blatant jealousy. To which, his aunt kept muttering, "The thunderbolt, fer sure."

But Justin wasn't the only visitor. J.B. and Maddie came uninvited—heck, no one in this crowd waited to be invited. They were overly enthusiastic about the documentary that she hadn't sold and René hadn't yet agreed to.

Tee-John arrived last. He looked at René, looked at her, then let out a hoot of laughter. "Who's been having wild monkey sex?" Then to Tante Lulu he inquired, "Got anything to eat, Auntie?"

Tante Lulu beamed. "Is the Pope Cath'lic?"

They sat around the living room now, taking voluminous notes on the documentary. Tante Lulu was in her glory in the kitchen, cooking up enough food to feed an army. She had sent Tee-John out for groceries soon after he arrived, and he was helping her prepare "a little snack."

René was brilliant in giving a passionate description of the destruction of his beloved bayou. He had a way of reducing dry, complex ideas down to the ridiculous. That talent would be appealing on camera, if they were able to talk him into doing it. For example, he wouldn't just say that it was a monumental problem involving the land in Southern Louisiana sinking or the massive erosion caused by oil company canals. Nope. He would say, "Every twenty minutes a landmass the size of a football field is disappearing in Southern Louisiana."

And surprisingly, J.B. and Maddie were equally eloquent in expressing their feelings about their beloved land.

"That writer Mike Tidwell said in his book that this was the greatest untold story in America, and it is, by God. But dammit we can't get people to listen," said J.B

"Even the big environmental groups don't join up with us. Partly because they think of us as backwards people, and partly because we ain't got no cute animal that's endangered, like a grizzly or a fox."

"People get all het up over the rain forests in Brazil or the Everglades in Florida, but they jist don't realize what effect Southern Loo-zee-anna has on the rest of the country," Maddie added.

Even Tante Lulu threw her two cents in from the kitchen. "I cain't hardly find haf' the herbs I need for healing. They's buried underwater now, or dead from the pollution." As annoying as she could be, Valerie admired the tough old bird.

Justin went out to his truck for a minute to get some kind of camera equipment he wanted to show them. J.B. and Maddie went to the kitchen to test Tante Lulu's gumbo, at her insistence. René leaned over on the couch and pinched Val's thigh. "Wanna scoot upstairs for five minutes of hanky-panky?"

"Get real."

"I don't like that Justin."

"You've made that obvious."

"I think he's gay."

She laughed. "Where would you ever get that idea."

"He wears a ponytail."

"Ozzy Osbourne wears a ponytail and he has three kids."

"Great example, toots." He chided her.

"David Beckham then. He has a ponytail."

"No, no. You already said Ozzy."

"Ponytail does not equal homosexual," she argued, even though he was probably kidding.

"He's not your type," he threw in, no doubt figuring new tactics were needed.

"What *is* my type?" she asked before she had a chance to bite her tongue.

He winked at her. "Me, baby. Me."

That's what I'm afraid of.

After another hour of brainstorming, they decided on a rough plan for the documentary. Valerie would contact and interview various Louisiana conservationists, including members of the Coast 2050 committee, along with scientists and oil company employees and executives. Justin thought, and he was right, that they needed visuals of the bayou's deterioration, and that meant that they needed to go deep into the bayou to get the real story. They decided they would take J.B. and Maddie's shrimp boat and travel along various bayous that led out to the Gulf. It was impossible to make the whole journey in that one boat, however. Some parts would be over land, where they would pick up their journey in another vessel. J.B. and Maddie had numerous friends who worked or lived on the water. They would interview people along the way—the people most affected by the bayou's deterioration: fishermen, farmers, storekeepers.

"Tante Lulu should come, too," Justin said.

"What?" Val and René said at the same time.

"Now, hear me out. You need color in this piece, and she is colorful to say the least. Plus, she's a *traiteur.* More color. And she knows lots of people . . . the born-and-bred Cajuns who could tell us stories of the old days."

Valerie whimpered. She thought she heard René whimper, as well.

She took a deep breath and said, "You're right."

"Well, if Tante Lulu is going, I am, too," Tee-John interjected from the kitchen doorway. "I can do all the grunt work on the boat. And fish for our food, and stuff."

"Dad would have a fit," René pointed out. Their father owned a part of Cypress Oil, having sold them family lands about thirty years ago. He would, indeed, have a fit if not just one, but two, of his sons were working on a project that could affect him adversely.

"*Pfffff!* Half the time he doesn't know or care where I am," Tee-John contended.

"This documentary project is getting totally out of hand. It's not at all what I envisioned," René said. That probably meant he would allow Tee-John to come along.

"That's not the half of it," Justin told René, then looked pointedly at Val.

"What now?" René asked, looking not at Justin, but at Val.

"You have to be the figurehead for this piece," she pleaded. "You're good-looking and charming, when you want to be, and . . ."

René waited for her to finish. When she didn't, he prodded, ". . . and?"

"And virile," Justin finished for her.

"Oh, no! Not that again!"

"Really, René, if we want big-time publicity, there has to be a hook. I'm talking *Oprah, Good Morning America, Dateline, 60 Minutes,* if we hope to really nudge the politicians."

"When Val told me about the Juju plant and male virility, I knew we had a hook," Justin continued. "And, let's face it, René, you exude male virility."

René gave Valerie a look that said, "See? Gay to the bone."

Which he was not. Valerie knew that for a fact. One of her coworkers at TTN had dated him at one time and had given glowing reports on his prowess.

"Get someone else. How about J.B.?"

Everyone turned to look at J.B. with his scruffy hair and scruffy beard and bleary eyes. He was eating a beignet at the moment and had sugar everywhere.

It was J.B.'s wife who exclaimed, "Get real!"

"I could do it," Tee-John asserted, thrusting out his chest.

"You probably could, but you're too young," Justin said.

Attention came back to René. "No, no, no!" he reiterated.

"Were you lying about the plant?" Valerie asked René.

"No. Not exactly. But I have no scientific proof that it really works. It's probably just an old wives' tale."

"It works," Tante Lulu yelled from the kitchen.

"Look, even the hint of such a plant will be enough," Justin said. "It's the old bait and switch of television. Pull them in with one thing and they'll stay for the rest of the story."

"*Mon Dieu!* We'll have herds of people tramping through the swamps looking for the plant. So much for protecting the environment!" René could easily see this whole plan backfiring.

"We'll find a way to get around that," Valerie said. "In fact, maybe we can get my aunts Margo and Madeline on our side in the process. They could get the trademark on Juju herbal tea, or some such thing. People won't be out tramping through gator-riddled swamps if they can buy the same thing in town or by mail in a tea."

"This is a freakin' nightmare." *Hmmm. Maybe it could work.*

Valerie patted his hand. René cared too much about the bayou to put his personal concerns above the greater good, and so it was no surprise that he agreed to work with them in the end. But he didn't like it. Not one bit.

"I promise, everything will be done tastefully," she assured him.

His only response was a grunt. When everyone headed out of the room for "a little snack," which covered every inch of space in the kitchen, René pulled Val out of hearing, and said, "You are going to owe me big-time for this, babe. And I'm not talking a little hanky-panky. I'm talking a marathon of world-class, eyeballs-rolling, heart-stopping sex."

She just smiled.

Chapter 14

Ahoy, maties!

A week later, everyone boarded J.B. and Maddie's fifty-foot, wooden shrimp trawler, *Swamp Sally,* on one of the smaller bayous that led out to the Gulf of Mexico. René wasn't sure if he should pull out all his hair now or after this circus parade was over.

J.B. and Maddie wore matching PROUD TO BE A COONASS T-shirts. "Coonass" is an affectionate, sometimes controversial, ethnic slur used among Cajuns. No one knows for sure the origins of the word. Some say it came from the French *conasse,* slang for a diseased whore; others say it came from the presumed habit Cajuns had of eating raccoons. Many Cajuns employ the term as their own way of poking fun at their allegedly ignorant ways.

Lots of people thought J.B. and Maddie were a little bit wacko, but they were just eccentric. And, man, did they love each other! They couldn't pass each other without touching—a squeeze of a shoulder, a pat on the butt, short kisses. And they had to be in their fifties, maybe late forties.

Tante Lulu arrived with enough food to sink the boat. A foot-high St. Jude statue, magnetized on the bottom, was also among her supplies; she put that in the wheel-house. She was dressed in her version of what a shrimp fisherman would wear if he was modeling for *GQ*. A BITE ME BAYOU BAIT COMPANY baseball cap covered her curly hair, which was jet-black today. A snow-white T-shirt, which wouldn't be white for long on this boat, was tucked into a brand-new pair of jeans with a designer patch on the butt. The jeans were tucked into the rubber boots known as "Coonass Reeboks" among fishermen here.

Stepping on board, after her second trip back to her car for supplies, she announced, "I've decided what I'm gonna do on my birthday."

That damn birthday party again! "I thought we were throwing you a big birthday party. And Charmaine was getting you tickets to see Richard Simmons," René said.

"Sure, but what am I gonna give myself? Well, re-member how President Bush—the first President Bush—jumped out of an airplane on his eightieth birth-day? Thass what I'm gonna do."

Oh, God! What next? "Tante Lulu, you are not going skydiving," he said as gently as he could.

"Why? Are you afraid I'll have a heart attack or sumpin'?"

"No, I'm afraid I would have a heart attack."

She went off in a huff then to the below-deck kitchen galley.

Some little blonde chippie who looked sixteen going on thirty dropped Tee-John off, rock music blaring from her red convertible Trans Am. He leaned over the driver's door and gave her a way-too-long kiss before waving good-bye. Then he picked up his duffel bag and started toward them, smiling like the tomcat he was. "Yo, Tante Lulu, my stomach, she's agrowlin'. You got anything to eat?"

His aunt smiled as if the scamp had just told her she'd won a date with Richard Simmons.

Then there was Valerie. Lordy, Lordy! She wore a plain ol' black tank top and shorts with white tennis shoes, but there was nothing "plain ol'" about her. She wore a baseball cap like the rest of them with a ponytail sticking out the back. Her cap proclaimed: WOMEN RULE. She could rule him looking like that, for sure.

"You better put on plenty of sunscreen and mosquito repellant," he advised her, taking in all that exposed skin. The heat wave continued in Southern Louisiana, never going much below 110 degrees daytime. Sweat rolled off all of them, and it was only 9 A.M.

"Maybe you can put it on for me later," she answered saucily.

Guar-an-teed!

Justin, meanwhile, was taping everyone and everything, Val at his side doing the interviews to go with the film. René was impressed with her professionalism . . . and, okay, with Justin's expertise, too. Even the guy who owned the bait shed along the road, which also advertised alligator meat, got his chance to vent for nationwide TV. René noticed Justin doing a few close-ups of Val, which tempted him to do something foolish, such as knock out his perfect front teeth. But Justin also gave equal film coverage to him and other members of the crew. René was deliberately keeping his shirt on, just in case he found himself on some poster someday. He could see it now, himself as "The Very Virile Cajun." Heck, they might even put such a picture on Juju tea. Yeah, that's what he needed—his naked chest on tea bags around the world.

They planned to spend a week or two filming the bayous, the marshland, and the barrier islands. Then Justin and Val would go off by themselves—*which pleased him to no end . . . not!*—while he took care of personal business, including some job interviews. It was time to think about what kind of work he wanted to do in the future. Justin and Val at this point would only be developing a proposal for the documentary to be shown to some big shot named Anderson in New York City. If he didn't buy it, there were a few other cable channels that might be interested.

It sounded well-organized and as if it were running according to plan. Not so. Not with seven people involved, all having strong opinions to express.

Most of all, though, he worried about the danger. Not for him and J.B. and Maddie, but the others. They weren't accustomed to the anti-environmentalist sentiments that abounded, even from their own people, who viewed their efforts as a potential trigger for a loss of jobs.

Val, himself, J.B., and Maddie had all gotten voice mails threatening their lives if they proceeded with the documentary. Water had been poured into the gas tank on the boat, which caused delays. His bank called in the mortgage on his town house, which he already put on the market. But he had to have Luc file orders to "cease and desist" with their threats of a sheriff's sale until the structure was sold. Val's mother claimed she was disinheriting her daughter if she continued with this "foolishness." The windshield of J.B.'s truck was shattered by what appeared to be a bullet.

He'd discussed the danger with all of them. J.B. and Maddie would die for the cause so this latest threat didn't faze them. Tante Lulu said, "I'm almos' eighty years old. Let 'em take me iffen they wants." Tee-John considered it a great adventure. Justin said that he'd faced worse in Iraq. And Val, bless her heart, said she felt alive for the first time in five years. Let them try to stop her.

I hope I have something to do with her feeling alive, too. That's what René thought, but he wasn't about to say that to her, not with five sets of ears listening in.

So now they were off, chugging down the bayou, heading slowly toward the Gulf. This was backcountry at its best. Along the way they saw fields of golden green marsh grass. Pink blooming mimosa trees added a bit of color. What habitation there was, outside the small towns, came in the form of fishing camps or clapboard cottages on pilings, always trying to escape the encroaching sea. Several times they saw gators in the water and on the banks, some of them as much as ten feet long, just staring at them with their googly eyes for daring to intrude into their world. There was even the occasional porpoise, romping playfully in the water; they came inland to feed on the crabs and fish.

One of the problems was the saltwater intrusion that was being caused by the coastal erosion. In essence, as the saltwater moved farther and farther inland they were pickling the swamplands. As a result many animals were pushing north, like gators and oysters.

Traffic was light on the bayou today, but still there

were fishing boats going out and coming in. All the vessels were manned by deeply tanned fishermen who waved happily at them as they passed.

René walked over to stand by Val, who was leaning on the rail. The moving boat created a slight breeze that offered some relief from the intense heat. She was watching the landscape pass by—a landscape he considered beautiful. But what did she think?

There were things that could be done. Filling in oil company canals. Rebuilding barrier islands. Rerouting the Mississippi River for controlled flooding as a first step for dumping new sediment.

In the meantime, a disaster of horrific magnitude that would affect the entire world was taking place here, but he didn't know if he had the ability to *show* her and Justin how bad it was. The coastal wetlands were vanishing at such a shocking rate, there would eventually be no shield at all against the hurricanes that assaulted this area routinely, thus leaving two million people exposed. *How do I get that point across? I could use a little help here, St. Jude.*

You're doing just fine, that voice in his head said.

"So what do you think so far?" he asked Val, looping an arm over her shoulder.

"Some of these people are so poor, and yet they seem so happy," she remarked.

"They are happy. And why not?"

"They barely eke out a living."

"True, but they're continuing a family tradition of living off the water. They feel the same way about the bayou as farmers do about their land."

"I suppose so."

"Many of their children have gone off to work in town, no longer willing to struggle so hard, always at the whim of the tides. But for those able to stay, it's a good life. Perhaps not by Beverly Hills standards, but—"

"Oh, don't go getting your back up. I wasn't criticizing or being condescending. One of the first things a jury analyst is taught is not to judge people by first impressions."

He wasn't so sure about that. "How about that fisherman you interviewed yesterday in Houma? What did you think of him?"

"The guy with one hand and crooked teeth?"

He nodded.

"Well, on first glance, I would have thought, why doesn't he get a prosthesis and why didn't his parents put braces on him as a child?" She put up a hand to stop him when he was about to speak. "But immediately, I realized they both cost money, which they probably didn't have. Nor medical insurance."

"What else?"

"His name is Clarence Dubois. His nickname 'Speedy' was given to him for his ability to sort bycatch from shrimp so fast, before the accident. What sticks with me about him is his love for his family. Every other sentence he mentioned his wife, Rose, who works at a convenience store to supplement their income, and his three-year-old son Sam. I believe he is probably a hard drinker, but never at the expense of his family."

"Not bad, but what you don't know is that Speedy was an All-American high school quarterback at one time. He was offered athletic scholarships to a number of colleges. He chose this, instead."

He could tell that she didn't understand why a man would have made such a choice. Maybe by the end of this week she would.

"Oh my God! Look at that . . . over there. What is it?"

"A graveyard," he said. "Those stones you see sticking out of the water are grave markers or sarcophagi."

"Look at that stone angel. It must have sat on top of a large tombstone at one time. And look at that marble cross." Val was clearly astounded.

"Holy shit!" Justin remarked from the other side. "Hey, J.B., can you stop this wreck so we can get a better look?" With his camera up to his eye he was already filming the marshland off to the right, and Val took out the small handheld recorder she used to take notes. "Talk to me while I do the filming, René," said Justin. "And, Val, you're recording, right?"

René began, "All this used to be land, obviously. I keep telling you that the Louisiana coastline is being washed out to sea. This is clear evidence of that fact. Why else would you see telephone poles like those over there submerged in the water, not to mention giant oak trees? In Louisiana, because of the low water tables, we bury our dead above ground, but in this case the water caught up with the cemetery anyhow. Some fishermen love to work sites like this because there's an abundance of fish; they hide among the nooks and crannies of the grave markers."

"Eeew!" Tante Lulu interjected, having just come up from the galley kitchen, where it was probably 150 degrees. She wiped the moisture off her forehead and neck with a wet cloth. Her white T-shirt was indeed soiled already, both by perspiration and food. "Who'd wanna eat crabs or fishies what been feastin' on human remains?"

"The human remains are still in their stone caskets, Auntie," René said. *For now, anyhow.*

Succulent smells of crawfish etouffee wafted up to them. The crawfish, also known as mudbugs, had been caught by an age-old method just this morning before they embarked on their journey. Maddie had swung a leafy green branch over the water, and J.B. had used a net to scoop up the crawfish that clung to the branches. Raw chicken necks worked just as well, tied to a long string.

J.B. killed the engines and dropped anchor. Using a telephoto lens, Justin was filming like crazy. "This is unbelievable," he said with excitement. "I can see the letters on some of them, and they date back to the Civil War. In fact, one of them is for a Sergeant Jeremiah Delacorte, who died at Shiloh. God, the historical preservationists will have a field day with this."

"At one time, not so long ago, either, there was a small town here, and it was twenty miles from the Gulf," René noted. "I remember it well because it was a place where teenagers came to park. In fact, I lost my . . . oops!" He cut himself off. But too late.

Val flashed him a glare. "Was that before or after our big event . . . or, rather, nonevent?"

"Shhh!" he said. Again, too late.

"What event?" Tante Lulu wanted to know.

"Betcha I know," Tee-John offered, a wide grin on his face.

"See, the thunderbolt was already doin' its work on you two long ago. It's a sign."

"The thunderbolt was definitely not involved back

then. And it is not a sign." Just then, he noticed that Justin was filming their ridiculous conversation and Val's recorder was presumably still on. "I better not hear myself discussing thunderbolts on nationwide TV or losing my virginity in a freakin' cemetery."

Justin just smiled.

Tante Lulu made a *tsk*-ing sound at his language.

He decided to change the subject. "Back to this watery graveyard. The townspeople left, but they couldn't take their dead with them. Eventually this area will probably be part of the Gulf itself, totally underwater, if nothing is done to save the coastline."

Just then, some egrets rose from the marsh grass in a white cloud, like ghosts rising to the sky, or angels. A mystical silence overtook the scene. They were all stunned by the beauty of it. Luckily, Justin got it all on tape.

During the rest of the morning and afternoon they passed some small towns, often only a bait shed, a couple of trailers and fishing camps on stilts near the water, usually with patched tin roofs. Aside from those meager signs of habitation, it was mostly a solitary journey. Other boats, everything from small outboards to large trawlers, were on the water, usually passing them by, since they were going so slowly. Early in the afternoon, they saw a shrimp boat coming back in. The captain slowed almost to a standstill and yelled out to J.B., who was apparently a friend, that the catch was meager that day, not worth going out for. He tossed over a bag full of freshly caught shrimp packed in ice.

"Do you like sushi?" René asked Val and Justin.

They both nodded.

"Try these then." He cracked open and peeled a couple of shrimp, handing them the meat.

"I don't know about this. Eating raw shrimp," Val said, scrunching up her nose.

"Sushi," he reminded her.

Justin tried his and made a swooning sound. "Mmmmmm. That is delicious."

Val tentatively tried hers. She, too, said it was wonderful, just the right amount of salty taste.

J.B., Maddie, Tee-John, even Tante Lulu, were partaking of the delicacy now, as well. There was nothing in the world like shrimp fresh from the water.

René used his thumb to wipe Val's mouth after her third shrimp. Just that small touch ignited something between them. He knew how he felt, deep in his gut, but it gave him immense pleasure to see Val's dark Creole eyes burn with the same awareness.

It had been a week since their night of lovemaking. They'd both had to go separate ways to get this project going. One night was not nearly enough. And there was going to be little chance of them connecting on this journey with so many other people around.

"I miss you," he said in an undertone so others wouldn't overhear.

"I miss you, too," she said, and dammit, she didn't keep her voice low.

Unfortunately Tante Lulu overheard. "Of course you two miss each other. The thunderbolt never misses."

Val looked at him and crossed her eyes.

"Will ya be wearin' white or beige at yer weddin'?" his aunt inquired sweetly of Val. Before Val could sputter in outrage, his aunt went on. "Charmaine wore red to her weddin'. What a hoot that was. Mebbe ya could wear red."

"Tante Lulu, there is not going to be a wedding," René said as gently as he could.

His aunt slapped her thigh with glee. "What a kidder!" She was still laughing as she returned to the galley kitchen.

Val arched her brows at him. "A kidder, huh?"

He arched his brows back at her. Let her think what she wanted.

You could say he got a little behind

Supper that evening was a spectacular event, something Valerie would remember for the rest of her life.

They were docked at Stop Off, a small community along the bayou. René had told her that Stop Off was one of the towns that would disappear completely someday if drastic measures weren't taken now.

They would stay that night in a nearby cut-rate motel, the type of place Valerie normally would not step in, let alone sleep in, but the proprietor assured them that there would be clean sheets. And no roaches, since they'd been fumigated the week before. *I do not need to hear about roaches. Lordy, Lordy!* The only saving grace was that the rooms had air-conditioning and showers.

They'd spread a plastic tablecloth over the built-in table in the middle of the boat, the place where they sorted shrimp from the bycatch. On paper plates, with plastic cutlery and disposable cups filled with white wine, they dined on food that would do a four-star restaurant proud. Crawfish etouffee, a loaf of French bread that had been purchased that morning fresh from the oven, dirty rice, fried okra, sliced tomatoes from Tante Lulu's garden, liberally sprinkled with salt, pepper and olive oil, and rum-soaked bread pudding for dessert.

The old lady beamed at all the well-deserved compliments tossed her way. Valerie had to give her credit, not just for the meal, but for her healing arts, as well. On several of their stops today, she had regaled them with stories about her herbal remedies as she gathered plants, which she put in labeled Ziploc bags. She would dry and package them when she got home.

Where Tante Lulu got her energy at her age was a wonder. In fact, Valerie had asked her just that. To which, Tante Lulu had replied, "Me, I only gots so many years left, and I wants to fill every minute." A good philosophy for anyone.

Justin was having a great time including Tante Lulu in the documentary. She would be a celebrity of sorts if this thing ever aired.

But now they were all replete. Tante Lulu and Tee-John gathered up all disposables and other trash into the tablecloth, which apparently was disposable, too, and went off to a nearby Dumpster. J.B. and Maddie went off to their motel room. René was rooming with Tee-John. And Val got to sleep with Tante Lulu once again. *Oh, joy!*

She and René watched the sun set on the horizon. It would be dark soon. He stood behind her at the rail, his arms around her. They were watching a flock of ibises return to their rookeries. These were snow-white birds with black wing tips, probably one of the many species made famous by Audubon.

"I want to be with you," René murmured against her ear, then nipped at the lobe with his teeth.

She shivered, which was remarkable considering the high temperature and humidity. "I want you, too, René. But not here. And not without taking a shower. I probably stink."

René laughed and squeezed her tight. "Darlin', sweaty sex has an attraction all its own. Trust me."

"I'll take your word for it."

He ran his hands down her sides from under her arms, over her waist and hips, then back up to rest under her breasts.

"René," she cautioned.

"I jus' wanna play a bit, *chére.*"

"No," she said, pushing his hand down to the more safe territory of her waist. "I am not playing any more of your near-sex games."

"Hey, I give good near-sex."

"Too good."

"Maybe I could slip into your room after Tante Lulu falls asleep."

"Yeah, right. She probably has a motion detector on the door. She already propped a St. Jude statue on my headboard."

He laughed. "You're probably right."

"I know I am."

"We could have closet sex. There is a closet, isn't there?"

She went stiff with horror at the prospect of such a thing. "No closets."

Her voice must have been shrill because René sensed her alarm and asked, "Why no closets?"

"My mother used to lock me in a closet," she revealed, then wished she hadn't. She never talked about that. Never.

"Val," he said sadly. "What could you possibly have done to merit such a punishment?"

She thought about declining to answer, but that was silly. It was a long time ago. "Getting a B on a test, instead of an A. Getting mud on the carpet. Being disheveled when I came home from school. Once, she locked me in the closet because I got a zit. Oh, and okra, if I failed to eat all my okra. I hate okra."

"I noticed you didn't eat any at supper." His voice was soft with sympathy. Thankfully all he added was, "Poor baby."

She leaned back to relish the feel of his breath on her skin . . . and to drop this distasteful subject.

"How about the bathroom?" he tried again.

She smiled. "Give it up, boy."

"We could go in there and lock the door."

"Have you seen the size of those bathrooms?" There was barely room to turn around with the sink, toilet, and shower stall all crammed in there.

"I don't need much room."

His roaming hands played with her breasts.

She didn't have the heart or inclination to stop him. Just yet. Instead, she arched her back to give him more of a playing field.

"You are killing me," he whispered hoarsely.

She could feel against her back just how much she was killing him. Temptation was a potent thing, and Valerie was sorely tempted.

He cupped her mound now and undulated himself

against her. "Betcha we could make love with you just standing there. Anyone walking by on shore wouldn't suspect a thing." Luckily the side of the boat covered them from the waist down.

"How?" she squeaked out, feeling embarrassed and very much aroused.

"Just hold on, sugar. We're off to the races."

Before she could say, "Holy moley!" he had her shorts and undies down to her ankles. Likewise for his own shorts and jockeys. She was about say, "Wait a minute, I changed my mind," but he already had a finger stroking her down below testing her readiness.

I'm ready, I'm ready, she wanted to scream, but she was still too shy to do that. Amazing that after what she did with him last week she still had any modesty left.

"Are you ready, babe?" he asked huskily against her neck, as if reading her mind, then bit her shoulder, like a stallion about to mount a mare, for goodness sake. She'd read that somewhere in a book.

She tried to tell him that she was more than ready, but it was too late. He'd taken her silence for assent. Lifting her to tiptoe, he bent his knees and entered her from behind. She grabbed the railing tight for balance, and found herself in the vulnerable position of being unable to touch him. But he could touch her. And, boy oh boy, did he ever!

His hands were everywhere. Her breasts. Her buttocks. Her exposed folds. She was in a frenzy of excitement trying to concentrate on each of the separate places he was setting afire. And the whole time he plunged himself in and out of her. Forget about embarrassment! They both glistened with perspiration and panted with their exertions in this intense heat.

"You folks havin' a problem?"

Valerie and René's heads shot up to see a man walking from the bar close to the dock, probably heading home to one of those cottages on stilts.

"No, we're just fine," René said, even as he did something really naughty to her between her legs. "We're just enjoying—"

She smacked him.

"—the moon." René was chuckling. The lout!

"Oh, I thought I heard some moanin'."

Valerie began to climax, and, yes, she did moan.

"Must be the wind," René said. She leaned back against his chest, and he whispered in her ear, "Shhh, he'll be gone soon."

"Well, have a nice evenin'."

"We will," René replied. Then, under his breath, "Guaranteed."

No sooner did the man pass the boat than René began to plunge in and out of her with short hard strokes. When he grunted out his own orgasm, Valerie spasmed around him again.

Once their breathing was back to normal and their shorts pulled back up, Valerie told him, "You have no idea how out of character this is for me."

"What?"

"Casual sex."

He shook his head at her. "Didn't you know? This is not casual sex."

What is it then? she wanted to ask, but didn't have the nerve.

But a voice in her head answered for her. *You know.*

Chapter 15

She wore an itsy-bitsy teeny-weeny

The next day they continued down the bayou, out to the Gulf, and Grand Isle, the largest of the barrier islands and the only one still inhabited today.

René sat on the beach, alone, just enjoying the view. J.B. and Maddie were doing some motor stuff on the fishing boat. Tante Lulu had forced Tee-John to accompany her to a market, even though he'd wanted to check out a bikini-clad girl he'd spotted on the beach. Justin and Valerie were off interviewing and taping some older residents who had stories to tell about "the old days."

René loved Grand Isle.

In the 1890s Creoles made it a posh resort, complete with fine hotels, bathhouses, gambling halls, an observatory, and a mule-drawn tram. It was the site of Kate Chopin's famous novel *The Awakening*. All that ended in 1909 with a hurricane that whipped 150 mph winds and fifteen-foot storm surges, causing the death of 350 people. Even today, it is the benchmark storm to which all other storms are compared. At that time, most of Southern Louisiana was affected by the size of the surge. René couldn't imagine the devastation today if a similar storm occurred because most of the buffers were now gone.

Val and Justin were practically googly-eyed at the first sight of this island, even though they'd both grown up in Southern Louisiana. The contrast was stark between the natural beauty of the island, despite its tacky souvenir shops and modern restaurants, and the numerous oil wells visible out on the Gulf. Many people didn't realize there were several thousand oil platforms and drilling rigs out there, serving more than twenty-five thousand wells. They represented money and power.

Only cottages and motels existed here now, used by fishermen, bird-watchers, and sun worshipers. It could no longer continue as a fancy resort island with high-priced hotels due to the many lashings by hurricanes over the years. But there was a charm in this battered survivor of times past.

Val came up and dropped down to the sand beside René. She wore her hair in a knot atop her head, sunglasses, a Trial TV T-shirt, and white shorts. To him, she looked sexier than hell.

He leaned over and gave her a brief kiss. Funny how natural that came to him! He was getting awfully comfortable with Valerie Breaux, and that made him uncomfortable.

Justin was standing a short distance away making conversation with a twenty-fiveish woman who worked in one of the shops. The body language between the two of them was clearly man-woman.

Val took off her sunglasses and turned to look at what he was staring at. "Still think he's gay?"

"Could be. You never know today," he said obstinately. "Did you and Justin get everything you wanted?"

"More than! This one old guy could remember his grandfather talking about the big hurricane here, and he has pictures he's going to let us copy."

"Good for you!" Her enthusiasm was a joy to watch.

She gazed out over the water, taking in the not-so-scenic view of oil platforms on the horizon. "Do you hate the oil companies?"

"No, of course not. Oil is a necessity. And, to be honest, nobody knew decades ago how devastating the effect would be on the environment. It's almost like the cigarette companies in that they fight tooth and nail over paying to correct their prior acts, and they have to be watched constantly or they revert to old ways. Actually, much of the coastal erosion is due to honest human error. In particular, the levees."

She cocked her head in question.

"For centuries people have been trying to tame the lower Mississippi River, which we now know was a mistake. They built levee after levee to prevent flooding when, in fact, the annual flooding and alluvial depositing is what created the coastline. Some scientists say that it took seventy centuries to build up the Louisiana we had in the nineteenth century, but in the past hundred years we've depleted one-third of that."

"So, if you—meaning the scientists and environmentalists— know about this massive erosion, why isn't something being done?"

"Money, pure and simple. There are good plans to correct the problem, but it would cost millions. That means matching funds from Congress, which is having a hard enough time paying for the war on terrorism, social

security, and other social ills. We need to stand in line . . .
usually at the end of the line."

"That's why you gave up on the lobbying work."

He nodded.

"So what if nothing is done? A lot of the people we've
interviewed so far think the problem is too overwhelming
or they have an air of fatalism about it."

"If nothing is done, it would cost billions in lost jobs,
infrastructure, fishing, wildlife, hurricane damage, just to
name a few."

She frowned with confusion. "Who is the enemy in
this war? Who would threaten you, us, for doing this documentary?"

"Probably the oil companies or the residential and
commercial developers, or the politicians who'd rather sit
on their behinds and wait for a solution to land in their
laps, cost-free. It's money, money, money." He stopped
and shook his head. "I'm lecturing you, aren't I?"

"Yeah, but you're good."

Good is . . . well, good, I guess. Yep, I am good. "So,
do you miss New York?"

"Not yet. I'm having too much fun."

He grinned.

She punched him in the upper arm. "I wasn't referring
to that. I'm enjoying the work."

"Don't you always enjoy your work?"

She paused, as if she needed to think before answering. "Not lately."

"Maybe you should move back to Louisiana," he offered before he had a chance to bite his fool tongue.

She laughed. "No way! Then I would have to be

226 *Sandra Hill*

within visiting distance of my mother and the rest of the family. Talk about hell on earth!"

René was oddly hurt by her reply. At the same time, he recalled what she'd said about her mother and a closet. He loathed anyone who would do that to a child. The treatment he and his brothers had suffered under Valcour LeDeux was nothing compared to that, mainly because they were little boys who could run fast and because they had Tante Lulu as a safety net.

"How about you? Would you ever move to a city again?"

It was his turn to laugh. "I would die if I had to plant myself in a city on a permanent basis. It's suffocating even on short visits."

They held eye contact for a long, poignant moment.

He was the first to speak. "It doesn't say much for our future, does it?"

An expression of surprise swept over her face. "Did you think we had a future?"

Yeah. Pitiful of me, huh? "Of course not."

Now she looked a little bit hurt.

Tante Lulu came slogging through the sand then in her bare feet. Her hair was still jet-black, which was a wonder; she usually changed it on a daily basis. She wore a black-and-white polka-dot skirted bathing suit with a sheer black cover-up. A huge straw hat covered her black curls. There were liver spots and wrinkled white skin everywhere, he noticed sadly. He didn't want to look closely for fear he'd be struck dead for seeing his aunt in such a state of undress.

Instead he glanced over at Tee-John who was—

surprise, surprise—hustling Ms. Bikini. *Good Lord! Was I ever that full of myself?*

Yep! that nagging voice in his head remarked.

"Why the bathing suit?" he asked his aunt.

"I was gonna take a quick dip, but I changed my mind. J.B. 'n' Maddie are ready to go." Tante Lulu swiped sweat off her forehead with her sleeve. He should get her out of the sun as soon as possible. "I saw J.B. touchin' Maddie's hiney when they din't know I was lookin'." She narrowed her eyes at him then.

Oh no! She wouldn't.

"You ain't bin touchin' Val's hiney, have you?"

Yep, she would.

Val made a choking sound beside him.

He cleared his throat and came up with the perfect answer. "Let's get out of here."

"My feet is burnin' in this sand," Tante Lulu complained. "You'd best carry me."

Val looked at him and smiled.

Sometimes he really liked her smiles. Not at this moment, though.

So they left the beach on Grand Isle with him carrying an eighty-year-old woman wearing a polka-dot bathing suit that she'd probably bought in 1950. And, actually, he loved it.

The big bang

Valerie was ready to move on to the next stage of their project.

For the past week, they'd cruised up one bayou and

down another. Bayou Lafourche. Bayou Petit Caillou. Bayou Teche. Bayous that had no name.

Sometimes they traveled in J.B. and Maddie's boat, sometimes in other boats. René never seemed to get tired of showing off the swampland he loved, but Val and Justin were about bayoued out. Tante Lulu was making noises about weeding her garden, and Tee-John had a "hot date" coming up soon. J.B. and Maddie were content as long as they were together. Val swore they were the touchingest people she ever did see, which was kind of nice, really.

They'd even interviewed a number of Vietnamese fishermen. After the fall of Saigon, many Vietnamese people sought refuge in this country and many of them, fishermen back home, came to this area. How unfortunate that the haven they'd sought here might just be melting away . . . not really a haven after all.

Now they were all tucked in, or about to be tucked in, at the Nighty Night Motel. She of course got to room with Tante Lulu. *Lucky me!* Her brain must be melting in this heat because she was coming to think the old lady wasn't so bad.

Speak of the old lady! She came out of the bathroom wearing a child-size terry cloth robe, white cream all over her face, and her now red hair rolled up in pink foam rollers. That must be what had taken her so long in there. She'd been dyeing her hair. *Lordy, Lordy!*

"What are yer intentions?" she asked right off the bat, sitting down on the other twin bed in the room, across from her.

"About what?"

"René."

Oh, good Lord! She laughed. "Isn't that the question that's supposed to be addressed to the male in a relationship?"

Tante Lulu shrugged. "I'm a women's liver."

It was probably a bad sign that she actually understood her. "You mean, women's libber?"

"Thass what I said," she snapped. "So, spit it out, what are yer intentions toward that boy? I doan want him hurt."

"Boy?" I don't think so. In fact, I know so. "Tante Lulu," she said, as gently as she could without giving in to her inclination to tell her it was none of her business, "René and I are just . . . friends."

Tante Lulu made a snorting sound of disbelief. "That boy looks at you like yer a snow cone on a hot N'awlins day. And you ain't no better. I swear you ogle him like he's eye candy."

He is eye candy. But I don't ogle. I definitely do not ogle. "He's an attractive man. That's all."

She made the snorting sound of disbelief again.

"Listen, I've grown fond of René, and—"

"No, no, no! This ain't 'fond'. This is love."

Valerie threw her hands in the air. "René and I are thirty-five years old. I think we're old enough to know our own minds."

"Thass another thing. The men in the LeDeux fam'ly are womanizers fer sure, but when the right one comes along, even when they's thirty-five years old, they grab and hold on tight. Once the thunderbolt hits, yer a goner, girl."

"I don't believe in thunderbolts of love."

Tante Lulu put both hands up in the air in front of her face as if to ward off some evil. "Doan you be sayin' such things. Mercy! I knew a lady once who said she din't believe in voodoo. Next day her tongue stuck to the roof of her mouth and stayed that way till she died."

"She probably licked Krazy Glue," Valerie said under her breath.

But Tante Lulu heard her and wagged a finger in her face. "Alls I'm sayin' is doan hurt that boy, or I'll put a voodoo curse on you myself."

Aaarrgh! Talking to her is like talking to a cypress tree.

Their conversation was cut short then by a loud explosion outside. Tante Lulu screamed. Valerie jumped off the bed and ran outside. People were swarming out of the motel, half undressed, and from other buildings in the little town. In the distance, down by the dock, they saw the source of the explosion.

J.B. and Maddie's boat was up in flames.

Quack, quack, quack!

By 10 A.M. the next morning, René was knee-deep in red tape and drowning fast.

He'd sent Tante Lulu and Tee-John home, despite their protests that they wanted to stay. Valerie and Justin had gone off to his place outside Houma—something René did not like but conceded was the best alternative at the moment. They would be cutting and editing all the material they'd gathered and whipping it into a TV documentary proposal. He'd stayed behind to help J.B. and Maddie talk with the police, the ATF, the FBI, and even the CIA. With all the threats of terrorism in the world today, they couldn't ignore any bombing, even if it was only dynamite in this case.

Luckily no one had been hurt. Luckily Justin had all his film equipment back in his motel room and not on the boat. Luckily J.B. and Maddie were insured, which was a miracle in itself. Luckily the news media was finally waking up to the fact that there were serious issues here that might interfere with the nefarious plans of some Louisiana big shots. Luckily he'd finally calmed down some locals who were blaming them for bringing trouble to their midst.

Luc and Remy walked up to him once the news media dispersed and left him alone. They came as soon as they'd heard about the bombing.

"How you doing, buddy?" Luc asked, squeezing his shoulder. Always the big brother.

"I'm fine, now that the shock is over."

"I think they timed it so that no one was aboard as sort of a warning," Remy said.

"Hah! How did they know for sure that no one was aboard? A pretty risky chance just for a warning." René shivered inside at the prospect that one of the people in his group could have been killed. J.B. and Maddie, his good friends. Tante Lulu, his precious aunt. Tee-John, the loveable scamp. And Val . . . oh, man, Val! He didn't know how to categorize her, he just knew she was important to him, and losing her would have crushed him.

"You're not dealing with rocket scientists," Luc remarked. "Probably some thugs hired by the oil company."

"Where are you heading from here?" Remy asked. "Do you need a lift?"

"Back to Baton Rouge to settle some stuff related to my town house, then I'll stay in your houseboat for a few days till I get settled, if that's okay with you," he told Remy.

Remy nodded. "Sure."

As the three of them walked toward the motel parking lot, Luc laughed. "Trouble does seem to follow you, Brother."

"You think?" He laughed, too. Then he said, "Guess what Tante Lulu did yesterday?"

"I can only imagine," Remy offered.

"Did it involve a woman?" Luc asked.

"Oh, yeah."

They both waited expectantly.

"She asked me if I've ever touched Val's hiney?"

"Hiney?" they both guffawed.

"Did you?" Luc wanted to know.

He ignored that question. "And then she told Val that, if she didn't fall in love with me and treat me right, she was gonna put a voodoo curse on her. Val told me about it this morning before she left. Guess she was trying to cheer me up. Voodoo, for chrissake! Talk about!"

Luc and Remy's jaws dropped open before they all burst out in laughter.

"You are a dead duck," Luc finally concluded.

"Guar-an-teed!" Remy agreed.

René wondered idly—or not so idly—if Val had a taste for duck.

Just call her Sarah Jessica Breaux

Valerie hadn't seen René for two days, but he was coming over now to look over the film proposal.

She stood on the deck of Justin's cottage as he pulled

up in a black Jeep Cherokee. He got out of the vehicle just as she came down the steps.

He smiled at her.

She smiled at him.

He opened his arms.

She made a flying leap that landed her in his arms with her legs wrapped around his waist and her face tucked in his neck, which smelled of soap and René-skin. She felt like a teenager with a crush, giddy and so very happy.

He spun them around a little, laughing. "Now that's a welcome!"

"Did you miss me?" she asked, leaning back to look at him.

He gave her a quick kiss and said, "Not at all." Then he gave her a not-so-quick kiss that about curled her toes and proved that he had, in fact, missed her a lot.

About ten minutes and twenty kisses later, they went inside on wobbly knees to look over the film.

"Hey, René," Justin said.

"Hey, Justin."

An hour later, René sat back on the leather sofa and just stared at the two of them. "You are amazing. I can't believe you pulled this all together . . . the scenery, the interviews, the facts, everything. You even made Tante Lulu look good. And Tee-John . . . hell, his head's gonna get so big when the girls see this."

"What did you think about the segments dealing with the Juju plant?" Val asked him tentatively.

"Well, you managed to shoot me without my shirt, which I didn't want, but it was okay. And Tante Lulu with her *traiteur* talk made it all seem believable."

"Let me show you something," Justin said. He kept

fast-forwarding and stopping, fast-forwarding and stopping, to highlight a number of scenes. All of them had René and Val together. Laughing. Looking at each other. On one, he'd put a hand on her butt, and it appeared as if she was chastizing him. On another one, he was leaning down to kiss her, and if she hadn't known it was her, she would have wanted to be the woman who was the recipient of this hunk's attentions.

"Very nice," René said, "but what's your point?"

"You two are hot together. Steam heat in the bayou, and then some. I think, if we manage to pull this off, it's going to have to be a package deal."

René grinned.

Valerie cringed. She had viewed herself as a behind-the-scenes person. "I don't know about that."

"Hey, if I'm gonna be the hunk of the month, you're gonna be the hottie of the year," René contended.

"Let me go one step further," Justin continued. "I'm not so sure we couldn't propose a series. Something like 'Bayou Travels' but more provocative. You two would be in each of them."

"Yeah, and each segment could be a different issue or location," Val said enthusiastically. "Like Grand Isle and the other barrier islands. Like Tante Lulu and her swamp healing. Like the Vietnamese here, and what remains of the Indian tribes indigenous to the area. Even those videos you gave us of The Swamp Rats playing rowdy Cajun music. By the way, if I didn't mention it before, you play a mean accordion, sweetie."

He waggled his eyebrows at her.

"All of them would have to be lively and colorful and fun. And the Juju plant could be a thread through all of them, sort of a teasing joke," Justin added, equally enthusiastic. "We're not trying to be a *National Geographic* copycat. More like *National Geographic* with humor and sex appeal."

"You're turning this into a 'Sex and the Bayou' version of *Sex and the City*," René protested.

"No, we're not, honey," Valerie assured him. "I promise you everything will be done with good taste. You liked what we did so far, didn't you?"

He nodded.

"But where would all the environmental concerns come in?" René wanted to know.

"That's the beauty of it," Justin explained. "We don't hit them over the head with it. We make them fall in love with the people and the area, and slip the environmental concerns in there like hidden messages. At the end of each program, we could put an address or Web site where people could go to learn how they can help. By contacting politicians. By contributing money. Whatever. Education is a powerful tool."

"It could work," Val said, looking to him for approval.

He hesitated for a long time. This wasn't at all what he'd expected, obviously, but Val hoped he would realize that maybe it was better. *Maybe* being the key word. Finally, he shrugged. "You're the experts. Go with it."

She launched herself at him, settling herself on his lap. Hugging him warmly, she said, "Thank you, thank you, thank you."

"One thing is for sure. This is going to be one special birthday for Tante Lulu," René said. "We're making her a TV star. She'll be the Cajun Joan Collins."

Everyone laughed, but it was probably true.

Chapter 16

Happy wedding to you, happy wedding to you

"Tante Lulu! You can't plan a surprise wedding for someone."

Sylvie Breaux-LeDeux was shaking her head adamantly as she made that pronouncement to her great-aunt-by-marriage. They were sitting at the kitchen table of the old lady's cottage, along with Rachel Fortier-LeDeux and Charmaine LeDeux-Lanier. Tante Lulu had just proposed that they organize a surprise wedding for René and Valerie in the middle of her eightieth birthday celebration.

"Why not? People have surprise birthday parties."

"It's not the same thing," Rachel said. "Both parties have to agree ahead of time."

"I don't know about that," Charmaine offered. "If the two parties are in love and just need a little nudge to tie the knot, why not?"

"A nudge. Yep, thass what this would be. A surprise nudge." Tante Lulu beamed.

"I think you need to obtain a marriage certificate signed in person by both parties," Sylvie said. "I don't see any way around that."

"*Pfff*, I know someone in the county offices. Not to worry." Tante Lulu probably did know people there. Heck, she knew everyone.

"Isn't that illegal?" Sylvie asked.

No one paid any attention to her. LeDeuxs never did pay much attention to the law, except for Luc, who helped them get out of legal scrapes.

"There's not enough time to plan a wedding," Rachel complained.

"It could be really romantic," Charmaine added.

"Or a disaster," Sylvie countered. Sylvie always was the cautious one.

Charmaine, on the other hand, never learned the word *cautious*. "Why not make tentative plans, don't tell anyone but us, and then play it by ear the day of the event?"

"Okey-dokey," Tante Lulu said, rubbing her hands together with enthusiasm. It was always a bad sign when Tante Lulu said, "Okey-dokey".

"What about the banns?" Sylvie inquired, smiling as if she'd just discovered a roadblock for the runaway truck that was Tante Lulu. "You'll never get a priest to marry them without calling the vows in church ahead of time."

"Hah! I got connections at Our Lady of the Bayou Church, too." She had been a member there her entire life. But it was one thing to bend the civil law with a forged marriage certificate and quite another to bend Church law. That was kind of like defying God.

He's all for it, Tante Lulu swore a voice in her head said. Probably St. Jude.

"Rings?" Rachel threw that in, but not with much hope.

"Thass the best part. I still have my grandma's and

grandpa's rings. They can use those." Tante Lulu seemed to have an answer for everything.

"Your birthday bash is supposed to be a casual affair, auntie. How are we going to get Val and René to come in wedding attire?" Charmaine propped a forefinger under her chin as she pondered the problem.

"I'll prod Val to spiffy up for the day 'cause of all the pictures we'll be taking, but iffen she doan . . ." Tante Lulu shrugged. "Then we has us a casual weddin'." She cocked her head as if a sudden thought occurred to her. "Mebbe Richard Simmons could be René's best man iffen he comes."

"Tante Lulu, I already told you that there isn't a chance in hell that Richard Simmons will be there," Charmaine said.

"You never know. Val knows 'im. Betcha she'll talk him into comin'."

"Val doesn't exactly know . . ." Charmaine started to say and then gave up.

"Will you invite Val's mother and her aunts?" Rachel asked.

Tante Lulu groaned. "Do we hafta?" Then she smiled widely. "Simone Breaux would have a diarrhea fit."

"This will never work," Sylvie concluded. "There are just too many complications that could screw it up."

"It'll work," Tante Lulu assured them all. "I'm gonna say a novena to St. Jude. He'll make it happen."

It appeared that the four of them were actually going to be in cahoots to plan a surprise wedding for Val and René. Each of them put a right hand on the middle of the table and did a communal hand squeeze.

"Oh, God! Luc will kill me," Sylvie said.

"Remy will say we've gone off the deep end," Rachel added.

"Rusty won't care," Charmaine said with a laugh. "He'll probably say I've gone off the deep end so many times, I've become a world-class swimmer."

Tante Lulu clapped her hands together to get their attention, as if she didn't already have that. "Here's the plan . . ."

Shades of Joan Crawford

"I hope you're not planning on marrying that . . . that swamp agitator."

Simone Breaux practically spat the words out to Valerie as they sat at a Houma restaurant. Val had agreed to have dinner with her mother before heading to New York with Justin to present their proposal to Amos Anderson. She'd foolishly thought she could mend some fences.

"Where did that idea come from, Mother?"

"It's no secret that you've been hanging around with that riff-raff."

"Who exactly are you calling riff-raff?"

"René, the LeDeux clan, that whole low-down Cajun bunch."

"Mother! One of our ancestors was Cajun. Breaux is a Cajun name. Are we low-down?"

"Don't be ridiculous. We only have a smidgeon of Cajun blood in our veins." Simone breathed in and out several times as if to calm herself. Her mother's motto had always been: never show emotions in public. "I spoke hastily," she conceded. "There are many good Cajun people. Of course there are. But not the LeDeuxs."

"Your niece Sylvie, my cousin, is married to a LeDeux," Valerie argued.

"And what a mistake that was! She crawled right down to their level."

It was no use arguing with her.

"What are your career plans?" her mother asked, switching the subject.

"I'm leaving tomorrow for New York to present a proposal to a television executive for a bayou documentary. After that, I'm not sure. I could go back to Trial TV if I want. I just don't know yet."

"That documentary. *Pfff!* Do you have any concern for how it will affect me? Do you even care? I'm about to start phase two of the Bayou Paradise development. I have a great deal of money invested that could go down the drain if those environmental crazies start up again."

"Mother, this documentary isn't about you, or any one problem . . . like overdevelopment," she explained tiredly. "It's about the whole ecosystem and what man has done to change it for the worse."

"Where are you staying?" Her mother was a master at changing the subject when the conversation wasn't going in the direction she wanted.

"On Remy LeDeux's houseboat."

"Alone?"

She refused to answer.

"How do you think that looks? People will talk."

She raised her chin haughtily in the manner her mother had taught her so well.

"You are just like your father. Stubborn to a fault."

Valerie rolled her eyes. The same old song her mother had been singing for years. "Sometimes I wonder how my . . . our lives would have been different if he had stayed."

"Well, he didn't stay. He dumped the both of us and went off to Paris where he's lived ever since. Got himself a new chippie of a wife, probably some floozie, and he probably had other children. He didn't care, he doesn't care, and he never will care. It's about time you stopped wallowing in self-pity over that man."

Her mother's words cut deep, but she refused to let her see her pain. That would just give her mother another weapon to use against her.

"I loved him, Mother. I still love him. He's my daddy."

"Then you're the fool."

Things aren't always as they appear

Tante Lulu cornered Val as she was leaving the restaurant.

Her mother had already left for another appointment, and she'd stayed to pay the bill. Tante Lulu, wearing a Hawaiian-style floral muumuu and flip-flops, was on her way to Charmaine's beauty spa for an after-hours hair treatment.

"Whass the matter, honey?" Tante Lulu asked. "I kin see yer upset."

"Just the usual reaction to my mother. She always manages to rattle my chain."

Valerie sank down on a street bench. She was five-foot-eight and the old lady couldn't be more than five-foot-nothing. It was awkward talking down to her.

"What was it this time?"

"My father." She sighed, wondering why she bothered to explain.

"What about Henri?"

Valerie raised a brow at Tante Lulu's use of his given name.

"He was about the age of René's mama, bless her soul. I knew 'im."

"Tell me about him."

"Gentle. Thass the first word what comes to mind. He din't have a mean bone in his body, even as a young'un. He liked books. Seems to me he studied lit-ra-chur at the university. Wanted to be a poet or teacher or sumpin', but yer mother wanted 'im to take over the family real estate concerns. They was allus fightin' and that was one thing yer father hated—harsh words." Tante Lulu paused and thought a moment. "One thing is fer certain, he loved you dearly."

Tears immediately smarted her eyes. "How can you say that? He abandoned me."

"He never did! Fer shame, sayin' such a thing!"

"It's the truth. My mother was not always nice. She—"

Tante Lulu patted her arm. "René tol' me 'bout the closets. She's a witch, fer sure, to do that to a little girl. But the worst thing, iffen you ask me, was keepin' you from yer dad."

Shivers went up Valerie's spine, and the fine hairs stood out on the back of her neck. She turned fully on the bench to look at the old lady. "What do you mean?"

"Well, there was that big custody fight. Whoo-ee! Ever'one was talkin' 'bout it at the time."

Valerie's heart began to race. "What custody fight?"

Tante Lulu tilted her head in question. "Yer daddy wanted to take you with him, but yer mother wouldn't 'low that, no way. Then he went to court to get part custody . . . whatever they call it."

"Joint custody?"

"Yep. Thass it. But yer mother wouldn't stand fer that, either. Said that iffen he wanted a divorce, he had to leave you fer good."

"So he chose his freedom over me?"

"I'm sure he kept in touch with you. I'm sure he was hopin' you'd contact him once you were of age."

"Not once."

Tante Lulu put a fist under her chin and pondered what she'd been told. "This is what I'm thinkin'. If no one tol' you 'bout the custody thingamajig, how do you know that he never tried to contact you over the years? He loved you, chile. Thass a fact."

Sudden hope rushed through Valerie, and tears spilled over her eyes and down her cheeks. She leaned over and kissed the old lady soundly on the cheek. "Thank you, thank you, thank you."

"I doan need no thanks. Jist make sure you come to my birthday party. Yer gonna be a . . . special guest."

"Huh?"

"Never mind. Jist be there. And if Richard Simmons happens to come with you, even better."

At the end of a long day, a guy just wants to . . .

By the time René arrived at his brother's houseboat that night, he felt as if he'd been wading in knee-deep shit all day, and what he needed most was a hot shower to wash it all away.

That shit had come in the form of, first, a meeting with some oil company executives along with his father, who had tossed out his usual threats and recriminations. "You always were a rotten kid. No wonder you turned into such a troublemaker." The other guys were more subtle. "Why stir up questions again? It's not going to do any good in the long run. And, besides, it could be to your advantage, financially, to step back from this ridiculous project." That last was meant as a bribe, of course.

"Did you guys have anything to do with the explosion on J.B. and Maddie's boat?" he'd asked point-blank. They'd all denied any involvement, of course, but his father's face had turned redder than its usual alcoholic hue.

"How about my mortgage being called in at the bank, and the threatening phone calls?" More denials, though those deeds might have come from other parties.

The second load of crap came from a group calling itself the Southern Louisiana Development Corporation, a group comprised of Realtors, bankers, landowners, and various others who stood to profit from overuse of the dwindling land resources. Simone Breaux was among the group, and the expression on her face boded ill for him.

René decided it was this bunch that had leaned on his lending bank. Simone probably had a personal hand in the dirty tricks.

The gist of that meeting was that he and Bayou Unite and the planned documentary were going to deprive honest working people in Southern Louisiana of much-needed jobs. And he better be prepared for the backlash once that happened.

Simone Breaux had stayed behind and issued her own threat. "Stay away from my daughter, or be prepared for the consequences. You and your whole low-down family will suffer, believe you me."

He had stood and towered over the woman, barely managing to control his temper. "Lady, you lost the right to have any say in your daughter's life the first time you locked her in a closet."

"Wh . . . wh . . . what do you mean?" she had sputtered, looking right and left to make sure no one was listening.

"You know what I mean. Everyone else is gonna know if you dare to interfere in Val's life again. Do you get my meaning?"

She'd scurried off like the rat she was.

On and on his crap-laden day had gone—police continuing the investigation into the bombing, J.B. and Maddie riding his tail about the documentary, the broker selling his town house, another broker wanting him to look at a place on Bayou Black—on and on and on, culminating with the strangest visit from his great-aunt.

"I jist wanna make sure yer comin' to my birthday bash."

"Of course I am. But it's not till next month."

"Jist makin' sure. Oh, and by the way, make sure you dress up real nice. Mebbe even wear a tuxedo."

"Huh? I thought this was supposed to be a casual event."

"It is, but I want you to look 'specially nice."

"Why?"

"Stop askin' why. Jist do it," she'd snapped.

"Well, I am not wearing a tuxedo."

She threw her hands up in surrender. "It's yer wed—funeral."

But now his day was over. He parked his Jeep near the stream and headed toward the houseboat. He saw lights on in the log home Remy and Rachel had recently built up on the hill; it was a big house for the two of them, but they were about to adopt two nine-year-old boys, Evan and Stephan, twins who had been deemed difficult-to-place foster children. René decided not to go up and visit; he wasn't in the mood for small talk tonight. Before going into the houseboat, he tossed a few gingersnaps to Remy's pet alligator, Useless, from a metal box he kept on the dock.

As he entered the houseboat, he heard Val singing some Aerosmith song in the bathroom. She was probably in the high-tech shower, which had a built-in sound system. Remy had put the shower stall in last year when he'd been trying to impress Rachel, then a feng shui decorator, by having her work on his houseboat.

Today had been a lousy day. Tomorrow René would be going to New York City with Justin and Val to present their proposal. But there was still tonight.

For the first time that day, he smiled.

Sometimes cleanliness is next to godliness, and sometimes not

Val was relishing a warm shower in the houseboat's spiffy glass shower stall, which sprayed water from a dozen different faucets. A hedonistic luxury item, to be sure.

Meanwhile, Aerosmith was wailing out "Jaded" from the built-in wall radio, and she was singing along, something she almost never did. She had the musical pitch of a parrot, a teacher had once told her, as in *squawk, squawk, squawk!* But who cared? She was alone. She was happy. And her future was looking bright.

Singing, "J-j-j-jaded," she lathered up her hair. She almost jumped out of her skin when she heard a more melodious voice behind her croon.

It was René, of course, finally back from his day of meetings. And, he was—Lordy, Lordy—bare naked and by a quick observation, more than ready, entering the shower stall behind her.

"Hey, baby," he said, stepping into the shower spray with her.

"Hey, baby," she said back, stepping into his embrace, smiling against his mouth.

"I missed you," he said.

"I can tell," she said, pressing her belly against his.

His erection jerked against her. He nipped at her earlobe and breathed into her ear, "Tease!"

The radio was now playing "Hit Me with Your Best Shot," but neither one of them was singing anymore.

"You're late," she said as he ran his fingers through her hair, helping to rinse the lather out. "How did your meetings go?"

He rolled his eyes. "You don't wanna know. I'll tell you later."

Looking at him with his wet black hair and spiked eyelashes and water running all over his splendid body, she gave herself a silent pat on the back for being able to attract such a man. "You look tired. Why don't you let me take care of you?" She was reaching for the liquid soap and a loofah sponge.

"Uh-uh. First, I have something to show you."

"I've seen it before."

"Not that, silly. It's the shower. Bet you don't know all it can do." He began fooling with some knobs and dials, changing the direction and the type of spray. "Now, stand just like this." He posed her against the wall, made her spread her legs and put her hands over her head. Then, oh my God, he hit her in all her best spots, just like the song. A short time later, she reciprocated. Then they both stood under the shower and let nature take its normal course, without any outside stimuli . . . just mouths, hands, and intimate body parts.

A short time later, they sat in the small kitchen galley booth, eating oyster po'boys that he'd picked up on the way here, followed by cold Dixie beers. Who knew a gal like Val would go for beer, but she did.

He'd already told her about his lousy day, ending with his meeting with Tante Lulu. "She asked me to wear a tuxedo to her birthday bash. Can you beat that?"

"Yeah, I can. She called a little while ago to ask me once again if I could give Richard Simmons a personal invite."

They smiled at each other, both knowing that it was par for the course with his aunt.

Then he looked at her and said, "I think I need another shower."

Business is business

The next morning, on the way to the airport, they stopped at the office of her aunts, Margo and Madeline Breaux. They were maiden ladies, over sixty-five she would guess, never married. They were sharks in the business of mail-order teas, in particular the well-known Southern Tea Company.

She and Justin entered their large conjoined offices, leaving René in the car. Knowing how much her aunts and her mother hated the LeDeux family, she figured it was best not to antagonize them right off the bat.

"Valerie, dear," her aunts greeted her, coming up and giving her air kisses on both of her cheeks.

They were twins, and they dressed the same, in stylish business suits and sensible pumps. They also styled their dyed brunette hair in the same French twist they'd worn as long as she could remember.

"Aunt Margo. Aunt Madeline," she said, giving them air kisses back. She noticed their eyes sweep over her, examining the black pants suit she wore for travel, and apparently deemed her satisfactory. "This is Justin Dugas, a videographer friend of mine."

Both ladies shook hands with him, then pointed them toward a casual sitting area in front of a window overlooking the outskirts of Houma. Years ago they'd tried to expand to the lot next door but failed, thanks to the legal efforts of Lucien LeDeux, who had the rundown place declared a national monument or some such thing. That had pretty much clinched the Breaux/LeDeux family ill will.

"What can we do for you?" Aunt Margo asked her.

"You did initiate this meeting," Aunt Madeline added.

Both were cool but clearly interested.

Val leaned forward and began. "You know that I'm working on a bayou documentary, possibly a series."

"We know," they both said, frowning their disapproval.

"After our meetings tomorrow in New York, we will have a better idea of what we can do, but I believe there is a business opportunity in this for your company."

"How so?" Aunt Margo asked. Both of them looked disbelieving, but still interested.

Valerie motioned for Justin to proceed, and a very nice job he did, too, looking extremely sharp in a white golf shirt and khaki pants, even with the ponytail, which they would not like. "A playful thread through all our tapes would be the Juju plant and how it has been contributing to male virility in Cajuns for more than a century."

"Male virility? Cajun? I never heard of such a thing," Aunt Madeline sputtered.

"I never did, either, but apparently lots of Cajun women have been giving the Juju herb to their husbands and sons for years, just to rev up the old engines." He waggled his eyebrows at them.

They were not amused.

"How did they give them the herb?" Aunt Margo wanted to know. "In what form?"

"Lots of ways." Val picked up the ball at the nod from Justin. "Sprinkled in sauces, in salads, but mostly . . ." She paused for a ta-da moment. ". . . in teas."

"Well I never!" the twins said as one.

Then Aunt Margo narrowed her eyes at them. "Is there really such a plant?"

"There is," Val answered, "but truthfully no one has ever tested it. Maybe it's just an old folktale."

"Why have you come to us?" Aunt Margo had her arms folded over her chest and was eyeing them suspiciously.

"We're afraid that if this documentary airs and people

get wind of this special plant, they'll be traipsing all over the swamplands searching for it, thus defeating the whole purpose of saving the environment," Justin explained.

"Why isn't that swamp agitator with you?" Aunt Madeline asked Valerie.

"Who?"

"Don't be pert, young lady. René LeDeux, that's who."

"He's down in the car," Valerie replied truthfully.

Both aunts smiled then, small smiles but smiles nonetheless. Aunt Margo observed, "Wise decision."

"You still haven't explained where we come in," Aunt Madeline reminded them.

"If we get you started on a new tea line—Juju tea, to be specific—and we mention it on air, then people would order it from you, rather than running up and down the bayou." Valerie looked at them closely when she finished, trying to read their reactions. She didn't have to use her jury analyst skills at all. It was obvious they were interested.

"It's a deal," Aunt Margo said and Aunt Madeline nodded her agreement. "Come talk to us when you get back from the city."

"In the meantime, we would appreciate your not discussing this proposition with anyone," Justin urged.

"That would be foolish of us, wouldn't it?" Aunt Margo said disdainfully. "We are smart business people. Why would we want to breed our own competition?"

"Riiiight!" Val and Justin concurred, not daring to look at each other for fear they would laugh.

"It occurs to me," Val said, "are you at all concerned

that there is no scientific research backing up these claims?"

"Hell, no," Aunt Margo said. "Half of the claims on our teas have no scientific foundation. Good heavens, we've got cures for sleeplessness, upset stomach, diarrhea, weight loss, and so on."

"Besides," Aunt Madeline added, "we could always ask Sylvie to help us with research. She's a chemist. But that probably won't be necessary."

"One last thing. Can I ask you both a personal question?"

They arched their well-plucked eyebrows at her as if personal questions were in poor taste. Even so, she plowed ahead. "Have you kept in touch with your brother, my father, over the years?"

Her question surprised them, she could tell.

"Occasionally," Aunt Margo said.

"More often when he first left," Aunt Madeline explained. "Not so much in recent years. He remarried, you know."

Valerie did know, but only because she'd overheard her mother one time when she was in high school. She hadn't dared ask about it, though, because her father's name was forbidden in the house.

"Did he want me?" Valerie immediately wished she hadn't asked such a pitiful question.

"Of course he did. What a foolish question!" Aunt Margo looked uncomfortable discussing the subject in front of Justin.

Still, Valerie persisted. "Did he fight for custody of me? More important, did he ever attempt to contact me over the years?"

Her two aunts exchanged worried glances.

"I think these questions should be addressed to your mother," Aunt Madeline said in a voice that brooked no argument.

Valerie smiled because, in essence, her aunt had answered her questions. Her mother had a lot to answer for. But not just yet.

She and Justin said their good-byes, and once they were out in the hall, with the closed door behind them, they gave each other high fives.

"At least two of the enemy are on our side," she said.

"We did well," Justin agreed.

When they exited the building, they saw René leaning back against the car talking to a pretty, young police officer. He wore jeans, a blue pinstriped oxford collar shirt, a navy blazer and low-heeled boots. Hot, hot, hot! The girl, in her early twenties, was giggling at something he said.

"Grrrr," Val growled in an exaggerated fashion.

Justin laughed.

"Maybe there's such a thing as too much Juju," she said.

René looked up and noticed them. He winked at her, a wink she felt all the way to her toes, and some other significant places.

"Then again, maybe not."

Chapter 17

Taking a bite of the Big Apple

They flew into JFK later that afternoon.

Justin went off to stay with a friend in the Village, while René and Val took a taxi to her apartment. They would meet the next morning in Anderson's office.

René had been in the Big Apple on several occasions, but he felt particularly suffocated this time because he could see that Val wanted him to love her town as much as she did. *Impossible!* He was putting on a mask, pretending to be impressed, while all he thought was, *I can't breathe.* The smell of auto exhausts, garbage, body odor, perfume, fried grease from restaurants, and pungent garlic from the cab driver—all combined to make his stomach roil.

He glanced over at Val beside him, about to say, "How can you stand this?" He stopped himself at the expression on her face. She was smiling and gazing raptly at the passing scenery. *This is home to her. How stupid of me not to realize that!*

He looked out his window of the cab, trying to see what she saw. What he saw were homeless people mixed with the crowds, the same sight that had greeted him each time he had visited Manhattan. *Mon Dieu,* there were homeless people in Louisiana, too, but they were so out in the open here, and people just walked by, not seeming to care.

Then there was Val's building, where they'd just arrived. A skyscraper, as far removed from his Cajun homeland as anything could be.

She greeted the doorman warmly. "Lewis, how are you? And your family?"

"Just fine, just fine. Nice to have you back, Ms. Breaux. I saved your mail for you."

They went up to the tenth floor on an elevator and soon entered her apartment. He could tell that she was proud of it, of the location overlooking Central Park and the fine furnishings. She kept glancing at him to see his reaction. *Man oh man, it's so freakin' small. I better not turn too quick or I might knock something over. Didn't I leave this behind in Washington, D.C.?* Living room, kitchen, bathroom, a closet-sized office, and one bedroom, all of which would have fit in his cabin. He guessed that every square inch of living space in Manhattan was comparable to a square yard in the bayou.

"Very nice," he said, looking at the red Oriental carpet and the furniture arranged around a low coffee table, sort of a settee on curved wooden legs and two wing-back chairs. There wasn't one single place where a guy could stretch out and watch a ball game on TV . . . if there was a TV. "Where do you eat?"

Her face flushed. "I don't eat at home much. When I do, it's standing up at the kitchen counter, or on the coffee table, or I pull out that gate leg table against the wall over there."

That's just great. An apartment that probably costs an arm and a leg, and it doesn't even have a place to eat. "Oh. That's nice." *That's ridiculous.*

"What do you think of this?" she asked brightly, pointing to a chair that sat in one corner.

It looked old. He didn't want to offend her by saying it would be uncomfortable for a guy his size. "Great. Is it an antique?"

"Yes. It's a violet ebony piece made by a New Orleans furniture maker named Seignouret about the time of the Civil War. I inherited it from my great-grandmother."

What do I say to that? "Must be expensive. Betcha it would go for at least a thousand dollars." *What a stupid thing to say!*

"Hah! More like twenty."

"Twenty what?"

"Thousand."

For chrissake, she has a chair that costs as much as my car. Talk about! "You're kidding." He immediately took his hand off its back, not wanting to get fingerprints on it or anything. Jeesh, he hoped he didn't trip and knock it over.

"Let's freshen up and go out to eat," she suggested. "We can walk to my favorite restaurant."

He used her tiny bathroom and came out wearing the same clothes he'd worn on the plane, except for exchanging his dress shirt for a white T-shirt under the jacket. She came out of her bedroom wearing a white dress that resembled a tank top with full skirt reaching to her calves. It was the fabric that about did him in. Sort of a T-shirt material that clung to her body like it was magnetized. If he didn't already know the shape of her champagne breasts, he did now. And when she turned to grab a purse, he saw her heart-shaped ass clearly delineated. *Maybe I could grow to like the city if this is how they dress here.*

She turned and said, "Why are you smiling? Is something wrong with my dress?"

"No, baby. Something's right with your dress." He made sure she walked in front of him to the elevator.

Her favorite restaurant turned out to be a Moroccan one. They sat on rugs on the floor before low tables. The menu included a bowl of soup that cost *twenty dollars. A meal for the two of us will cost three hundred dollars, if we're lucky.* It wasn't that René didn't know about expensive restaurants, couldn't afford to spend the money or didn't appreciate fine food, but jeesamighty this was a ridiculous waste, in his opinion. Not that he was about to voice that opinion to Val, who was beaming with pleasure.

They both ate the spiced lentil soup. *I should tell Tante Lulu again that her gumbo would bring in a fortune here.* Val ordered lamb shank tagine with apricot couscous—a fancy name for leg of lamb. He ordered simple beef kebobs, which pretty much amounted to beef and veggies on a stick, after declining the brains with sauce or calf foot entrees which were also on the menu. They sipped at an alcoholic drink that resembled curdled milk in funny cups.

Actually René was not a picky eater and this food was delicious. A belly dancer moved about the rooms of the restaurant, scantily clad and undulating nicely to the beat of her tambourine and some Arab music in the background. The dancer had a very nice navel, he happened to notice, especially with that pigeon-egg-sized jewel in it; he thought about asking Val how the woman kept the stone there, if she used glue or what, but one look at Val's frown, and he decided not to. The dancer took a particular liking to him, twirling her scarves around him and swaying her hips in front of his face. He pretended to be really interested just to be nice, and when the dancer moved on, he winked at Val and said, "Remember what Charmaine said about belly dancers and orgasms? Do you think I should ask this one if it's true?"

"Don't you dare."

"She has nothing on you." He was still fixated on that clingy white dress of hers, which was sexier any day than a flimsy harem outfit.

"Tsk-tsk-tsk," she said, but he could tell she was pleased.

On the way home, they walked hand in hand. It was nice. He didn't even mind the smell of garbage coming from some of the alleyways. When they passed a below-street level nightclub with big band-style music coming from its open door, he suggested they go in. René loved music of all kinds, except maybe rap, and he smiled with appreciation as they entered. They sat at a table near the small dance floor. He ordered a beer, she ordered white wine. At first they just watched the six-piece band with singer, and a half dozen couples, mostly older folks, on the dance floor move to the slow and swing tunes made popular in the 1940s: "Sentimental Journey." "In the Mood." "Chatanooga Choo-Choo."

"Wanna dance?" he asked, nudging her sandal with his boot.

She smiled. "Sure."

For the next two hours they danced and danced. Slow dances to songs like "It Had to Be You" and "Don't Get Around Much Anymore" and jitterbug-type dancing to songs like "Sixty Minute Man," "Mack the Knife," and "It Don't Mean a Thing." René was in his element on the dance floor, and Val followed well. People watched them move expertly to the beat and sometimes even clapped. He was hardly aware of all that, he was more interested in watching the movement of Val's body in the white clingy dress.

To him, dancing—specifically, dancing with Val—was foreplay at its best. They looked into each other's eyes. They brushed body parts. They held each other close in a dance embrace. They moved in a sexual rhythm. Hell, he was a walking half-hard-on for a full two hours. If he were a betting man, he'd say Val was in a similar condition, whatever they called it for a woman.

They walked back to her apartment with her tucked under his right arm and her left arm around his waist.

"That was fun," she said.

"Ummmm," he replied. "Have I told you how much I like your dress?"

She laughed and he felt the movement against his chest. "Only about fifty times. You look pretty good yourself, Mr. LeDeux."

"I know."

She swatted him playfully.

He kissed the top of her head and squeezed her tighter. When they got back to her apartment, he took off his jacket and tossed it on a chair, not the antique one, God forbid. Following her toward the bedroom—he already had his T-shirt off and over his head—he asked, "Is that bed an antique?"

"No. Why?" She turned halfway to look at him, which gave him a nice profile view of her breasts and butt in the fuck-me dress.

"Because I plan on giving it a good pounding, and I don't want to have to worry about the bill." Before she had a chance to ask him what he meant, he picked her up by the waist and tossed her onto the bed. Then he crawled up and over her, cat-style. "Leave the dress on, baby. I've been fantasizing about this all night."

To his surprise, she replied, "Me, too."

They were a hit

The meeting with Amos Anderson was going very well.

Val looked around the conference room where they were showing their proposal on a flat-screen wall TV, with her and Justin providing the commentary and René answering questions about the bayou when they came up.

She was so proud of them all. René and Justin looked so New York casual in their T-shirts, jeans and jackets over well-worn boots. She was wearing a beige silk suit with a brown tailored blouse and alligator high heels. They'd each taken turns presenting portions of the proposal—verbally, with poster boards and video—as they'd practiced. René's passion for the bayou ecosystem brought tears to her eyes. Justin's camera expertise showed through beautifully.

She could tell that Mr. Anderson was impressed, but did that translate into a go-ahead? He ordered them to hit pause at a point where she and René were smiling at each other while eating raw shrimp. "Do you see what I see here?"

They all looked, but no one spoke.

"You two," he said, glancing pointedly at her and then René, "throw off more sparks than a Fourth of July sparkler."

"Mais, oui," René responded, waggling his eyebrows at Val. "That is the truth."

"That's what I keep telling them," Justin said.

Valerie folded her arms over her chest, waiting for Mr. Anderson to make his point.

"There are several important things to consider here. The bayou is and always has been a character in itself, whether it be as the backdrop to a movie or an investigative piece. I agree that the Juju plant stuff is a great hook, which might very well merit some network and national media attention. That old Cajun lady with the herbs is a pistol. But in the end, you two add the sizzle that would sell this piece."

Valerie crossed her fingers in her lap, hoping.

"I have to talk with some of my associates, but I'm thinking you have enough material here for a six-segment program. Do you agree?"

They nodded, all of them smiling.

He mentioned a sum of money that was astounding even to Valerie, who was used to overblown television salaries. "Do you all have agents?"

She spoke for all of them. "We're all using my agent. We're having lunch with her today. She'll contact you about negotiations."

Mr. Anderson leaned back in his swivel chair. "The sweet part of all this is that we might have an open slot in the fall. One of the shows we had planned down in the Everglades fell through."

That was the best news of all. Valerie knew how urgent time was in René's opinion when it came to the coastal erosion. The sooner this played the better.

He called in some of his associates, and they did their presentation again. Everyone was enthusiastic, giving suggestions that would make the series even more appealing.

For the next few days, they were involved in details that hadn't occurred to her, even with all her experience in television. Everything from voice overlays, choosing which film went in each segment, taking publicity photos, the whole works.

In the evenings, she and René ate out in a different restaurant each night. Sometimes they went dancing. Once they saw a Broadway show, a musical, which they both enjoyed. And then, oh my, then they made love. She didn't delude herself that René had fallen in love with the city, but he had adjusted very well. She could see him here.

At the end of the week they decided that she would stay here in New York to handle this end of the program, while Justin and René went back to Louisiana to get additional footage that was deemed important.

Before they left, Mr. Anderson said, "You realize this series is going to upset a lot of people."

"Oh yeah!" they all said, smiling at that prospect.

"That fire on the boat is probably just the beginning."

"As my Tante Lulu always says, you've got to stir up the flour if you want a good roux," René said.

Everyone laughed at that homespun wisdom.

Before they left the building, Mr. Anderson pulled Val aside. "Do you have any plans to return to Trial TV?"

"Do I have a choice?"

"Oh yes. A few heads are going to roll shortly, and I have an idea. Well, we can discuss it later."

Valerie got a call on her cell phone, just as they were about to leave the building. It was for René, from his brother Luc.

"No! When? How bad? Oh shit. Shit, shit, shit! No clues, I assume? That figures. Those sonsabitches just never let up, do they? All right. I'll be back soon. Keep in touch. Bye." He clicked the off button and stared at the phone.

"What? What is it?" she asked. Justin was equally alarmed by the one-sided conversation.

René took a deep breath, then looked at her. "The bastards burned down my cabin . . . the one I was building."

"Oh, René."

"I was afraid of this," Justin said. "They'll stop at nothing."

They all nodded sadly. What could she say? She knew how much René loved that place. She squeezed his arm in sympathy and made noises about being able to rebuild, but she doubted he had insurance on the place.

The two guys flew back to the bayou that night, and Valerie stayed behind, as planned. Little did she know just how long the separation was going to be.

I'm not missing you at all

René was missing Val like crazy.

He was staying in Tante Lulu's guest room, lying on the bed, staring at the ceiling. *Is it too late to call her?*

For the past two weeks, he'd worked like the devil to finish the documentary filming with Justin, to complete the sale of his town house, and put out feelers for a new place closer to Houma, to decide about a new job, to clean up the fire debris from his bayou property, which was a total loss, and to help his family plan Tante Lulu's birthday bash. You would think he'd be too tired at the end of the day to think about anything but hitting the sack. Not so.

He hadn't said the words—out loud or to himself— but he was pretty sure he had fallen head over boots in love with Val. It was the first time in his life that René had ever entertained the notion so he couldn't be sure. But, yeah, he loved Val.

He smiled to himself. *Who would have thunk it?*

Justin was back in New York working with Val on the project. He should have gone back himself by now, but he kept putting it off. On the one hand, he wanted desperately to be with Val again. But he wanted them to be here, on his turf. Selfish of him, he supposed, but there it was.

Does she love me? he wondered. He thought so, but he couldn't be sure.

He glanced over to the St. Jude statue in the corner of the bedroom; Tante Lulu was an equal opportunity giver of St. Jude statues, and René had received his share, too. He thought he heard the statue say, *Absolutely*. It was probably wishful thinking on his part, but it made him feel good to think she might return his sentiments. *If she doesn't, I'll make her fall in love with me. Yeah, that's what I'll do. Seduce her into love.*

Just then, the phone rang. He picked it up on the first ring, not wanting to wake up his aunt, who'd gone to bed about nine.

"Hello," a sultry voice drawled out.

"Hi. I was just about to call you."

"Why?"

"I miss you."

"Come here then."

"I can't. I have work to do here." It was the truth. He had to protect his family and work with authorities to track down the culprits. He had job interviews scheduled for this week, too. He'd been offered several positions, but he wasn't sure yet what he wanted to do. In the meantime he'd gone back to working on the frickin' doctoral thesis. Luckily he'd had a copy back at his town house. "Why don't you come here? Besides, I have something to show you."

She laughed. "I've already seen it."

"Not that. I saw a small house out here on Bayou Black today that I'm thinking about buying. I'd like you to look at it first." *How's that for coming as close to saying, "I love you. Will you come live with me?"*

Unfortunately his words were met with silence.

"Val?" *Oh, my God! She doesn't love me after all.*

"Why are you buying a house on the bayou? I thought when you sold the Baton Rouge town house that you would . . ." She let her words trail off.

"You thought what?"

"That you would move here."

Is she nuts? "To New York City?" he asked, disbelief ringing in his raised voice. "Why would I do that?"

"Because I live here," she said softly.

Tone it down, big boy. No need to be offensive. "Oh, baby, I do want to be where you are, but I felt like I was suffocating in the city. I would die there."

"I thought you enjoyed yourself here."

"I did." *Well, the part where we made love a lot.* "But only for a visit." *Like once every ten years or so.* "Why can't you live here?" *We could make love a lot here, too.* He knew his question was foolish before it left his mouth.

"My work is here."

"You were able to work on the TV documentary here," he argued. "Maybe there are other documentaries you could work on. Or you could practice law. Bet Luc would hire you."

"René," she chided him gently. He could hear her take a deep breath. "I was offered another job at Trial TV today. Elton was fired and I have free rein to develop my own nightly show. They're giving me five hundred thousand dollars a year with an escalator if the ratings do well."

His heart sank. *She's making plans without consulting me. Hell, I'm making plans without consulting her. What does that say about our relationship? Do we have a relationship?* "Well, I can't compete with a half mil so that's that." His heart sank even more.

He heard her gasp as if he'd sucker punched her. "That was unfair, René. It's not about money."

Then why did you mention it? "Ambition, then."

"What's wrong with ambition?"

"It doesn't warm the cockles on a cold night."

"I'm not the one with cockles."

"I was making a joke." *You gotta laugh sometimes, or else you'll cry.*

"Guess I'm not in the mood for jokes."

Me neither, actually. "Val, you can't be serious about me living in the city. What kind of work would I do there?"

"That's the good part. With my new job, if I accept it, I would have the authority to hire people."

"Me? On TV?" *Frankly, I don't give a rat's ass about TV. The only thing I ever watch is the news and ESPN. And, you, of course.*

"Mr. Goodman did say you are very photogenic."

Uh-huh. Me, the Fabio of Trial TV. Giving commentary without my shirt on. "Give me a break. That was a film about the bayou, something I know at least an iota about. What would I do on a court TV show?"

"Maybe you could be the average guy on a panel. You know, each program would discuss the hot trial of the day. We could have defense and prosecution lawyers, a jury analyst, and you, the average guy giving his opinion."

I think I'm gonna puke. "Nice to know you consider me average."

"You know what I mean. You're just being difficult."

No kidding! "Val, I am willing to compromise on lots of things, but there is no way in hell I am ever going to live in a city again. I did it in DC and hated it."

"So what then? A long-distance affair?"

"No. I'm too old for that crap. Can we talk about this, in person?" *Oh, shit! Now, I'm thinking of marriage.*

What the hell's wrong with me? I want marriage; she wants sex on the hoof.

"What's there to say, René?"

A lot! "I could say why I was calling you tonight, but I guess it's too late for that now." *Don't say it, René. Do not say it now.*

"What?" she snapped. "You may as well tell me anyhow."

Oh, go ahead, the voice in his head urged.

"I love you," he said, and hung up.

He loves me, he loves me not, he loves me, he—

Val stared at the dead phone in her hand.

Did René just say what she thought he said? *It couldn't be. Could it?*

And did he hang up on her? *No, he wouldn't do something so immature. Would he?*

She pressed speed dial. He answered on the first ring. Before she could say hello, he blurted out, "Forget I said that. It was a slip of the tongue."

"Oh, no, no, no. Those are words that cannot be taken back once they leave your lips. Tell me again."

"No."

"Please."

"I love you. God help me, I love you."

There was a long silence.

"Val, if you don't say something soon, I am going to crawl through these phone lines and wring your neck."

"I love you, too," she said in a voice hardly above a whisper.

"Are you crying? Dammit! Don't you dare cry."

Then she hung up on him. Really, what more could she say?

He loved her, she loved him, but they could not be together.

She cried in earnest then.

Tears on her pillow

"Now I'm mad," René said the second Val picked up the phone.

"Why?" She sniffled.

I cannot stand to see a woman cry. I was only a little kid, but I still remember my dad making my mother cry. I do not want to become my father. "Because you pulled the typical girl trick. Cry and you can get whatever you want." *You are a piece of work, LeDeux.*

"That was not a trick. It was real," she sobbed.

I know. "Well, then, I'm sorry if I made you cry."

"You should be. It's your fault. You made me fall in love with you, and now you're going to dump me."

I apologized, but I am not going to let you run all over me. "Uh-uh. I am not doing the dumping. You are dumping me."

"No way!"

"Okay," he said, exhaling with disgust, mostly at himself. "So we aren't dumping each other. What *are* we doing?"

"Talking."

"Are we getting anywhere?" *Because it sure feels like we're stuck in idle.*

"No. I think we need to talk in person."

Hallelujah! "That's what I said from the beginning. But I can't come there right now. I just can't."

"You're worried about your aunt?"

"Yeah, I am. Come here, Val. Please."

There was a long pause. "I do want to meet with my mother. We have things to resolve."

"About your father?" She'd told him about the news her aunts had imparted to her. Sounded like her mother had a lot of answering to do.

"Yes. And I need to know whether she had anything to do with the bombing or the fire."

"When?" *How about tonight?*

"Next week."

"I can't wait." *And I mean that just like you think I do.*

"Me neither."

"I love you, babe."

"I love you, too, René. Are we going to be able to work this out?"

My gut says no, but my heart says yes. That infernal voice in his head advised, *Go with your heart.*

What he said was, "I don't know. I honestly don't."

_____

Chapter 18

Shot through the heart

"Valerie! I didn't know you were back in Houma."

Simone stood and came around from behind her desk in the plush office of Breaux Real Estate. Her mother was wearing a pearl-gray silk shirtwaist dress and even lighter gray pumps. There were pearls at her ears and at her neck. Her dark hair was impeccably groomed. The epitome of successful businesswoman.

"I came here from the airport. My luggage is in the outer office."

"Shall I have it sent to the house?" She was about to reach for the phone.

Valerie shook her head. "No. I'm not sure how long I'll be in town, and I'm staying at a hotel tonight."

"How does that look, that you don't stay in your own home?" She glared at Valerie in a way that in the past would have made her cower. No more!

"I really don't care about appearances at this point. And, frankly, it hasn't seemed like home to me for a long time." *If ever.* She sank down into a chair in front of the desk and set her purse and a folder on the floor.

Her mother was about to say something more, probably something cutting, but then seemed to think better of it. She went back to her chair behind the desk. "Why are you here, Valerie?"

"I came primarily to see you."

Her mother arched her perfect, dyed eyebrows. "You've done enough harm by barreling ahead with that . . . that propaganda piece. What next? A *National Enquirer* exposé?"

Valerie ignored the venom in her mother's voice. "There are two reasons I want to talk with you. Did you have anything to do with the boat bomb or the fire at René's cabin?"

"No," she said without hesitation, "but I must say that I think both were well-deserved."

Valerie gasped at her mother's insensitivity. "How can you say that? Someone could have been hurt or killed. I, your own daughter, could have been on board that boat."

Her mother dismissed that possibility with an airy wave of her hand. "It was no accident that the boat was empty when the dynamite was set off." She paused, then to avoid culpability added, "In my opinion, anyway."

"You know who did it, don't you?"

She shrugged. "I have my suspicions."

"Have you told the police?"

"Of course not. Why would I do that?"

"Because it's the right thing to do?"

"It depends on what your definition of what right is, doesn't it?"

"How about the telephone calls and René's mortgage being called in? Did you have anything to do with those?"

Her mother just smiled smugly.

Valerie shook her head at the hopelessness of trying to reach her mother. "There are things I know about you . . . and our family. If you do one more thing, just one, you are going to read about yourself in the local newspapers."

Her mother's face reddened with anger. "Are you threatening me?"

"Damn right I am." She picked up the folder from the floor and held it up for demonstration. "There's stuff in these folders that would blow the lid off this town."

"You are an evil child."

"Think so? How do you think your colleagues would treat you if they knew you used to lock your child in a closet, repeatedly? What do you think the press would do if I led them to some files that show exactly how you got permits for Bayou Paradise? I wonder how Aunt Inez's career as a congresswoman would go if it came out that Grandmother Dixie filtered oil money into her campaign coffers? And that's just for a start."

"Get out," her mother said in a level voice. She never shouted so this was the equivalent of her shouting.

"Not until I finish. Do you promise there will be no more dirty tricks?"

Her mother looked as if she'd like to spit on her, but finally she nodded. "Now go, and I don't care if you ever come back."

"Not yet. There's one other thing. It's about my father."

Her mother rolled her eyes. "That bastard!"

"All my life you told me that Daddy didn't want me . . . that when he left, he was leaving both of us."

"So?"

"I learned recently that my father waged a custody battle for me."

"It was just to get back at me. He didn't really want you."

"Why didn't you ever tell me that he wanted custody, even partial custody?"

"Why should I have? He was a weak man. He backed down the minute I threatened to fight the divorce. That's how much he wanted you."

Valerie winced at what was probably the truth. "Has he ever tried to make contact with me over the years?"

Her mother studied her fingernails and did not answer.

"Did he ever come back to Houma?"

"Several times when you were little," she admitted.

"And?"

"It wasn't convenient for me to arrange any visits. Besides, it would have just set you to whining again for your father once he left. Separations are best when the cut is final."

Best for whom? "Telephone calls? Letters? Anything?"

The pink tinge of her mother's pale cheeks told her plenty. "The letters were returned to sender. They would have only upset you. It was best that your father thought you didn't want any contact with him."

Best for whom? Tears welled in her eyes at the tragedy of it all. "You said most. What do you still have?"

"The lawyer insisted that I save the letter your father wrote at the time of the divorce and that I should give it to you at age eighteen or whenever you asked."

Hey, Mom, yoo-hoo! I've been over eighteen for a long time now. "Where is it now?" She could barely restrain herself from leaping over the desk and slapping her own mother.

Simone regarded her with disdain, then walked over to

a filing cabinet where she removed a thick envelope. She tossed it in Valerie's lap and went back to her chair.

Valerie just stared at it as tears streamed down her face. Finally, she stood and tucked the envelope in her folder and picked up her purse. "Did you hate him that much, Mother?"

"More than you can know. He rejected me. No one does that."

"Really? Guess what? I'm rejecting you now."

With those words she left and did not look back.

It was an ending of sorts, but a good ending.

René to the rescue

There she was.

René was parked along the street, waiting for Val to come out of the real estate office. When she hadn't called him to pick her up at the airport, he'd figured out where she would have gone. To confront her mother.

And by the looks of her, tears streaming down her face, it was not a good meeting. He got out of his Jeep and went around to the sidewalk, picking up her luggage. "Get in, honey."

Her head jerked up. She was surprised to see him. "Thank God you're here."

"Where else did you think I'd be?"

"I never cry," she blubbered, taking a tissue out of her purse and wiping her face.

Right! That's just sweat running down your cheeks.

"My mother is a bitch."

You took the words right out of my mouth. "What's

that?" he asked as he maneuvered the vehicle out into traffic and headed out toward Bayou Black. She had just taken a sealed envelope out of a folder on her lap.

"A letter to me from my father. It was written at the time of the divorce."

Uh-oh. I predict more tears.

She read it aloud:

Dear Valerie:

I'm going away for a while, sweetie, but I will come back to see you whenever I can. You are the light of my life, always have been, always will be.

When I think of you—and I will think of you every day of my life—I will remember the day you were born, how precious you were. The first time I held you, you looked up at me, and I swear to God you smiled. Your first steps were into my arms. Your first word was "Papa." I loved reading you books and teaching you to read. You danced on my shoes when I played music. Remember the times we went fishing on the bayou.

I have so many dreams for you. Most of all I wish you love. I was the first man in your life. May the Good Lord grant you a husband one day who will love you half as much.

I will try to be in your life as much as possible. If I am prevented from doing that, please come to me when you are of age.

With much love,
Papa

At the bottom of the letter there was the address of a legal firm in Paris for making contact.

Valerie began weeping again. Hell, he had tears in his eyes, too. She swiped her face with tissues and reread the letter in silence.

When he pulled to a stop about fifteen minutes later, she looked up with surprise. "Where are we?"

"This is the house I'm thinking about buying. I want to show it to you."

"René," she chided him. "You already know how I feel about this."

"C'mon. Humor me," he said. "It'll take your mind off . . . other things."

They both got out of the car and headed toward the front door. It was a spectacular house and very unusual for Southern Louisiana. Made of cypress logs, it was modern and comprised of many levels, all of them raised high off the ground. Huge windows looked down on a wide stretch of Bayou Black. It was Frank Lloyd Wright-ish in design, built by an architect for his own family ten years ago, but they'd moved to the west coast. There were two acres, and immediate neighbors were not visible through the heavy foliage.

"René! It's beautiful," Val said, once they entered the house. It was empty, of course, which made it appear even bigger than it was. The random plank hardwood floors gleamed. The kitchen had ultramodern features. An office/library off the living room had wonderful cherry paneling. There was even a dining area, which should be a novelty for Val. A gas fireplace in a carved wood fireplace would be a delight on those rare cold winter nights.

He kept watching Val's face to get her reaction. She

loved it, he could tell, and at least her mind was taken off the day's sad events.

"Can you afford this?" she asked at one point.

"Yeah, I can, actually. I've made good money at times over the years and never lived extravagantly. Plus I made a mint in the stock market a few years back during the dot-com boom and had the good sense to get out early."

She nodded with understanding.

The house had three bedrooms, and he told her, "That's the master bedroom and the other two would be children's bedrooms." She was unnaturally quiet, and he turned to look at her.

"Children?" she squeaked out.

He tilted his head in question. "Yeah. What do you think of children?"

"I never think about children."

"Never?"

She shook her head. "You?"

He nodded. "I would like to have three or four, but I'd settle for one or two." He smiled at her, hoping to get some kind of positive reaction. No such luck. Deflated, he asked, "Don't you want children at all?"

"I don't think so. I don't know. I've always thought I would think about it later."

"You're thirty-five years old, honey. You don't have that much time to think about it."

She gave him a hard look and turned on her heels, walking back to the living room and out on the deck. He joined her there.

"Are children a deal breaker for you?" she asked.

He thought for a while and answered, "No."

"No?"

"I could live without children. I'm not sure I could live without you."

"Oh, René!" She stepped into his arms. "You're pushing too hard," she said against his neck.

"I know," he responded, kissing the top of her head.

"You're making assumptions that I would live in Louisiana, and I've already told you I don't want to do that."

"I know."

"Why are you doing this?"

"Because I want you to see how it could be with us."

"You're scaring me."

"Oh, babe, I'm sorry. I feel as if we have so little time and I've got to make my case quick."

She put her face in her hand.

"Okay. I'll back off. Let's go to your hotel. This has been a long, eventful day for you. I've got just what the doctor ordered."

She arched her eyebrows.

"You take a bubble bath with a glass of wine. I'll order room service."

She sighed. "That sounds wonderful."

"I promise I won't jump your bones the minute we enter the hotel room." *Maybe five minutes later. Just not the instant the door shuts.*

"Thank you."

Don't be thanking me yet. I plan to bring out the big guns tonight, sugar. You don't stand a chance.

He was a dancing fool

René LeDeux was the best thing that had ever happened in Valerie's life. Even as she recognized that fact, she realized that they had been doomed from the start. This would probably be their last night together.

He drew a bath for her and filled it with some expensive department store bubble bath, which he must have purchased especially for her. He handed her a stemmed glass with white wine, then refilled it when it was empty. He wrapped her in a thick hotel terry cloth robe when she was done and led her to the dinner he'd ordered for them both, crab imperial with tiny roast potatoes and a garden salad. There were strawberries and whipped cream, which they set aside for later.

She ate heartily, not having eaten all day. He ate very little. He just sipped at his wine and watched her, like a hawk waiting for the perfect moment to swoop down on its prey.

His restraint was incredible to watch. And flattering. She knew how much he wanted her—his fingers trembled when they accidentally touched her—but he was waiting for the right moment. His right moment.

"I intend to screw your brains out tonight," he said out of the blue.

A sexual shiver ran through her body. "And how is that different from any other night?"

"It will be different," he promised her silkily.

"How? Why?"

"I want you to be addicted to my touch. I want you to dream of me night and day. I want you, body and soul."

Oh, sweetheart, don't you know that I already feel like that? "So that I will move back here?"

"So that you will want to be with me more than anything else in the world."

He's trying to change my mind about living here. "I thought we weren't going to talk about that any more today."

"We won't. What time does your flight leave tomorrow?"

"Noon."

"Ah, then we have roughly twelve hours together, babe. Are you ready?"

I've been ready for weeks now.

He held his hand across the table, palm up.

She put her hand in his. "Are we going to do something perverted?"

"I hope so," he said, then grinned. "What did you have in mind?"

They both stood, still holding hands.

"I would be too embarrassed to tell you about all my fantasies. They're silly." She could tell he was interested. *What a can of worms to open now!*

He led her over to the king-size bed and sat her down while he fiddled with the clock radio on the nightstand. He finally found a station playing rock music. Bruce Springsteen sang "Glory Days." Then he turned his attention to her. "You can't possibly toss out such a tantalizing remark and then back down. Come on, Val. Give."

She felt herself blush. *Should I? Heck, this might very well be my last chance. Go for broke, girl!* "Well, there is one thing. When I was in college, some of my sorority sisters rented an x-rated video. In it, this really hunky guy was in a shower or tub or something—the details are hazy. The woman stood outside watching while he soaped and touched and posed and stuff. It should have been sleazy, but somehow it wasn't. I told you it was silly."

"That's all. Hell, that isn't even perverted."

"Forget about it."

"Uh, uh, uh. Your wish is my command. I've never done this before, but I'm not shy and I think . . . yep, I'm *up* for the job." He winked at her.

He led her into the bathroom and sat her on the closed seat of the toilet. "Only the best for you, sugar. Front row center."

Standing in the middle of the room, he toed off first one boot then the other, in such a way that they twirled in the air and landed upright, next to each other. "It took me weeks when I was eleven years old to perfect that trick," he told her.

"It's an important talent to have," she remarked.

"Damn straight. It impressed the hell out of the girls."

"I don't like you impressing other girls."

"Okay, I'll 'fess up. This is the first time I've done it."

"Yeah, right."

The song on the radio changed to "Do You Love Me . . . Now That I Can Dance?" and they both laughed at the appropriateness of its lyrics.

René began to dance a little bit for her. Just swaying his hips from side to side as he pulled off his shirt. "Talk to me, darlin'. I need a little encouragement here."

"You have a nice body, René. I like that you have chest hair but not too much. I like your underarm hair, too."

"My underarm hair?" He raised one arm, then the other, sniffing. "I'm okay."

"You also have a nice butt."

Chuckling, he turned his back to her and did a little shake of his booty, looking back at her over his shoulder.

She let out a hoot of laughter. "That was a little too Chippendale-y."

He faced her again and opened the top snap of his jeans. He put his hands behind his neck and danced some more, rolling his shoulders and undulating his hips. Moving up directly in front of her, he urged her, "Unzip me, baby."

She did. Real slow.

He turned then and shrugged out of his jeans and boxers, not letting her see the front of him. Stepping into the glass shower stall, he turned on the faucet and stepped under the spray.

After that, he didn't look at her again. But, Lordy, Lordy, what a show he put on! All to the tune of Rod Stewart's "Do Ya Think I'm Sexy."

Oh yeah!

He shampooed his hair, tilted his head back, and let the lather run down his back in a stream that eventually made its way through the dead center crease of his tight buttocks. He soaped his arms and chest and belly, then used his hands to massage it in. Finally, he held onto the showerhead with one hand and leaned forward to lift his balls and touch his erection. After that, he turned, braced his back against the far wall and looked at her while he pumped himself, first slowly, then more rapidly. At the very end, he bared his teeth, arched his neck, and climaxed in front of her.

He turned off the faucets and came out of the shower soaking wet. "How'd that do for you?" Before she could answer, he picked her up and carried her into the bedroom. "René! You're wet!"

"The question is, *chére*," he whispered into her ear, "are you wet?"

She was.

Tit for tat, and then some

"Do you believe in good sportsmanship?" he asked Val when they returned to the bedroom.

"Huh?" He was still carrying her and her face was buried in his neck.

"You know, fair play?"

"Sure. Why?"

"Because, cupcake, it's time for my fantasy. And guess what? I had the same fantasy you did. Isn't that amazing?"

It took a couple seconds for her to realize what he meant. "Oh, I don't think I could do that." Her face looked really cute, all pink with embarrassment.

"Oh, well. If you can't you can't." He put a particularly hangdog expression on his face. "Guess I thought you were more daring than that."

She swatted him playfully on the face. "Don't try to trick me. I'll do it, but you better not laugh."

"I wouldn't think of it." He set her on her feet and gave her a quick kiss on the mouth.

"What should I do?" She was standing at the foot of the bed, still in her fluffy robe.

"It's your party, toots. Show me your moves."

"You're smiling."

"With anticipation."

Oh, boy! The Beach Boys started to sing something about California girls.

"Hey, that gives me an idea," he said. "I'll sit here." He pointed to the dresser that faced the bottom of the bed. He shimmied up there and sat, buck naked, with his legs dangling off the floor. Rooting through her makeup case beside him, he said, "Voila!" and handed her the small bottle of baby oil that she used to remove makeup and tossed it to her. "Okay, here's the deal. It's a really hot day, and you're going to the beach"—he pointed to the bed—"to sunbathe."

"And what are you?" she scoffed. "The horny lifeguard?"

"Whatever you want. A spectator. The lifeguard. A loose dog. The police. A wave."

Yikes! "Where's my beach blanket?"

"You're wearing it."

"Okaaay."

She crawled up on the bed, lay down, opened her robe, and spread it out blanket-style. Then she scrunched her eyes shut tight.

"Coward!" René laughed.

"You betcha. I always keep my eyes closed when I . . . sunbathe."

"So is it hot on the beach today?" he inquired. She could hear the amusement in his voice.

"Scorching." Truth to tell, she was feeling really hot. "I can feel the sun beating down. My skin feels tight. There are red colors behind my eyelids."

"Be careful you don't get a sunburn. You better put on some lotion."

"Oh, yeah." With her eyes still shut, she felt for the plastic bottle at her side and flipped the cap. By sense alone, she drizzled some on the middle of her chest, more than she'd planned. Setting the bottle aside, she began to spread it with her palms over her breasts, her abdomen, her belly. Then she returned to her breasts, massaging them to hard points.

"Oh . . . my . . . God," he muttered under his breath.

"What did you say?"

"Nothing. Go on."

"I'm imagining that you're kneeling between my legs and you're the one oiling me up," she admitted.

"Then spread your legs to let me in," he recommended.

She did.

"If I were really there, I would be drizzling oil on those curls so it would seep down and mix with your own . . . oil."

She still had her eyes shut, so she had a little trouble aiming correctly. In the end, she accomplished her goal.

"Lift your knees and spread wider. I want to see you, all of you," he said huskily. When she did, he said, "Mercy!"

"Is that mercy good or mercy bad?"

"Definitely good. Now, show me how you like to be touched. I'm a slow learner so a little vocal instruction would help."

She groaned. "I am not that uninhibited."

"Yes, you are. You would do anything for me . . . anything to please me."

"Gentle, at first. Along the sides." She used a middle finger to show him, over and over.

"This is the hottest thing I have ever seen. Keep going."

She stuck one finger inside herself, then two, and moaned. "I am imagining you doing this, not me."

"Make yourself come. Make your body hum."

At her first touch there, she moaned softly and felt her inner muscles clench. The mattress moved as René eased himself onto the bottom of the bed. Her eyes were closed, but she sensed him watching her.

"That's the way, that's the way."

She was flicking her finger rapidly back and forth till she was arching her hips off the bed, and she climaxed in ever increasing spasms.

Holy freakin' hell! He had never seen anything so hot in all his life. She was a regular sex goddess, every man's wet dream, Playmate and girl next door mixed into one. *And the night is still young.*

The minute she opened her eyes, he was up and over her.

"Oh, sweetheart, you were wonderful. Did you like it?" He lifted his head so he could see her answer.

"I did, but not as much as having you."

"Your wish is my command, *chére*." With those words, and no preliminaries, he slid inside her.

"Aaaaahhh!" she screamed, climaxing fiercely around him. *Thank God for multiple orgasms.* Blinking at him in astonishment, she said, "You must think I'm a slut."

He would have laughed or teased her about that silly statement, but he was too busy concentrating on what was going on down there. He filled her and then, when he began to move out of her, nearly all the way, the tight friction was almost more than he could bear.

Before he lost his mind and his control, he wanted to say something. "Val, honey?"

Her eyes were glazed, staring up at him. "Hmmm?"

"I love you." He slammed into her.

She made a little squeaking sound that he took to be pleasure and said, "I love you, too."

Over and over, they repeated the procedure. He told her he loved her on the withdrawal. She told him she loved him on the deep plunge. After a while, as the strokes came harder and faster, their words blurred together, and their bodies seemed like one.

In the end, he lifted her hips off the bed and pounded into her one last time. They both yelled out "Yessssss!" at the same time as they were swept away on a mutual orgasm.

When they came back to normal breathing, René rolled off of her and tucked her into his side, kissing her lips lightly first.

"That was nice," Val said, snuggling closer.

"Nice?" he protested.

"For an appetizer. What do you do for a main course?"

He laughed and said, "Wait and see."

Chapter 19

Fighting the clock

René was a desperate man.

Val slept soundly in his arms. Hell, it was no wonder. He'd kept after her, over and over, hour after hour, till he lost track of how many climaxes each of them had.

He'd started them off on those silly sex fantasy games because, frankly, he was afraid of himself and how very much he wanted her. Not that he hadn't enjoyed those games. He had hoped to cut the edge on his massive appetite; instead, the games had whetted his hunger for more.

She was worn out, unable to stay awake. He was hyped, unable to fall asleep.

As if a time clock was winding down in his brain, he constantly checked his watch, aware that his time with Val was melting away. He'd become insatiable, unable to keep his hands off of her, unable to stop telling her that he loved her. He kept thinking there must be something else he could do to make her stay. He was trying too damn hard, like a pathetic nerd pestering the prom queen.

It was pointless, really. Val had to go back to New

York, at least for now. But he knew, he just knew, that if they didn't make a commitment before she left, their relationship would end. Neither of them would want to drag out an inevitable sad parting.

She must not love him as much as he loved her.

Breaking up is hard to do

Valerie was a desperate woman.

René had finally fallen into a dead sleep after practically killing himself making love to her repeatedly. He was a bleepin' sex machine, or trying to be.

He was wearing her down . . . with love. It was sex, to be sure, that he used on her, but more than that. He showed her his love in every little gesture, from a butterfly kiss on her fingertips to a mind-blowing orgasm.

She could not make a decision under this kind of pressure.

No, that wasn't quite true.

She'd already made a decision. She couldn't change that decision under this kind of pressure.

He was too damn tempting.

Imagine us married.

Yeah, like he even asked me.

Imagine having him to come home to every day.

What is he, a puppy or something that would be at my beck and call?

Imagine living together, sharing our lives.

Sex, sex . . . and more sex.

Imagine growing old together.

Imagine having children together.

Good Lord! Where did that thought come from?

Bottom line: René couldn't live in the city. She realized the foolishness of her ever imagining he could. And Valerie felt absolute terror at the prospect of moving back here.

Everything that was bad about the first eighteen or so years of her life, she associated with this place. All the family members she wanted to avoid were here.

Her entire identity was tied up with her career. It was who she was. She would lose herself if she gave up her ambition, her dreams of success, her sophisticated world.

She would be a failure.

So it was with great pain that she slipped out of bed, dressed quietly in the bathroom, and packed her luggage. She left the folder on the dresser along with a note. Only then, with tears flowing freely, did she allow herself to look at him.

"I love you," she whispered.

And then she left.

Hello, heartache

René awakened to sunlight streaming through the windows . . . and a sudden panic.

He soon realized that his panic was warranted. Val was gone. For good, presumably.

"Son of a bitch!" he yelled, throwing a pillow across the room. Walking over to the dresser, he read her short note.

René: I love you more than I can say. But you and I both know it would not work. Please don't call me.

This is the hardest thing I've ever had to do. Good-bye, my love.
    Valerie

"Bullshit!" he swore, ripping the note into shreds and tossing it onto the floor.

Next, he flipped open the folder and discovered all the evidence he would need to end the harassment by the oil companies and developers on his tail. He supposed she considered it a good-bye gift to him. He tossed that to the floor, too.

When he left the hotel a half hour later, his tears were gone, and his face was a steely mask of bitterness. Unfortunately he ran into Luc heading toward his law office.

"René, what's wrong?" his brother asked with concern, running to catch up with him.

"Not a damn thing." He shoved the folder, which he'd had the good sense to pick up at the last minute, into Luc's hands.

"Where are you going?" Luc asked, without even looking inside the folder.

René stopped and looked at Luc. "To hell, I suspect."

Attack of the killer LeDeuxs

Three weeks later, Tante Lulu tracked him down.

He'd bought the Bayou Black house after all, figuring it would make a good investment, but the only furniture in the place was the mattress on the floor of his bedroom and some patio furniture that had been left on the deck by the former owners. It was from that mattress that he now staggered to the front door where all the banging was taking place. His head felt about the size of a basketball.

Opening the door, he moaned. "Tante Lulu! What are you doing here?"

"Pee-yew, you stink," she said, waving a hand in front of her face. "And when was the las' time ya did any laundry?" He was wearing sweatpants and that's all. She was right. He couldn't recall the last time he'd done laundry. Holding a palm in front of his mouth, he blew. Yep, he did stink. Must have been those ten—or was it twenty?—Dixie beers he'd downed last night.

The first week after Val had left, he'd been a walking zombie. Inconsolable. Pathetic.

The second week, he did a little better. He accepted a position teaching science in a local junior high school, starting next month. The job offer had come out of the blue. It was something he never thought he'd see himself doing. But for some reason it seemed right . . . for now. Was there any more fundamental way to improve the bayou ecosystem than to educate the young? It wasn't a yuppie kind of job that Val would admire, though. Not enough money. Not enough prestige. Maybe, in the end, that's why he took it. A last act of defiance.

He even had a date. A local court stenographer. What a disaster that was! He apologized for his distraction and took her home early. She was beautiful and intelligent, but she was not Val. He obviously needed more time.

This week, he'd met with Luc to discuss the settlements the oil company and Realtors association had made, under threat of exposing the contents of the folder Valerie had left for him. J.B. and Maddie would be getting a new boat. And he would be given just compensation for the loss of his cabin. He hoped the thugs would lie low once the documentary came out in the fall, at least for the short term. Otherwise they could still file charges.

The thing that had sucker punched him last night was Valerie. Again. He'd stopped at Swampy's for a beer and muffaletta, early, before the night crowds. While sitting at the bar, someone flicked the TV channel, and, lo and behold, there was Val on the screen hosting her new TV show. She looked great. He felt like shit. Apparently the break-up hadn't affected her like it had him.

After that he drank more beer than any sane man should. He entertained the crowds with his accordion playing. He might have even danced . . . by himself. Yep, he had a vivid image of himself leading the crowds in a wild rendition of "Twist and Shout," then leading a conga line to some rowdy Cajun song. The life of the friggin' party, that's what he had been. He had no idea how he'd gotten home, but he vaguely recalled someone driving him while he belted out one Cajun song after another, in particular "*Parlez-Nous Boire*" or "Let's Talk About Drinking."

So here he was, hungover, at his front door with Tante Lulu when suddenly a strikingly beautiful woman, wearing only his boxer shorts and his Tulane T-shirt, walked toward them from the kitchen. It was Francine Pitre, the woman he had once been engaged to be engaged to. *Son of a gun! How did I hook up with her?*

Tante Lulu took one look at Francine and exclaimed, "I thought you was happy."

René tried to smile but his lips hurt. "She means gay," he interpreted.

"Thass what I said."

"I am," Francine told Tante Lulu.

His aunt must have somehow found out that Francine was a lesbian. He hadn't told her.

"Then, what you doin' with this boy? Oh, no! Francine, bless yer heart, I hope you din't talk René into one of them threesome thingees like I read about in one of Charmaine's *Cosmo* magazines."

He and Francine both laughed. And, boy, did it hurt!

"I brought him home because he had too much to drink," Francine told his aunt. "As a friend."

"Thass a relief. I din't want him doin' anything perverted like . . . more'n usual, leastways."

"Tante Lulu, what are you doing here?"

"I come to straighten ya out. And doan ya be givin' me that black look. Ya been wallowin' too long."

I can wallow if I want to. "I'm all right."

"No, you are not. Now, go get those groceries outta my car. I'm gonna make ya breakfas'. Then we gonna talk."

As she made herself at home, and Francine kept laughing, and he stomped out to her pink Thunderbird to get five, *five,* bags of groceries, Tante Lulu called back to him, "By the by, yer brothers is comin' with a truck to unload yer furniture from yer ol' place. We's gonna have us a reg'lar *fais do do* right here. Ain't that nice?"

Just super! René's head just grew bigger. He was pretty sure it might explode.

"One more thing," she yelled from the kitchen.

I cannot take one more thing. I really can't.

"Me and Charmaine is takin' a li'l trip to New York City."

It felt as if his head did, in fact, explode then.

It was a family affair

Three hours later, René's furniture, such as it was, was in place, half-filling his new home. All thanks to the most meddlesome, endearing family in the world.

The women were in the kitchen preparing an everyday LeDeux-style supper, which meant enough to feed the Confederate army. He and his brothers were out on the deck, watching a proud gator papa-to-be building a nest for its mate out of mud and grass and other yucky stuff. It was a good distance from the house, no reason for concern.

"Why are you all here?" he asked.

"Hah! Where else would we be after the show you put on last night?" Luc said.

He winced. Apparently his hazy memory had been accurate.

"Dancing on the table! Only you would do that." Remy was laughing as he relayed that information.

"I liked the part where you were lap dancing some babe," Tee-John interjected. "Can you show me how to do that?"

René's jaw dropped. "Oh my God! Am I facing a sexual harassment lawsuit or something? Who was the babe?"

"I was the babe," Francine yelled through the window. "And not to worry, there was nothing sexual about it for me."

René should have been insulted, but actually he was relieved.

"You've got to get your act together." Luc put a hand on his shoulder and squeezed.

"I know that, and I will. Yesterday was just a bad day, a bump in the road."

"Can't you work it out?" Rusty asked. "Nothing's hopeless, you know?"

"This is."

Tsk-tsk-tsk! he thought he heard someone say from the other end of the deck, but when he looked over there all he saw was the life-size, plastic St. Jude statue his aunt had brought as a housewarming gift. His hope chest had been burned in the cabin fire, but she promised to put together another one for him. *Oh, joy!*

Before they ate, everyone sat around the table holding hands while Tante Lulu said the grace. "Dear God, bless this food and our fam'ly and friends. And tell St. Jude to help René 'cause he sure is hopeless."

He groaned, but everyone else just laughed.

Once they started eating, Tee-John asked Francine, who was sitting next to him, "How exactly do lesbians do it?"

Tante Lulu smacked him on the arm with a wooden spoon and said, "Hush yer mouth, boy." She would probably ask Francine the same question later when they were alone.

"How are the plans going for the birthday party?" Rachel asked. The party was to be held in one week.

"Just great. I'll tell you everything after we eat," Charmaine answered. She waggled her eyebrows in some meaningful way, which René feared somehow involved him, and added, "*Big* plans."

"Do you still want me to play? If so, I need to contact the other members of The Swamp Rats." René looked to Charmaine and his aunt for confirmation.

Tante Lulu said, "Iffen you wants to, although yer gonna be mighty busy."

"I am?"

He could swear that a grin passed around the table.

"Yep, and I still think you oughta wear a tuxedo," Tante Lulu said.

"Why? Is everyone else wearing a tux?"

His brothers shrugged and looked to Tante Lulu, as if she was the ringleader of this circus.

"Well, mebbe you doan need a tuxedo, but dress nice."

After the meal and the cleanup, René shooed everyone out of his house. He grabbed hold of his aunt at the last minute.

"This was nice of you, but you are not to worry about me anymore. I'm a big boy. I can take care of myself."

"To me you'll allus be a little boy." She patted his hand and reached up on her tiptoes to give him a hug.

"You are not going to New York City."

"I kin go if I wanna. Besides, I allus wanted to see the Statue of Liberty and the naked cowboy on Forty-Second Street."

Some combination! "You are not to go near Val under any circumstances."

"Why not?"

Because you'll make things even worse than they already are.

"You don't even like her."

"I din't like her at first, but now I like her."

He rolled his eyes. "Why do you like her now?"

"Because you love her."

Invasion of the mind snatchers

Valerie should have been on top of the world. Instead she felt like she was in the pits.

She had a primo job in a primo show that could very well soon rival the best of Court TV. In fact, she'd already had feelers from some of their execs trying to steal her away.

Any day of the week there were cocktail parties and important events she could attend. Two very eligible men had asked her to go out this week alone.

So what did she do?

She worked ten to twelve hours a day and went home alone to eat take-out food, standing up at her kitchen counter. Everything was the same and yet everything was different. She had this odd suffocated feeling when she walked down the street. Her apartment seemed too small. Her coworkers seemed artificial. She knew it was all in her mind, but she couldn't help herself. She was miserable.

She missed René so much.

And not once had he even tried to call her. She knew because it was the first thing she checked on her answering machine when she got home. She jumped every time the phone rang at work or at home.

Of course she hadn't called him, either. Of course she'd told him not to call her. Of course nothing had changed. Still . . .

She had to be out of her mind.

That's why when, in the middle of the afternoon, her secretary beeped her to say, "You have company," she responded in a mindless fashion, "Company?"

"Yes. They talk just like you do. Southern."

I thought I got rid of my Southern accent.

"And the guy . . . whew! Every woman on this floor is fanning herself. The South could surely rise again if they have men like that down there."

René! was her first thought. She smiled—probably goofily—and said, "Send him right in." She stood and was about to go around her desk, but immediately sank back into her chair with disappointment.

It wasn't René. It was Raoul Lanier, René's brother-in-law with his wife, Charmaine. And, oh my God, Tante Lulu.

"Surprise!" Tante Lulu said and came up and around the desk to give her a hug.

Surprise didn't begin to express how she felt. Crushed. Shocked. Puzzled.

"Sorry to barge in on you like this." Charmaine gave her a little hug and sank down into a chair in front of her desk. "Tante Lulu insisted on coming, and we couldn't let her come alone."

Raoul half-sat on the arm of his wife's chair. Ducking his head sheepishly, he added, "I'm just here for the ride." And, yes, the man was drop-dead gorgeous in his cowboy hat and boots and tight jeans. She could see why all these city women would swoon over him. *He isn't René, though.*

"Oh, no! Did something happen to René?" That must be why they'd come all this way, to tell her in person.

"He's fine." Tante Lulu was walking around the large office, examining everything from the silver water carafe on the sideboard to the coffee in the high-tech cof-feemaker, which she sniffed and seemed to deem inferior.

"Bought himself a house, got a new job, and had a pretty woman sleepin' over las' time I saw 'im."

Charmaine and Raoul gave Tante Lulu a questioning look, but said nothing. So it must be true.

"René is dating?" She could barely get the words out over the lump in her throat.

"Sure. Ain't you?" Tante Lulu asked, a sly expression on her wrinkled face. The old lady was wearing her going-to-the-city clothes today. Outlandish, as usual. Her hair was a mess of blonde curls. She wore a red pantsuit. Polyester, of course. White orthopedic style shoes. And she carried a canvas bag decorated with cartoon alligators that proclaimed, CAJUN PROUD.

"I've been too busy to date." *But I will, you can be sure of that. The two-timing rat!* "What brings you to the city?"

"You," Charmaine and Raoul said together.

"I wanna see the Statue of Liberty and the naked cowboy before I die," Tante Lulu replied at the same time.

Uh-oh! "Are you planning on dying anytime soon?"

"Ya never know. I'm almos' eighty. By the by, you are comin' to my birthday party next week, ain't you?"

"Oh, I don't know. Considering the circum—"

Tante Lulu shook her head fiercely. "You promised."

"But the situation was different then."

"You promised."

"Look, it would be awkward for me with René there."

"There's gonna be three hundred people. Surely, a smart girl like you can avoid him if ya want to," Charmaine offered, even as her husband gave her a disbelieving look.

"I really want ya to come," Tante Lulu said sincerely. "Cain't ya do it fer me?"

"Oh, all right," she snapped. "But I better not be running into René, and I sure as hell better not be seeing some bimbo hanging all over him."

"He'll be alone," Tante Lulu assured her. "And you kin hide from him all you wants."

They all smiled then, even Valerie. For some reason, a weight was lifted off her. *I'm going back. One last time. Doesn't matter why. I'm going back.*

"I doan suppose you called Richard Simmons yet?" the old lady asked. "We have a special exercise area set up outside the hall with speakers and everythin' fer 'Sweatin' to the Oldies'."

That's just great.

Valerie took off the rest of Friday and spent the afternoon and all day Saturday showing off her city to the three visitors. She did all the touristy things she'd never done herself—Statue of Liberty, Empire State Building, St. Patrick's Cathedral, Rockefeller Center, strolls down Broadway and Fifth Avenue, and, yes, even a little ogling of the underwear-clad cowboy. She'd heard a few women mutter that they'd rather see Raoul naked than that guy out there. Charmaine just grinned at a red-faced Raoul, as if to say, "This naked cowboy is all mine."

Valerie really enjoyed herself, seeing the city through their eyes. Oddly, she was the one making the comparisons. The air was sweeter down on the bayou. The flowers were more lush. The people were more genuine. The life was more simple.

More than once that weekend, she felt as if she were losing her mind. Her world was turning upside down. Everything she believed in and valued seemed suddenly unimportant. Yep, her mind was melting under the barrage of Southern folk.

More than anything, she kept looking at Charmaine and Raoul and how their love for each other was apparent in everything they did. How they looked at each other often. How they touched each other often. How they tried to please each other often. Charmaine thought Raoul walked on water; Raoul thought Charmaine was God's gift to men. And yet they were so very different from each other—in their looks, lifestyles, dreams, everything.

"How?" she asked Charmaine when they were in the ladies' room at a restaurant. "How could two people so different from each other manage a life together?"

Charmaine shrugged. "We love each other. True love finds a way."

That enigmatic answer told Valerie nothing. It was like a Hallmark card. Love conquers all. Which in her mind translated to "Bull!"

On Sunday afternoon, Valerie was saying good-bye to the three of them in front of their hotel where they were waiting for a limo to take them to the airport. Tante Lulu was sitting on a stone bench next to her.

"Promise you'll come to my party next week," Tante Lulu urged her for about the hundredth time.

"I promise."

The old lady nodded. "Jist one thing I want to know. Do ya love René?"

Valerie didn't have to think. "Yes, but—"

"Thass all I need to know." Tante Lulu squeezed her hand. "Everything's gonna work out. You'll see."

"No, it won't."

"Shhh. It's all in the hands of St. Jude now."

Chapter 20

Happy birthday to me

Louise Rivard surveyed the grounds of the Veterans Club and all the people who had come to celebrate her eightieth birthday.

There was a bar and dance floor set up inside, all decorated in a festive manner with a huge banner proclaiming, HAPPY BIRTHDAY TANTE LULU. Outside there were tents all around and rented tables and chairs. Highfalutin stuff. All kinds of Cajun foods were offered: crawfish in a dozen different dishes, three kinds of jambalaya, four kinds of gumbo, red beans and rice, boudin, andouille, blackened redfish, catfish fingers, ham and red-eye gravy, buttered grits, a big ol' mess of collard greens, Limping Susan, Lazy Chicken, dirty rice, fried okra, pralines, beignets, Tipsy Cake, Lost Bread, bread pudding, beaten biscuits, cornbread, even alligator steaks.

She wore party clothes today—a pretty purple flowered dress she'd bought special for the event at Wal-Mart, matching purple shoes, which pinched her toes and would soon be replaced with slippers once the dancing began, and pearls, which had been a gift from Luc and

Sylvie. Charmaine had done her hair up in soft brown waves and applied "subtle" makeup, whatever that meant. Even her finger- and toe-nails had been painted a soft pink color, despite her having wanted "Wanton Red."

She'd brought her exercise clothes in a plastic bag, just in case you-know-who showed up. Everyone told her not to get her hopes up, but she'd prayed to St. Jude. He could do anything.

René's band, The Swamp Rats, was alternating with another Cajun band in providing entertainment for the crowd. They would probably get rowdy later; she hoped so. What was a Cajun party without a little rowdiness?

Three hundred people had come to wish her well, most of them good friends. She'd touched many lives over the years, both as a *traiteur* and as a longtime resident. Most important here were all of her children and grandchildren. That's how she considered the LeDeux boys and Charmaine, even though she'd never given birth to them herself. She'd been as much a mother to them as any woman could be, having decided long ago that it must have been God's plan for her.

And speaking of God's plan and St. Jude's miracle working, where was Valerie? She'd promised to come. See, there was René coming over to her, dressed in nice tan slacks, a blue button-down shirt and a dark blue blazer. Acceptable wedding attire, in her opinion. Not a tuxedo, but good enough. He smiled at her, but she could see his pain.

"How you doin', sugar?" he asked, leaning down to give her a warm hug.

Looking over his shoulder she saw something, looked up to the sky, and whispered, "Thank you."

"What did you say?" René asked, straightening the collar on her dress.

"Jus' that I have a present for you, sweetie."

"For me?" He frowned. "It's your birthday. You're the one getting presents. Not me."

She shook her head. "Uh-uh! At my party, I likes to give presents, too. There's yer present right over there."

René turned and gasped.

It was Valerie. And she was wearing the perfect dress for a birthday/wedding party. It was white.

Will you marry me, baby . . . RIGHT NOW?

René's heart constricted, his blood raced, and his eyes burned as he looked at Val across the grounds. She was wearing the clingy white "fuck me" dress that she'd worn on his last night in New York. Oh, that was a low, low blow! Especially since it was a humid day, and the dress was clinging like crazy. *Un-be-freakin'-lievable!*

She hadn't noticed him yet. She seemed to be scanning the crowd for someone, probably Tante Lulu, who had suddenly disappeared from his side. *I am going to kill my aunt if she had something to do with this. Doesn't she know how hard this has been for me? Doesn't she know that this is going to set me back?*

He'd never in a million years thought she would come. Not after their breakup. What was she thinking? She was the one who had emphasized the importance of clean breaks. *Does she have a cruel streak? Could she possibly be an "Ice" Breaux after all? No, that can't be it.*

Still, she looked great.

Just then, her eyes caught his . . . and held. They started to walk toward each other, slowly. It gave him time to notice the swirl of her dress around her body, the sheen of her red lipstick, the tears in her eyes. *Tears? Why is she crying? I'm the one who should be crying.*

"Val . . ." he said.

"René . . ." she said at the same time.

Don't make a fool of yourself, René. Get your act together and act like a man. "What are you doing . . . I mean, I never thought . . . why . . ."

"Your aunt made me promise to come. When she came to New York last week." Her dark eyes darted from side to side. She was as nervous and embarrassed as he was.

He groaned. "She actually went to New York? Shit! I'm sorry if she bothered you." *I can only imagine my aunt in the city. The Big Apple might not ever recover.*

Val waved a hand. "No problem. I enjoyed having her."

"You look good." *And, man, is that an understatement.*

"So do you."

I do? I don't feel good.

"I hear you've been dating."

"Huh? Who told you that? Forget it. I can guess." *Is she jealous? Or just making conversation?* "Truth is, I went out once and it was a disaster."

She raised her eyebrows. "She slept over."

He almost laughed at the obvious machinations of his dear old aunt. Too bad they were wasted. "Oh, that! It was just Francine. She drove me home 'cause I was too drunk to drive."

"Francine? The lesbian?" Her eyes went wide with surprise.

He nodded.

Val smiled as if that made her happy.

What the hell is going on here? Val has to be here for Tante Lulu. If it was for me, she would have called first. Don't get your hopes up. Just be casual. Friends. That's all we are now. Hah! "I bought the house." *Brilliant. Why don't I talk about the weather?*

She seemed to approve, though why she would or why it would matter couldn't make its way through his foggy brain.

"I quit my job," she told him.

"Why? What are you going to do now?" *Mon Dieu! Will I ever be able to figure out women? She dumps me because her job is so important, rips me to pieces, and now says she quit her job. What the hell is going on here?*

"I don't know. It depends . . ."

"On what?" His heart was really racing now.

She had no chance to answer because everyone was being called inside to sing "Happy Birthday" to his aunt. As they walked side by side, Val slipped her hand into his and intertwined their fingers. He glanced over at her but she was staring straight ahead. She looked as scared as he felt. But where their palms were joined, he swore he felt their two hearts beating together.

For the first time in weeks, he started to feel hopeful. *Please, God, please, St. Jude, the whole bunch of you, please . . . please . . . please . . .*

Tante Lulu was up on the stage with Luc, Sylvie, Remy, Rachel, Tee-John, Charmaine, and Rusty. He supposed he should have been up there, too, but it was too late now. A giant cake with eighty candles were lit, and all three hundred-plus of them began to sing "Happy

Birthday." It was a moment out of time. Something they would all remember, and not just because a photographer was snapping away.

He noticed an odd thing then. All his brothers and Rusty were wearing suits and the ladies had on very respectable dresses, even Charmaine. And there was a priest standing in the background, too.

When the singing was over and Tante Lulu, with the family's help, blew out all the candles, she stepped up to the microphone and called for quiet. "Thank you, ever'one, fer comin' to my party. But I have a surprise fer you today. We're gonna have us a surprise weddin'. Right here and now."

"Huh?" This was news to him. Besides, how did someone have a surprise wedding? *Oh, my God!* Everyone was turning to look at him. *They wouldn't. They couldn't. Oh, shit! I just got punked by my family. I hope it's just a joke.*

"René?" Val asked. "What's going on?" There was panic in her eyes.

He felt a bit panicked himself. "I think they planned a wedding for us." *Is there a crack in the floor somewhere that I can fall through?*

The crowd was starting to clap and call out congratulations and rebel yells.

Val made a sort of whimpering sound and huddled closer. Or maybe it was him.

Meanwhile an aisle was being cleared and chairs were being set up in rows, and the stage was being transformed into an altar. The women suddenly had bouquets in their hands, and Luc and Sylvie's little girls, dressed in pretty long white dresses, joined them.

Is it possible? Does my dopey family actually think they can spring a surprise wedding on someone?

Val was just beginning to comprehend what was about to happen. "What?" she shrieked. Turning to René, she said, "They can't do this, can they?"

Who the hell knows? "I'll take care of it. I'll take care of it," he said to assure her.

"How?"

Who the hell knows?

Everyone was quieting down, staring at them expectantly.

"René?" she prodded. "What should we do?"

"I don't know. Give me a chance to think."

Tante Lulu was heading toward them with a big smile on her face, carrying a bridal bouquet. Charmaine was next to her carrying a bridal veil; her smile was a nervous one. *It oughta be.* Luc, presumably his best man, the traitor, was carrying a ring box. Luc shrugged at the glower René shot his way.

"Let's go outside where we can settle this in private," he suggested. *Then maybe we can make a getaway . . . like to Nebraska.*

Val nodded.

He put up a hand to his family who were about to follow them. They stopped, but Luc handed him a parchment paper and the ring box. "Just in case," he said, patting him on the shoulder. "Give it your best shot, Bro. You can do it."

No, I can't. I am not that smooth. "Are you people nuts?" he said, shaking his head as he walked outside with Val.

They went around the side of the building and back

behind a giant oak tree. They were hidden from view. She pulled her hand out of his. *Not a good sign.*

"How could you, René?"

He put up both hands. "Hey, I'm as surprised as you are."

"How could they?"

Because they are who they are. "I'm sure their intentions were good, but I'm gonna kill them anyhow."

She nodded and glanced at the paper in his hand. "What's that?"

He opened it and laughed. "Our marriage license, all signed and notarized, legal-like."

Being the lawyer she was, he half expected her to say it couldn't be legal. But she didn't. *Whoo-boy! It must be real. We should probably be laughing about this, but I suddenly feel like crying.*

She wasn't laughing, either. "And that?" She pointed to the old-fashioned jeweler's box in his other hand.

He knew what it was without opening it. Inside was a female engagement and wedding ring, along with a man's wedding ring. "They belonged to my great grandparents."

She sighed and touched them in an admiring fashion. "What are we going to do?"

"I'll go in and announce that it was a joke, that there won't be a wedding after all." His heart felt like a lead weight in his chest. Talk about putting a world-class closure on a relationship!

"Tante Lulu will be so disappointed," she said.

Ain't that the truth? Big deal! "Yeah, well, what else can we do?"

Her eyes suddenly welled with tears.

I cannot freakin' handle tears at this point. I just can't. He reached over and wiped a big fat one with his thumb.

"We could get married," she suggested in a voice so soft he barely heard her.

Suddenly he got lightheaded, and his heart beat so fast he could hardly breathe. *This would be the time, St. Jude.*

I hear you, that voice in his head replied.

"Don't tease me, Val. I'm a little bit fragile these days. No telling what I might do. Like . . . like get down on my knees and beg you to marry me."

She tried to smile, but failed. "That might be . . . interesting."

It's happening. It's happening. Thank you, God! "Val, do you love me?"

"That was never in question."

He was beginning to think . . . he was beginning to hope. *Oh, hell! What do I have to lose?* He dropped down to his knee on the grass, took one of her hands in his, and asked, "Valerie Breaux, will you marry me?"

She dropped down to her knees in front of him, uncaring of grass stains, and took his other hand, as well. "I thought you'd never ask."

He slipped the engagement ring on her finger. There were tears in both their eyes now.

"We're going to be married. Today," he declared with absolute amazement.

"Yeah. Cool, huh?" she responded.

He kissed her, lovingly, to seal the promise. Then they stood, leaning back against the tree.

"How are we going to handle this marriage? Long distance?"

"No. That wouldn't work. I'll try moving back here and finding work."

They couldn't stop touching each other as they talked.

"Okay, that's a huge compromise. On my end, I'll agree not to have kids. I'll get a vasectomy." *Oh, shit! Oh, well!*

"René, I never said I didn't want a child with you."

"You didn't?" *I've got to clear my brain. I keep getting all these mixed signals.*

She shook her head. "I stopped taking birth control pills the day I quit my job."

Understanding and hope bloomed in him. "Then the only thing I can offer you is me." *That sounds corny as hell, but I mean it.* "I will love you every day of your life. I will make you smile when you wake up and when you go to bed, and in bed. I will bring music into your life. I will give you a baby, if you want."

She touched his cheek.

"Val, let's try and make this work."

They kissed again. And kissed. And kissed.

Before the ceremony took place, there was discussion on who should do what. It was decided that Luc would be René's best man, and the other brothers would be ushers, along with the nine-year-old boys Evan and Stephan, who Remy and Rachel were in the process of adopting. Charmaine, Rachel, and Sylvie would be maids of honor. Luc's little girls, Blanche Marie, Camille, and Jeanette would be flower girls.

René and Val could have cared less who did what. They kept smiling at each other because they were really going to do this outrageous, wonderful thing.

The biggest surprise to everyone—except Tante Lulu,

of course—came when someone asked, "Who will give away the bride?"

A gray-haired man, impeccably dressed in a European-styled suit, stepped out of the crowd and said, "I will."

It was Val's father. The father and daughter hugged warmly and tried to express how much they'd missed each other.

René mouthed the words, "Thank you" to Tante Lulu across the way, and she just nodded. *I love the old bat. I really do.*

Henri Breaux had come back to Louisiana at Tante Lulu's urging to reconnect with his daughter. There was much kissing and crying, but it was decided to put off the explanations till after the wedding took place. The priest was tapping his foot up on the "altar." He had to get back to the church for evening mass.

And so it was that Houma, Louisiana, had its first ever surprise wedding. No one was surprised. Those crazy LeDeuxs were always up to something. The newspapers would probably report that it was a low-down Cajun affair, which meant everyone had fun.

The oddest thing happened then. Richard Simmons showed up. But, no, that wasn't quite correct. Four Richard Simmons's showed up. René turned to Val in question, and she just shrugged. "I did contact Richard's manager, but he wasn't sure if he'd be able to come." It was René's turn to shrug. Turns out, Charmaine, Remy, and Luc had also, without knowing what the other was doing, hired Richard Simmons impersonators to come to the party. No one could be sure if the real Richard Simmons was there, because they all claimed to be him. Regardless, lots of people had fun exercising outside on the special mats provided. And the Richards then came to join the party inside. Tante Lulu was beside herself with joy.

Toward the end of the evening, René watched with amusement as Tante Lulu approached Tee-John, who was dirty dancing, Cajun-style, with some little chippie from up the bayou. He'd probably been sampling the adult punch bowl. "Well, yer next," she told him. "Best I get started on yer hope chest."

"Tante Lulu, I'm only sixteen years old."

"I've still got some snap in my garters. I guess I'm gonna hafta stick around fer another ten years or so, to make sure you pick the right girl."

Everyone laughed because she would probably do just that. And what a job that would be! Tee-John LeDeux was sure to be the wildest of the bunch, "wilder than a hog in a peach orchard," as his aunt would say.

At one point, Luc raised a toast to congratulate René for putting an end to Valerie's two-year sexual drought. Everyone laughed and remarked that those LeDeuxs were known for discussing intimate things in public. Valerie was getting used to it apparently, because she didn't even blush, just leaned into him for about the hundredth kiss of the day, which he liked . . . a lot.

After that, René serenaded his new bride with an accordion performance. He bragged that his performance was sweeter than bagpipes, which wasn't saying much.

An odd thing happened in the middle of the evening. René was apologizing to Val for not having a bride gift for her. "Not to worry, honey," she said. "I have one that will serve as both a bride and groom gift." Turned out it was a pair of pink velvet handcuffs she pulled out of her handbag. He hooted with laughter. *My Val always manages to get the last jab in.*

René had to admit that he and his bride were one hot couple at their own wedding. Hell, they began making love in their own special way even while they danced the night away. Little did they know then that their baby boy would be born nine months later.

His name would be Jude.

Epilogue

Five years later, and it's still damn hot

René and Valerie LeDeux were the perfect couple, but, more important, they still loved each other with a passion. Some people said they gave new meaning to steam heat on the bayou. They had two children, Jude and Louise, named after Tante Lulu, who was still going strong.

Their bayou documentary on IRC had been a big hit. Tante Lulu even had a Web site for her fan club for a while. Some changes were made as a result of their reports—not a lot—but every little change mattered in the race to save the wetlands.

Some charity had wanted René to pose for one of their calendars. He'd politely declined. But later he'd told his wife, "I'd pose for you anytime, *chére*." To which she'd responded, "Only if you're wearing the velvet handcuffs."

René's bayou cabin was rebuilt two years ago with the settlement money from the oil company and developers. He and Val and the kids went there periodically to get away from the city, which these days was Houma.

René was teaching junior high school science and loving it. He'd earned his doctorate degree and just grinned when anyone called him Dr. LeDeux. He continued to work avidly for bayou restoration. He performed with The Swamp Rats on occasion, just for fun, he was teaching Jude to play the accordion and both of his children how to dance.

Valerie started her own jury consulting firm, headquartered in Houma, and she'd written a book on the fine art of reading people. She was often a guest on both Trial TV and Court TV.

Valerie's father visited them often in their beautiful home on Bayou Black. Valerie never reconciled with her mother, but she had a tenuous relationship with her aunts, who were making gobs of money on Juju tea.

At this, their fifth anniversary party, which, of course, was also Tante Lulu's birthday, they stood on the deck, admiring the bayou that they all loved. It was a gorgeous September day, not too humid, and the scent of magnolia and bougainvillea wafted toward them on a slight breeze.

"This is why God put us on earth," Tante Lulu proclaimed all of a sudden.

They all turned to look at her.

"Family . . . and love. Thass the most important things in life."

Who could argue with that?

About the Author

Sandra Hill lives in the middle of chaos, surrounded by a husband, four sons, a live-in girlfriend, two grandchildren, a male German shepherd the size of a horse, and five cats. Each of them is more outrageous than the other. Sometimes three other dogs come to visit. No wonder she has developed a zany sense of humor. And the clutter is never-ending: golf clubs, skis, wrestling gear, baseball bats and gloves, tennis rackets, mountain-climbing ropes, fishing rods, bikes, exercise equipment. . . .

Sandra and her stockbroker husband, Robert, own two cottages on a world-renowned fishing stream (which are supposed to be refuges), two condos in Myrtle Beach (which are too far away to be used), and seven Domino's Pizza stores (don't ask!). One son and his significant other had Sandra's first grandchild at home with an Amish midwife. Another son says he won't marry his longtime girlfriend unless they can have a *Star Wars* wedding. Another son at twenty-three fashions himself the Donald Trump of central Pennsylvania. A fourth son . . . well, you get the picture.

Robert and Sandra love their sons dearly, but Robert says they are boomerangs: they keep coming back.

Sandra says it must be a sign of what good parents they are, that the boys want to be with them.

No wonder Sandra likes to escape to the library in her home, which luckily is soundproof, where she can dwell in the more sane, laugh-out-loud world of her Cajuns. When asked by others where Sandra got her marvelous sense of humor, her husband and sons just gape. They don't think she's funny at all.

Sandra is a *USA Today, New York Times* extended and Waldenbooks best-selling author of seventeen novels and four novellas. All of her books are heavy on humor and sizzle.

Little do Sandra's husband and sons know what she's doing in that library. <grin>

Dear Reader:

Well, I did it. You asked for René's story and you asked that it be hot, hot, hot, befitting the sexiest rogue in the LeDeux family. I blush to say that I did just that. The tongue and hot pepper on the cover say it all.

Please let me know what you think. Did you like René's story? How about Valerie's? Did I go too far . . . or not far enough?

I've said it before, but it bears repeating: I love the Cajun culture. The bayou backdrop with its lush plants, eerie swamps and tropical heat, the spicy Cajun food, music and sense of humor, good men who are equally good lovers— that's what I see there.

Having said that, I want you to know that this is the end of the Cajun series . . . for now. I know, I know, hundreds of you have written saying you want Tee-John's story. Well, he and Tante Lulu may very well end up in another series of mine, or maybe I'll do another book in the Cajun series sometime later.

Instead I'm embarking on a new set of books, which I tentatively call the Jinx series, named after the female protagonist in the first book, Veronica Jinkowsky. She's a treasure hunter, and the male protagonist is her fourth (and only) ex-husband; they've been married and divorced four times. The thread that winds through the series will be the treasure hunting company. And of course humor. You cannot have a Sandra Hill book without my trademark humor.

Please know how much I appreciate your support. Some of you have been with me from the beginning, and believe me, I know who you are. Feedback is always welcome.

With much fondness,

Sandra Hill
PO Box 604
State College, PA 16804
e-mail: shill733@aol.com
Web site: www.sandrahill.net

THE EDITOR'S DIARY

Dear Reader,

Food is the spice of life. Whether it's chili that's so hot you're breathing fire or chocolate whose decadence indulges your senses, take a bite out of life—and love—in our two Warner Forever titles this April. After all, what fun is one without the other?

Jambalaya isn't the only thing that's spicy in the bayou. Check out Rene LeDeux in **Sandra Hill's** latest, **THE RED-HOT CAJUN**. Fed up with DC politics, Rene moved back to Louisiana with only one goal: to build his cabin in peace. But he'll never find peace here. His wacky, matchmaking great-aunt is determined to get Rene married and his activist friends devise a kidnapping scheme to bring media attention to their cause. Rene just never expected his friends to kidnap his high school nemesis Valerie "Ice" Breux, now a TV personality, and stow her at Rene's beloved cabin. And he certainly never expected the heat wave that began when she walked through his door. She swears she'll tolerate him when alligators fly, but he's always liked a challenge...and soon the weather won't have anything to do with the heat. Pick it up and see why *Publishers Weekly* raves "some like it hot and hilarious, and Hill delivers both."

Romantic Times Bookclub called her last book "dazzling" and "impossible to put down," so grab **Julie Anne Long's TO LOVE A THIEF**. The story of Pygmalion never seemed so romantic—or so sensual. Lily Masters has a silver tongue and the fastest fingers in all of

London. Skilled at picking pockets, Lily has provided for herself and her sister in the city's slums without being detected. But records are meant to be broken. When Lily is caught and threatened with prison, Gideon Cole comes to her rescue. A broad-shouldered barrister with a heart so charitable it leads him into trouble, Gideon can't resist buying the aquamarine-eyed beauty's freedom. In exchange, Lily must invade polite society and pose as the object of Gideon's desire to snare him a wealthy bride. Before the scheme can begin, Gideon must first teach her proper speech, dancing, pianoforte, etiquette—everything a lady knows. But does Gideon's pupil, with her stubborn and sensual nature, have something to teach him?

To find out more about Warner Forever, these titles and the authors, visit us at www.warnerforever.com.

With warmest wishes,

Karen Kosztolnyik

Karen Kosztolnyik, Senior Editor

P.S. Fate has a funny way of breaking the best laid plans in these two irresistible novels: Amanda Scott weaves the sensual and unforgettable tale of a Scottish lord whose scheme leads him to marry the wrong sister but fall in love with her for all of the right reasons in LORD OF THE ISLES; and Lori Wilde debuts her latest hilarious and sexy story of an impulsive PR specialist who teams with a brainy archeologist to reunite two Egyptian star-crossed lovers with a magic amulet in MISSION: IRRESISTIBLE.